ONCE THERE WERE WOLVES

Also by Charlotte McConaghy

Migrations

ONCE THERE
WERE WOLVES

Charlotte McConaghy

FLATIRON
BOOKS
NEW YORK

ONCE THERE WERE WOLVES. Copyright © 2021 by Charlotte McConaghy.
All rights reserved. Printed in the United States of America.
For information, address Flatiron Books,
120 Broadway, New York, NY 10271.

Designed by Donna Sinisgalli Noetzel

ISBN 978-1-250-24414-7

For my little one

One beast and only one howls in the woods by night.

—ANGELA CARTER

ONCE THERE WERE WOLVES

1

When we were eight, Dad cut me open from throat to stomach.

In a forest in the wilds of British Columbia sat his workshop, dusty and reeking of blood. He had skins hanging to dry and they brushed our foreheads as we crept through them. I shivered, even then, while Aggie grinned devilishly ahead of me, bolder than me by far. After summers spent wishing to know what happened in this shed I was suddenly desperate to be gone from it.

He'd caught a rabbit and though he'd let us stalk the woods with him he'd never shown us the act of killing.

Aggie was eager, and in her haste she kicked a brine barrel, her foot making a deep echoing thud, one I felt on my foot, too. Dad looked up and sighed. "You really want to see?"

Aggie nodded.

"Are you prepared for it?"

Another nod.

I could see the furry rabbit and all the blades. It wasn't moving; dead already.

"Come on over then."

We went to either side of him, our noses peeking over his workbench. From here I could see all the fine colors of its pelt, russet browns and dusky oranges and warm creams and grays and whites and blacks. A kaleidoscope of color, all designed, I supposed, to make it invisible and prevent this exact fate. Poor rabbit.

"Do you understand why I'm doing this?" Dad asked us.

We both nodded. "Subsistence living," Aggie said.

"Which means? Inti?"

"We hunt only what we need and we give back to the ecosystem, we grow food, too, we live as self-sufficiently as we can," I said.

"That's right. So we pay our respects to this creature and thank it for sustaining us."

"Thank you," Aggie and I chimed. I had the feeling the rabbit could have cared less about our gratitude. Silently I bid it a glum apology. But all the while something was tingling in my belly, right down at the bottom of it. I wanted to get out of there. This was Dad's realm, the furs and the blades and the blood, the smell he was always draped in, it had always been his realm and I wished it could stay that way; this felt like the opening of a door to a darker place, a crueler one, an *adult* one, and I didn't know why she wanted this but if she did, if she did want it then I had to stay. Where Aggie went, I followed.

"Before we eat it we have to skin it. I'll cure the pelt so we can use it or trade it, and then we'll eat every part of the carcass so there's no . . . ?"

"Waste," we answered.

"And why's that?"

"Waste is the true enemy of the planet," we said.

"Come on, Dad," Aggie complained.

"All right, first we cut from throat to stomach."

The tip of his blade went to the fur of the rabbit's throat and I knew I had made a mistake. Before I could slam my eyes shut the knife opened my throat and sliced my skin in one long swift motion to my tummy.

I hit the floor hard, cut open and spilling. It felt so real, I was sure there must be blood and I screamed and screamed and Dad was shouting now too and the knife dropped and Aggie dropped and she pulled me tight against her. Her heartbeat pressed to mine. Her fingers drumming a rhythm against my spine. And in her skinny arms I was intact again. Myself, with no blood and never in fact a wound at all.

I had always known there was something different about me, but that was the day I first recognized it to be dangerous. It was also the day, as I stumbled out of the shed into a long violet dusk, that I looked to the trees' edge and saw my first wolf, and it saw me.

Now, in a different part of the world, the dark is heavy and their breathing is all around. The scent has changed. Still warm, earthy, but muskier now, which means there's fear in it, which means one of them is awake.

Her golden eyes find just enough light to reflect.

Easy, I bid her without words.

She is wolf Number Six, the mother, and she watches me from her metal crate. Her pelt is pale as a winter sky. Her paws haven't known the feel of steel until now. I'd take that knowledge from her if I could. It's a cold knowing. Instinct tells me to try to soothe her with soft words or a tender touch but it's my presence that scares her most, so I leave her be.

I move lightly past the other crates to the back of the truck's container. The rolling door's hinges rasp as they let me free. My boots hit the ground with a crunch. An eerie world, this night place. A carpet of snow reaches up for the moon, glowing for her. Naked trees cast in silver. My breath making clouds.

I rap on the driver's side window to wake the others. They've been sleeping in the cabin of the truck and blink blearily at me. Evan has a blanket pulled over him; I can feel the scratchy edge of it against my neck.

"Six is awake," I say, and they know what it means.

"This won't go down well," Evan says.

"They're not gonna find out," I say.

"Anne'll flip, Inti."

"Screw Anne."

There was meant to be press here for this, government officials and heads of departments and armed guards; there was meant to be fanfare. Instead we have been hamstrung by a last-minute motion meant to delay us until the stress of this prolonged journey causes our animals to die. Our enemies would have us keep them caged until their hearts give out. But I won't have it. So we are four—three biologists and one vet—stealing, moonlit, into a forest with our precious cargo. Silent and unseen. Without permission. The way it always should have begun.

There's no more road for the truck so we're on foot. We lift Number Six's container first, Niels and I taking a back corner each while burly Evan carries the front on his own. Amelia, our vet and the only local among us, will remain here with the other two containers to keep watch.

It's a little over half a mile to the pen, and the snow is deep. The only sound Six makes is a soft panting that signals her distress.

A loon calls, distinct and lovely.

I wonder if it stirs her, that lonely cry in the night, a recognition of the same ancient call she makes. But if it does, then she doesn't reply in any way I can interpret.

It seems to take an age to reach the pen, but eventually I make out its chain-link boundary. We place Six's container inside the gate and head back for the other two animals. I don't like leaving her unguarded, but very few know where in the forest these pens have been placed.

Next we carry male wolf Number Nine. He is a massive creature, so this second hike is harder than the first, but he hasn't woken from his sleep so there is that, at least. The third wolf is a yearling female, Number Thirteen. She is Six's daughter, and lighter than either of the adults, and we have Amelia for this last journey. By the time we have carried Thirteen to the pen it's nearly dawn and exhaustion has set into my bones, but there is excitement, too, and worry. Female Number Six and male Number Nine have never met. They are not from the same pack. But we are placing them in a pen together in the hope they will decide they like each other. We need breeding pairs for this to work.

It's just as likely they'll kill each other.

We open the three containers and move out of the pen.

Six, singularly conscious, doesn't move. Not until we retreat as far as we can without losing sight of them. She doesn't like the scent of us. Soon we see her lithe form rise and pad out onto the snow. She is nearly as white as the ground she walks so lightly upon; she, too, glows. A few seconds pass as she lifts her muzzle to smell the air, maybe taking note of the leather radio collar we have placed around her neck, and then, instead of exploring the new world, she lopes quickly to her daughter's container and lies beside it.

It stirs something in me, something warm and fragile I have come to dread. There is danger here for me.

"Let's call her Ash," Evan says.

Dawn burnishes the world from gray to golden and as the sun rises the other two animals stir from their drugged sleep. All three wolves emerge from their containers into their single acre of glittering forest. For now, it's all the space they'll be given and it's not enough, I wish there didn't have to be fences at all.

Turning back for the truck, I say, "No names. She's Number Six."

Not long ago, not in the grand scheme of things, this forest was not small and sparse but strong and bursting with life. Lush with rowan trees, aspen, birch, juniper and oak, it stretched itself across a vast swathe of land, coloring Scotland's now-bare hills, providing food and shelter to all manner of untamed thing.

And within these roots and trunks and canopies, there ran wolves.

Today, wolves once again walk upon this ground, which has not seen their kind in hundreds of years. Does something in their bodies remember this land, as it remembers them? It knows them well; it has been waiting for them to wake it from its long slumber.

We spend all day carrying the remaining wolves to their pens, and return as evening falls to the project base camp, a small stone cabin at the edge of the woods. The others drink sparkling wine in the kitchenette to celebrate our having released all fourteen gray wolves into their three acclimation pens. But they aren't free yet, our wolves, the experiment has barely begun. I sit apart at the computer monitors and watch the feed from the cameras in the pens, wondering what they think of this new home. A forest not dissimilar to the one they came from in British Columbia, though temperate instead of boreal. I too came from that forest, and know it will smell different, sound and look and feel different. If there is any one thing I know best about wolves, though, it's that they adapt. I hold my breath now as big Number Nine approaches delicate Number Six and her daughter. The females have dug a groove into the snow at the very back of the pen and hunker down, wary of Nine's advance. He towers over them, shades of gray and white and black, as glorious a wolf as I've ever seen. He places his head over the back of Six's neck in a sign of dominance and I feel, with exquisite vividness, his muzzle pressing onto the back of my neck. His soft fur tickles my skin, the heat of his breath brings bumps to my flesh. Number Six whines but stays down, showing her deference. I don't move; any sign of defiance and those jaws will close over my throat. He nips her on the ear and teeth sink into my lobe, startling my eyes closed. In the dark, the pain fades almost as quickly as it struck. I return to myself. And when I look again Nine has gone back to ignoring the females, pacing round the perimeter of the fence. If I watch, I will feel the cold of the snow on my bare feet with each of his steps but I don't, I'm already too close, my edges have forgotten themselves. So I look instead at the dark ceiling of the cabin, letting my pulse slow.

I am unlike most people. I move through life in a different way, with an entirely unique understanding of touch. Before I knew its name I knew this. To make sense of it, it is called a neurological condition. Mirror-touch synesthesia. My brain re-creates the sensory experiences of living creatures, of all people and even sometimes animals; if I see it I feel it, and for just a moment I am them, we are one and their pain or pleasure is my own. It can seem like magic and for a long time I thought it was, but really it's not so far removed from how other brains behave: the physiological response to witnessing someone's pain is a cringe, a recoil, a wince. We are hardwired for empathy. Once upon a time I took delight in feeling what others felt. Now the constant stream of sensory information exhausts me. Now I'd give anything to be cut free.

This project isn't going to work if I can't create distance between the wolves and me. I can't get lost in them, or I won't survive. The world is a dangerous place for wolves. Most of them will be dead soon.

It's midnight when I next look at the time. I have been watching the wolves sleep or pace, hoping in vain that they might howl, that one would begin and the rest would follow. But wolves don't howl when they're stressed. The research base cabin is made up of one main room, in which we keep all the computer monitors and equipment, an adjoining kitchen, and a bathroom at the back. Outside is a stable housing three horses. Evan and Niels have clearly already gone home to their rented cottages in the nearest town—I'm so tired I don't even remember saying good-bye to them—while Zoe, our data analyst, is asleep on the couch. I should have left hours ago, and scramble to pull my winter gear back on.

Outside the air is biting. I drive through the forest and onto a snaking road, a couple of miles along the north-west of the Cairngorms, led only by the small orbs of my headlights. I've never liked car travel at night for it turns the thriving world into something empty and gaping. If I stopped and walked into it, it would be a different world altogether, filled with the shivering of life, blinking reflective eyes and the scurry of little feet in the underbrush. I turn the car down a smaller, winding road, one that leads me all the way to the valley in which Blue Cottage sits. Made of grayish blue stone and flanked by a couple of grassy paddocks, during the day its view is twofold: to the south lies thick, beckoning forest, to the north long bare hills that, come spring, will be covered in grazing red deer.

Inside the lights are out, but the fireplace glows orange. I remove all my gear, piece by piece, and then pad through the little living room to a bedroom not mine. She is motionless in the bed, a shape in the dark. I crawl in beside her; if she wakes, she gives no sign of it. I breathe her in, finding comfort in her scent, unchanged even now, even unmade as she's been. My fingers twine within her pale hair and I let myself fall asleep, safe now in the sphere of my sister, who was always meant to be the stronger of us.

2

Gently, he says.

Her small hands are gripping so tightly to the reins. She is too tiny up there, so tiny she must surely be flung.

Gently.

He slows her, a palm to her spine to press her flat.

Feel him. Feel his heartbeat inside yours.

The stallion was free not long ago and a part of him remains that way, but when she drapes herself upon him like this, gently, gently, as Dad says, he calms.

I am perched with one leg either side of the training yard fence, watching. There is coarse timber under my hands, a splinter beneath my fingernail. And I am on that horse, too, I am my sister, pressed to the warmth of the trembling, powerful beast, with my father's large, steady hand holding me still, and I am my father's hand, too, and I am the stallion, the light load he carries and the cold metal in his mouth.

All creatures know love, Dad says. I watch Aggie's embrace turn tender and fierce. She won't be flung free.

But the stallion's head lifts in the pink evening light; a scent has been carried to him on the wind and he paws at the earth. I twist on the fence, turning to scan the tree line.

Easy, Dad is saying, calming the horse and his daughter both. But I think it's too late for that. Because I've seen it now. Watching from the forest. Two unblinking eyes.

Our gazes meet and for a moment I am the wolf.

While behind me my sister tumbles from the rearing horse—

I wake disoriented from the dream, dreamt often, also a memory. For a few moments I lie warm in bed, remembering, but the day won't be denied, there is light streaming through the window and I have to get my sister up.

"Good morning, my love," I murmur, stroking Aggie's hair from her face and gently helping her rise. She is guided into the bathroom and allows me to undress her and sit her in the tub. "There's actual, real sun out there," I say, "so we'd better wash this mane in case you want to sit outside and dry it." She loves to do that, as much as she loves anything, but my words are a charade for us both: I know she won't be going outside today.

"The wolves are in their pens. They survived the journey," I say as I massage shampoo into her scalp. "They'll want to run home."

She doesn't respond. It's one of her bad days, which means I can talk and talk and she will do nothing but gaze listlessly at something beyond my capacity to see. But I will keep talking, in case she can hear me from that faraway place.

Aggie's hair is thick and long and pale, as mine is, and as I methodically work the conditioner through the tangles I wonder if she was right and we should have cut it all off. She is dispassionate about it now but despite the effort it takes to care for I couldn't bring myself to get rid of it, this mane she has always been known for, the hair I've spent my life brushing and braiding and trimming for her.

"If we hadn't taken them across an ocean they might have been able to." I help Aggie out of the bath and dry her off, then dress her in warm, comfortable clothes and park her in front of the fireplace while I make breakfast. "There's no love between Six and Nine yet," I say. "But they haven't killed each other, either." The words fall so casually from my mouth that I am startled. Is that the way of all love? That it should carry the risk of death?

But the words haven't reminded Aggie of the same things, she is too far distant to be reached. I want to follow her to wherever she's gone and I also fear that place more than anything. I fear, too, the day she stops returning from it.

She doesn't eat the eggs I leave at her elbow, too tired, too soul-exhausted to manage anything at all. I brush her wet hair slowly, gently, and I speak more of the wolves because they are all I have left that isn't rage.

Blue Cottage isn't far from the project base camp. Both cottage and camp sit on the edge of Abernethy Forest, one of the last remnants of the ancient Caledonian Forest that arrived here after the Ice Age. These old trees belong to an unbroken, 9,000-year evolutionary chain, and it's within them that we placed the closest wolf pen, the one containing wolves Six, Nine, and Thirteen. If they manage to form a pack, we will name them after their new home: Abernethy. There are few houses around here, but behind us sprawls vibrant green pasture for the many sheep farms dividing us from the closest town. This was not where I would have chosen to place a new pack of wolves. But there aren't many places in the Highlands upon which you wouldn't find sheep, and anyway the wolves aren't going to stay put. I only hope they prefer the shelter of forest. Beyond this stretch of wintry pine woods rise the Cairngorm mountains, and there, I'm told, is the wild heart of the Highlands, where no sheep roam and no roads enter. Perhaps this will be where the wolves like it best.

I have the heater on high in the car. The road is slippery with ice, and a light snowfall has begun, a gentle swirl of lace. The drive is beautiful; this is big country, sloping hills and sinuous frozen rivers, stretches of thick forest.

When the black horse blazes onto the road in front of me I think at first I have imagined it. Its tail is a dark comet trailing behind. My foot slams the brakes too hard and my wheels fishtail. The car spins half a circle and comes to a stop backward in the middle of the road, in time for me to watch the horse disappear into the trees.

My chest feels tight as I ease the car onto the side of the road.

A truck rumbles to a stop beside me. "You okay?" a male voice calls from the driver's side window, which is open only a pinch.

I nod.

"See a horse?"

I point in the direction it ran. "Ah shite," says the driver, and then the truck, to my astonishment, promptly heads off-road to follow it. I am horrified as it skids through the snow. I check the time and hop out of the car, following the tire tracks. It's not hard. He's left trenches in his wake.

The snow picks up; the world is falling around me. I'm in a rush now, late for work, but even so. I tilt my head to look up. Flakes upon my lips and eyelashes. My hand reaching to the cool papery bark of a silver birch. The memory of forty thousand aspens breathing around me, their canopy not naked but canary yellow and as vivid as his voice in my ear. *It's dying. We are killing it.*

A shout, from somewhere distant.

I let the memory slip away and start running. Past his truck and into thick snow only disturbed by his footprints and the hoof marks of a frantic horse. I'm sweating by the time I reach the river. A narrow, frozen stretch of ice between steep embankments.

The dark shape of him ahead. Below on the ice stands the horse.

Even at such a distance I feel the cold beneath its hooves. A cutting kind of cold. The man is tall, but I can't see any more of his shape beneath his winter layers. His hair is short, dark like his beard. There's a black-and-white collie sitting calmly next to him. The man turns to me.

"You know this is protected forest?" I ask.

He frowns quizzically.

I gesture to his truck and the mess it's made. "You don't mind breaking the law?"

He considers me and then smiles. "You can report me after I've dealt with the horse." He has a thick Scottish brogue.

We look at the animal on the ice. She's not putting much weight on her front hoof.

"What are you waiting for?" I ask.

"I got a bum leg. I wouldn't get back out. And that ice won't hold forever."

There are tiny cracks on the surface of the river, spreading with each shift of the horse's weight.

"Best get my rifle from the truck."

The horse gives a snort, tosses her head. The black of her coat is broken only by a diamond of white between her wide, darting eyes. I can see the quick rise and fall of her belly.

"What's her name?" I ask.

"No idea."

"She's not yours?"

He shakes his head.

I start climbing down the steep ravine.

"Don't," he says. "I won't be able to get you out."

My eyes stay on the horse as I slip and slide down the jagged edge. My boots hit ice and I edge my way out, watching for cracks. It holds me for now but there are sections thin enough to reveal the dark flow of water beneath. I see how easy it would be to step wrong, for that sheath to split and for me to slip silently through; I see my body dragged and tumbled head over tail until it's gone.

The horse. She is watching me. "Hello," I say, meeting her deep liquid eyes.

She tosses her head and stamps a hoof. She is fierce and defiant; I move closer and she rears, thundering hooves landing with a crack. I wonder if she knows her fury will kill her, if maybe she's fine with that, maybe she would charge toward oblivion rather than return to whatever she fled. A bit and bridle, a saddle. Some horses aren't meant to be ridden.

I lower myself into a crouch, making myself small. She doesn't rear again, keeping her eyes on me.

"You got any rope in your truck?" I ask the man without looking up at him.

I hear him move off to retrieve it.

The horse and I wait. *Who are you,* I ask her silently. She's a strong beast and, if I had to guess, newly broken. It's been a long while since I've ridden a horse and I'm a different kind of thing than I was. I let her see me, wondering what she will make of me.

The man returns with a coil of rope and throws it down. I don't break from her eyes as my hands tie the old familiar knot by rote, I keep her with me and rise to my feet. With a quick motion I loop the lasso over her head and draw it closed about her neck. She rears once more, furious, and the ice will crack, I'm sure of it. I let the rope through my hands so I'm not yanked from my feet but make sure to keep a good hold. When she lands I don't give her the chance to rear again, I pull on the rope to force her head down and then I move in close to lift her foreleg. The two motions cause the horse to bend her other front leg and almost with relief she lowers herself to the ice and tilts heavily onto her side. I drape myself over her body, stroking her forehead and neck, whispering to her. *Good girl.* Her heart is thundering. I can feel the rope about my own neck.

"The ice," says the man, because there are a thousand fine lines now.

When she's ready I slide my leg over her back and give her a squeeze with my knees, a few clicks of the tongue and an *up, up.* She surges and I slide onto her properly, getting my other leg into place and tightening my knees. The rope is still about her neck but I don't need it, I take hold of her mane and maneuver her toward the steep embankment as the cracks shudder beneath us. *This will hurt,* I tell her but she leaps up the edge, tilting me back. I'm ready for it, and I move with her, legs firm enough to keep my seat. She strains upward as her hooves scrabble for purchase and the ground gives way beneath her and then we are up and over, and the thrill that runs through her burns straight through me. Behind us the icy river has cracked open.

I press myself flat to her neck once more. *Good girl. Brave girl.* She's calm now, but I don't know for how long. She's not standing on her bad leg. Getting free might have harmed it beyond repair. I dismount and pass the rope to the man. It's rough in his bare palm, in mine. "Be gentle."

"Much appreciated," he says with a nod. "You're a horsewoman?"

A quirk of my lips. "No."

"Would you ride her home? She's from the Burns farm, not far north."

"Why'd you come get her if she's not yours?"

"I just saw her, same as you."

I consider him. "Her leg's injured. She shouldn't be ridden."

"I'll radio in a float then. You're not from around here?"

"I just moved here."

"Whereabouts?" he asks, and I wonder if he's one of those people who make it their business to know everyone in a hundred-mile radius. He has a heavy brow and a dark look about his eyes; I can't tell if he's handsome but there is something unsettling about him. "What brings you here then?"

I turn away. "Don't you have someone to radio about that horse?"

"You with the wolves?" he asks, and I stop. "We got told to expect an Australian lassie. Now how does that come about? Aren't there enough koalas for you to be cuddling?"

"Not really," I say. "Most have died in bushfires."

"Oh."

That shut him up.

After a moment he asks, "They free yet?"

"Not yet. But they will be."

"I'll alert the villagers to lock up their wives and daughters. The big bad wolves are coming."

I meet his eyes. "If I were you I'd be more worried about the wives and daughters going out to run with the wolves."

He gazes at me, taken aback.

I turn in the direction of my car. "Next time you've got an animal to track, call someone who's up to the task instead of bulldozing your monster truck through protected undergrowth." *Prick*.

I hear him laugh. "Yes, ma'am."

When I glance back it's at the horse. *Bye,* I bid her. And, *I'm sorry*. Because that damaged leg might mean freedom of a different kind.

3

For the first sixteen years of our lives, Aggie and I spent a couple of months each year visiting our father in his forest. Our true home, the place we belonged. A landscape that made sense of me. As a child I believed the trees of this forest our family. The tallest and widest had branches that began high above the ground: this was how you knew they were very old. The red cedars had stripes, almost, straight vertical grooves in their bark that ran up the lengths of them, but otherwise they were smooth, and their gray turned silver in the afternoon sunlight peeking its way through the canopy above. Elegant, the cedars, with their fern-like leaves. The hemlocks were different, darker in color, earthier, and the patterns in their rough bark were wriggly. Both had spatters of paint-like moss so green it was electric. There were many other trees here, too, littlies that wrapped around the bigger ones, these were younger, teenagers, maybe, and unruly. Some that snaked fingers along the ground for us to trip over, these were the cheeky ones, while some were bushy and fat, others thin and spindly. There was not one the same; they were unique and strange and varied, but they all had one thing in common: they spoke.

"The forest has a beating heart we can't see," Dad told us once. He lay flat on the earth and we copied him, placing our hands on the warm ground and our ears to the underbrush, listening. "It's here, beneath us. This is how the trees speak with and care for each other. Their roots tangle together, dozens of trees with dozens more in a web that reaches on forever, and they whisper to each other through their roots. They warn of danger and they share sustenance. They're like us, a family. Stronger together. Nothing gets through this life alone." He smiled then, and asked, "Can you hear the beating?" and we could, somehow we could.

On the day we turned ten Dad led us somewhere we hadn't been before. We'd camped in these woods all our lives but he hadn't ever brought us this far. For five nights we'd been sleeping out here in the green, five days we'd been walking. Aggie liked to wait for the deepest silence and then shout something so loud it shook the world. I liked the quiet better.

Dad would carry *Werner's Nomenclature of Colours* everywhere with him; he believed it was a book to live by. Aggie and I took turns poring over the pages, running our fingers over the little squares of color and their descriptions, learning them all by heart. For each hue was an animal that shared the color, plus a vegetable and a mineral. It was, my dad would say often and with pride, the very book that Charles Darwin used to describe the colors in nature that he saw while on his HMS *Beagle* voyage. It always struck me as wonderful that "flesh red," which to my eye looked a pale, brownish pink, was the color not only of limestone and larkspur flowers, but also some shades of human skin. Or that "Prussian blue" was the beauty spot on the wing of a mallard drake, the stamen of a bluish-purple anemone, and deep blue copper ore.

"It connects things, this book," Dad told us. "It makes everything the same, all just different shades of color. It makes us part of nature."

But Dad went quiet that day and we followed suit until instead of stepping over a rise into another copse of lush forest, we stepped out into an empty valley. The ground before us had been scoured, every tree hacked down and carried away.

"What happened to it?" Aggie asked, but Dad took it all in silently, took it upon himself and grew older as he did. His eyes fell on something in the distance. Hard to miss. A lone tree, the mightiest I had ever seen. A staggering Douglas fir, reaching right up into the sky, at least 80 percent of its trunk naked of any branches. It stood steadfast amid the wreckage.

Dad led the way down into the valley and across to the tree; it grew more enormous the closer we drew to it. With my back to the ground I watched distant leaves caress the sky.

Then Dad told us a story. "I wasn't always the man you know," he began. "A long time ago, long before you two were even a thought, I was a logger."

He told us of his walks through forests, so much like the walks he takes now and so very different. It was his job to show his colleagues where to fell and where to stop, using brightly colored tape to mark the trees and value their timber. Once he'd done his job the loggers would come in and start up their chain saws, and a place alive when he'd entered would be left dead.

One day he walked this land. It looked different in those days. He came up from the river we crossed this morning, measuring his distances and marking his trees. And he reached this one. This Douglas fir, which was to be the tree that would change his life.

He knew straightaway that it was special. Larger than any tree he'd come across, it would be worth a fortune. He marked it red, and carried on.

Only to return to gaze up at it, again and again throughout the day. It stirred something in him. Alexander Flynn, at twenty-five, got out his green tape and he marked the tree a second time, this time to "keep." And so ended his career.

"I left work that day and I never went back," Dad said. "Too late. Far too late." He gazed out at the stumps. "It's a threatened species now. Ninety-nine percent of old-growth Douglas firs have been cut down. Which makes this one of the last of its kind."

"Is it lonely?" I asked, aching for the roots that must be reaching to find nothing to hold.

"Yes," Dad said. Then he rested his forehead against the Douglas fir, and he did something Aggie and I had never seen him do, not before that day and never again after, he wept.

It was a long journey from Vancouver to Sydney and Aggie and I knew it well. A long journey from logger-turned-forest-dwelling-naturalist father to city-bound-gritty-crime-detective mother. Life with Mum a different world altogether. But even once I returned home to the concrete apartment building and the treeless sandy beaches and their crashing oceans I still dreamt of the lonely Doug fir, and I would wake certain its roots had been my own, reaching to find no others, not even Aggie's.

Mum didn't ask us how the trip went—she never did. In fact she never asked us much at all. It was usually me doing the questioning, wanting always to know more, no answers ever feeling like enough, a parrot who'd been taught the word "why" solely to send her mother insane, as Mum declared.

Most of my preoccupation was with my parents and why I'd never seen them in the same room, let alone *together,* together. *Why do you and Dad live so far apart?* Someone's gotta fund the airlines, she'd say, or something along those lines. So I'd ask *Where'd you meet?* In Canada. *Why were you in Canada?* Because sometimes people go to other countries, Inti. *How old were you?* Can't remember. *Did you fall in love?* When you're grown up that word means something different. *Was he happy when you got pregnant?* I'd never seen him happier. *Were you?* What do you think, you nut? *Why'd you break up then?* Because I wanted a career, and he didn't want to leave his forest. *Why?* Why what? *Why couldn't he leave?* I don't know, Inti, it's something I'll never understand, Mum would say, and then she'd pretend to tie a gag around my mouth which would make us both laugh and that would be the end of the interrogation for one day.

After the latest visit to Dad's, when the nightmares about dead trees had been going on for a while, she called me into her study and this was strange enough to make me nervous. Mum's study was a place of bruises and blood and death. Not entirely unlike Dad's shed. We weren't usually allowed in there.

"Sit up here," she said, pulling a second chair beside hers at the desk. I sat, glancing at the crack in the door where Aggie was eavesdropping. "What did you do with Dad this time?" Mum asked.

"Just camping and stuff."

"What unsettled you both so much?"

I considered the question. "There's all these trees got cut down."

She studied my face for what felt an age. "Inti," she said clearly. "You need to toughen up."

I flushed.

Mum stroked my hair once, then lifted me onto her lap with strong arms. On the desk were folders that opened with a flap. Inside, pictures. Women's smiling faces. "These," Mum told me, "are the women who have been killed this month by their husbands or boyfriends."

I didn't understand.

"It happens once a week in Australia."

"Why?"

"I don't know. What I do know is that worrying about trees is not a good way to spend your energy. Worry about this. Other people. Your mirror-touch makes you vulnerable and on top of that you're too kind, Inti. If you're not careful—if you're not *vigilant*—someone's going to hurt you. Do you understand?"

She took a pocket knife from the desk drawer. Her baton and Taser were in the same drawer, but the gun stayed at work. I had never seen her wearing it but Aggie used to draw pictures of her with it all the time, and asked about it constantly.

Mum flipped the blade open and without warning sliced her index finger.

I yelped in pain and grabbed my finger tightly, trying to stem the blood, only there wasn't any and I knew there wouldn't be any but still it had me tricked, every time.

Aggie charged into the room, shouting, "Don't!"

"Relax, Aggie," Mum said. "She's fine. Open your eyes," Mum told me and then, as I watched, she cut her second finger, cut my second finger, and then her third and fourth and fifth. I was crying as she said, "This isn't yours. It doesn't belong to you. When your brain tells you otherwise it's lying. So you must form a defense."

"I'll be her defense," Aggie said.

"I know that, but you won't always be together—she needs one of her own."

Aggie and I looked at each other and mutually dismissed that comment.

"How?" I asked Mum.

"Any way that you can, because people harm each other. I see it every day. You need to start protecting yourself. I'll cut myself until you don't feel it anymore."

And so she did.

The camera monitors in the base camp aren't doing it for me so I hike out to the pen and climb a tree. With binoculars I watch Number Six and Number Nine deciding how they feel about each other.

It isn't going to work. I'm sure of it. The world is not that kind; I am not so lucky.

And then it does. Because really it has nothing to do with me and my luck.

He pads over to her and she rises to meet him. I am sure they will finally fight, the fight to end one of them, undoubtedly the smaller female. But instead Number Nine touches his muzzle to hers and settles himself next to her, where their bodies will keep each other warm. They nuzzle and lick each other, then rest their faces together.

The first pair of wolves to mate in Scotland in hundreds of years.

It is easy to tell myself that what passes between them is only biology, nature, but then who said love does not exist in the nature of all things?

I climb down from the tree. Whether or not any of the females fall pregnant this season, we now have three breeding pairs, which means we are one step closer to returning the wolves to Scotland. Only then will the forest come back to life.

I take a detour home so I can stop and walk the hill on which this entire project is relying.

The first thing Evan did when I arrived in Scotland a few weeks ago was bring me to this hillside. It's the chosen spot for the vegetation survey that will eventually inform our report to the government. Evan, who was a botanist in another life, has been liaising with the botanist consultants independently running the survey.

A large transect of about a hundred meters has been set up, with smaller square intervals marked out. "These are four-by-four quadrants," Evan explained to me that first day. "They're monitoring the species diversity and abundance and they'll continue to do so over the next few years to see what physical impact the wolves are having on the habitat regeneration."

My eyes scanned the plant life on this windy patch of hill, just as they do again now. There are very few trees and only short grass beneath the ling and heather. A favorite grazing ground of the red deer that cover the Scottish Highlands.

"So this patch of land is going to determine if we've been successful or not," I'd said.

"Aye. And she better get on with it too because she's looking right hackit."

As I'm arriving back at base camp my phone rings. I'm in a bit of hot water with Anne Barrie from the Wolf Trust for placing the wolves in the pens without being given the go-ahead. I think mostly she's pissed because she wanted to be there to see it. She's worked so hard to make it happen, it was a bit of a shit thing of me to do, but then again, keeping them in those crates would have been negligent. I almost don't answer her phone call, not in the mood to be chewed out again.

"Hey, Anne."

"I trust you'll be at the meeting tonight?"

I sigh.

"You're going, Inti. The head of the project needs to show her face there."

"Yeah, fine."

"But you aren't going to say anything, okay? Leave that to Evan. He's charming and you're not."

"Cheers."

"I mean it. This is an opportunity to defuse some of the tension, not stir it up further."

"I was planning on taking a vegan power sign. Do you think that would help?"

"Please don't take the piss right now, Inti, I don't have time."

"Why are we pandering to the unions, anyway?"

"Oh, Jesus, don't even start with that. I know you are not that stupid."

I can't help grinning. She's easy to stir.

"Just, *please,* don't lose your shit."

"I won't, I've got it."

The school auditorium has no heating; the air within feels even colder than it does outside. My fingers are turning numb as I sink into a back-row seat beside Niels and Zoe. There is a woman in the audience holding a sign that reads CIGARETTES AND WOLVES, KILLERS THAT COME IN PACKS and a kid waving one that says WILL THERE BE ANY DEER LEFT WHEN I GROW UP? I roll my eyes.

On the stage sit a row of people. Evan is among them, our spokesperson, chosen not only because he is articulate and charismatic, but because he's the only one in our core team who is Scottish, and this, we've been told, is likely to land better with the locals. Niels by contrast is a stiff Scandinavian who has an almost encyclopedic knowledge of our field but zero people skills and a thick Norwegian accent, Zoe is an American data analyst who doesn't like the outdoors and makes no secret of this, while I am a bad-tempered Australian who finds it hard to hide contempt and sucks at public speaking. Next to Evan sits Anne, the warrior who singlehandedly got this project through Parliament and also a massive pain in my ass. I don't know who the rest of the people up there are, I suppose prominent members of the community. In the crowd I know there are members of the farmers union, the gamekeepers union, and the Hillwalkers group, plus dozens of landowners from the entire Cairngorms region—all of whom have opposed our project. And despite my teasing with Anne, I do understand why. There are no members of corporate agriculture here tonight. These people are mostly local farmers living under massive financial pressure, and a perceived threat to their hard-earned livelihoods is a frightening thing. It's Evan's job to try and ease some of that fear.

One of the men on the stage stands to speak, white-haired and pairing his traditional tartan kilt with a more casual knit pullover. "Most of you know me but for any who don't, I'm Mayor Andy Oakes," he says. "This meeting's been called to give you some necessary information and for you to voice your concerns and hopefully have them appeased. Here to speak to us tonight is Anne Barrie, head of the Wolf Trust, in cooperation with Rewilding Scotland, and Evan Long, who's one of the biologists with the Cairngorms Wolf Project."

Anne gives a little thank-you speech that could not be more brown nosing if she tried, then she yields the stage to Evan to explain the situation: that there are now three pens holding a total of fourteen wolves within the Cairngorms National Park and that come the end of winter the wolves will be released from these pens to live freely in the Scottish Highlands. They are here specifically for a rewilding effort in a broader attempt to slow climate change, and on an experimental basis.

"What we have here in Scotland," Evan says, "is an ecosystem in crisis. We urgently need to rewild. If we can extend woodland cover by a hundred thousand hectares by 2026 then we could dramatically reduce CO_2 emissions that contribute to climate change and we could provide habitats for native species. The only way to do this is to control the herbivore population, and the simplest, most effective way to do that is to reintroduce a keystone predator species that was here long before we were. The vital predation element of the ecosystem has been missing in this land for hundreds of years, since wolves were hunted to extinction. Killing the wolves was a massive blunder on our part. Ecosystems need apex predators because they elicit dynamic ecological changes that ripple down the food chain, and these are known as 'trophic cascades.' With their return the landscape will change for the better—more habitats for wildlife will be created, soil health increased, flood waters reduced, carbon emissions captured. Animals of all shapes and sizes will return to these lands."

I look around at the faces I can see; most appear somewhere between pissed off, bored, and plainly confused.

Evan continues. "Deer eat tree and plant shoots so that nothing has a chance to grow. We are overrun with deer. But wolves cull that deer population, and keep it moving, which allows for natural growth of plants and vegetation, which encourages pollinating insects and smaller mammals and rodents to return, which in turn allows the return of birds of prey, and by keeping the fox population in check the wolves also allow medium-sized animals to thrive, such as badgers and beavers. Trees can grow again, creating the air we breathe. When an ecosystem is varied, it is healthy, and everything benefits from a healthy natural ecosystem."

A man from the crowd stands. He's wearing a crisp white shirt and tie and holds his tweed flat cap in his hands. His gray handlebar mustache is a sight to behold, even from my angle. "That's all well and good for nature," he says in a deep, resonant voice, "but it's costing me land I could be grazing sheep on. Agriculture is the third-largest employer in rural Scotland. You threaten that and you threaten the entire community."

There are a few rumbles of agreement.

"It is unacceptable to me," he goes on, "that animals could be introduced that would destroy the Highlander way of life. I want to see a thriving community, I want to see glens dotted with sheep and people. People are the lifeblood of a place."

A whistle, a smattering of applause. I stare at the back of the farmer. This world he describes, empty of wild creatures and places, overrun instead by people and their agriculture, is a dying world.

"We propose that there can be both," Evan says. "Balance is paramount. I can assure you that societies cope economically with both wolves and farming, we see it all over the world."

"You've done this before," the farmer says. "You came here and convinced us it was in our best interests to reintroduce the sea eagles. I lived through that and watched those eagles eat the lambs. And now you want to add wolves on top of the eagles? You'll be the death of farming in the Highlands."

"There are methods of deterring wolf depredation," Evan says. "Guard dogs, llamas, donkeys, shepherds. Audio guard boxes emit wolf sounds to scare off any approaching wolves."

"They tried that in Norway," the farmer says. "It didn't work, not completely."

"They also tried it in America and the results have been excellent. The only reason we're even attempting this project here is because we have such a strong precedent. The reintroduction of wolves to Yellowstone National Park in America has been a staggering success. It's brought the park back to life, and there have been few negative impacts on the local people and agriculture."

"Do I need to point out that Scotland is a wee bit smaller than America?" the man asks, which causes a ripple of laughter throughout the hall.

Evan keeps his cool but I can see him growing frustrated. "But it is large enough to sustain this. Look, we have to expect a certain number of off-take by predators—it's normal! It happens all over the world. But unlike in many places, here you'll be financially compensated for your losses, which, statistical modeling tells us, are going to be extremely low anyway."

"And how will you compensate me," the farmer says, deep and slow, "for the tragedy of watching something I love, something I've spent a lifetime breeding, savagely slaughtered?"

"We're not asking you to watch that," Evan answers. "If you find a wolf attacking your livestock, you may shoot it."

There is silence at that. I don't think they were expecting it.

My eyes are drawn to the side of the auditorium, to where a man is standing by the door, the man I met by the river today but whose name I didn't learn. He's not watching Evan or the farmer, but the rest of the crowd of people, his eyes scanning each of their faces. I wonder what he is looking for among us.

"This population of wolves is small and experimental," Evan explains. "It is protected but up to a point. If you can prove the wolf was attacking your livestock then you're permitted to shoot it. You are also permitted to report it to us and we have a legal obligation to gather evidence on which wolf has done the predation and to go out and destroy it ourselves. But if you kill one for sport or simply because you've spotted it, that's punishable by fines and jail time."

"If you think I'm going to let wolves anywhere near my children then you're sorely mistaken," a woman calls out, and there are murmurs of agreement. "Will it take one of our kids getting killed before you decide the 'experiment' has failed?"

"The chance of a person getting attacked by a wolf is almost nonexistent," Evan assures them. "This is a shy, family-oriented, *gentle* creature. We should never have been taught to fear them."

"That is a lie, sir," says the farmer. "Predators are feared and hunted because they're predators—they're dangerous. My ancestors risked their lives to rid this land of those beasts and now you want to dump them back on our doorsteps. Are we expected to keep our children inside?"

Signs wave amid a lifting of angry voices. If Evan ever had control of the room he's losing it fast.

I stand. "What's dangerous," I say, "is the unwarranted spreading of fear."

The farmer turns to look at me, as do a hundred other faces. Anne's sigh of exasperation on the stage might be comical at any other time.

"If you truly think wolves are the blood spillers, then you're blind," I say. "*We* do that. We are the people killers, the children killers. *We're* the monsters."

I sit down within the silence. The cold seems to have deepened in the auditorium.

My eyes are drawn to the man by the door. He's watching me and I realize what he was searching for in the crowd because he seems to have found it in me. A disruption. A threat.

I push through the back doors and let them swing shut behind me. A sucking of air into my lungs. Trembling hands.

The others are emerging from a different set of doors and streaming toward the carpark. I lean against the cold brick of the auditorium and look up at the silver moon. I have a strange yearning for her that is as likely to disturb me as ease me. A large figure moves to block my view. I can't make out his face well, but I know he is the farmer who spoke up, the man the others allowed to speak for them. To match the impressive mustache is a set of thick, pointed eyebrows.

"Red McRae," he says, offering a hand.

I shake it. "Inti Flynn."

"My name's Ray but everyone calls me Red. I wanted to take the chance to introduce myself because mine's a name you're going to come to know well."

"Why do I get the feeling that won't be fun for me?"

Red leans forward so I can see his face under the shadow of his cap. It is weathered, leathery, might be appealing if it weren't so full of disdain. "Because if one of those wolves takes a bite out of a single one of my sheep," he says, "I will take myself and my people into that forest and I won't stop until I have hunted down every last one of them."

"Sounds like you might be looking forward to it, Red."

"Well now maybe I am."

In the following silence I take the measure of him, as he wants me to. But I see more than he might imagine. I've met him so many times I could laugh, except that I will not make the mistake of underestimating the damage an angry man can do, not again.

I straighten off the wall. "You went on in there like there's still something to be decided. It's done. The wolves are protected. You hunt them, you go to jail. I'll make sure of it."

Red tilts his cap to me and walks away.

I spot the other guy, the one from this morning, walking swiftly down the street with a pronounced limp. It is either a recent injury or a very bad one; every step causes him pain, watching causes me pain. "Hey!" I call, jogging after him.

He glances back and pauses when he recognizes me.

"How's the horse?"

"They're destroying her."

I stare at him, maybe looking for some sign that he gives a shit. I don't see it. "When?"

He looks at his watch. "Soon. Now. Might already be done."

I nod and turn for my car.

Then stop.

"Fuck," I mutter. "Where do they live?"

"What are you gonna do, girl, barrel out there and stop them yourself?"

"Sure, maybe. Where do they live."

He considers, then starts for his truck again. "You'll never find it in the dark. Come on."

The Burns farm is huge, I'm told, and there is a dirt road to reach the house and then another to the stables. That's about as much conversation as we manage in the car. That, and: "I'm Duncan MacTavish."

"Inti Flynn."

Duncan has an old two-seater truck filled with dust and cobwebs and grubby tools. We have to travel with the window down because a rat died inside the engine somewhere so it stinks, and his air system doesn't work. My nose is icy by the time we arrive. Duncan's amusement from this morning seems to have vanished. He is silent now, preoccupied.

The stables are lit from within, glowing eyes under the shadow of the mountain.

Three people are standing outside the horse's stall, and she is very much still alive, her eyes darting uneasily. I introduce myself to the Burns couple. Stuart is tall and carries a paunch that threatens to burst through the buttons of his shirt. Massive shoulders, fleshy, likable features, dusty blond hair under his flat cap. Lainey Burns is as small as her husband is large, but her grip when I shake her hand is stronger than I am expecting. The third I know already—Amelia, our vet—and she's holding a bag in which I can clearly see a syringe. They greet Duncan, who hangs back, and he tells them he is just my chauffeur, that he has no business here. "Inti's the one who rode your mare out of the ravine today."

Their interest kindles.

"Then we owe you a debt," Stuart says. "This one didn't latch the pen gate properly"—he gestures to Lainey without looking at her, and Lainey blushes—"and now we're down a mare. But at least thanks to you, Miss Flynn, we got some dog food out of it."

"That's why I'm here. There's no need to put her down."

"Amelia says the ligament in the foreleg is done for."

"That's not exactly what I said, Stuart," Amelia corrects. "I said it's torn."

"She can't be ridden, correct?"

"Not for a good while."

"Would she recover with rest and rehab?" I ask.

"Maybe," Amelia says. "She'll likely never run, or carry much load, and her emotional damage might mean she can never be ridden at all . . ."

"I'm sorry to say it," Stuart says, and he does indeed sound sorry, "but we don't have the time or the manpower to rehab a horse that may or may not ever work for us. Now if you'll excuse us, love, we'd best put the poor beast out of her misery."

My pulse is a whitewater rapid, rushing and uneven and filling my ears so I can't think straight.

Stuart is moving to the stable, Amelia reluctantly following. Lainey turns away, not wanting to watch, unwilling to argue.

"I'll buy her," I say.

"What's that, love?"

"How much do you want for her?"

"You want to buy an unusable horse?"

"Yes."

"Why?"

Because fuck all of you, that's why.

When I don't answer, Stuart looks to Lainey, then Duncan, and there's something suspicious in his gaze, like he thinks maybe he's missing something. But he shrugs. "Three thousand."

Amelia bursts out laughing. "Come on, Stuart."

He doesn't take his eyes off me and I realize he is much shrewder than he seems. "That's a prize mustang there, and I put a lot of time into her breaking."

Good job he did of it, too.

"And she's useless to you," Amelia reminds him. "To anyone."

"Doesn't make her worthless," he says. Because he can see I want her.

"One thousand," I say.

He turns back to the stable, motioning for Amelia.

"Fine. Three."

Stuart smiles and offers to shake my hand again. I don't have three thousand pounds. I shake anyway.

"I'll be out to pick her up in the morning."

"Lainey and I'll have coffee and cake waiting for you," he says cheerfully, as though he has not just swindled me outrageously. Lainey has nothing even close to a smile on her lips. I thought she'd be relieved and it disconcerts me.

"Everyone happy, then? Stuart?" Duncan asks.

"Over the moon," the big farmer replies.

"Lainey, you all right there, love?"

"Yes, thank you," she replies and there is her smile, radiant and sudden, and it strikes me that she's good at smiling when she doesn't want to. "If I hadn't been such an idiot we wouldn't be in this mess."

"No mess," I say.

"I've left pen gates unlocked a thousand times," Amelia says. "Everyone does it."

"Not on this farm we don't, do we?" Stuart asks his wife.

Lainey shakes her head.

We bid them farewell and walk to the cars, boots crunching. Infinite stars above.

"I'll be out to see you tomorrow," Amelia tells me.

"Cheers."

"How they looking?"

"Six and Nine have mated."

She lets out a whoop that scares the crap out of me, and then we both laugh before she waves goodnight and drives off.

Duncan and I climb into his truck, following Stuart and Lainey up the dirt path to their house. They disappear inside as we drive past. But instead of carrying on, Duncan stops the truck and turns off the engine and lights.

"What are we doing?"

He doesn't reply, just settles himself in as though for a stakeout.

It's confounding.

Until it's not.

Because there is a way of being that whispers fear and there is a way of being that has the hard edge of anger in it, and I saw both of those tonight. Since Alaska I have felt them both more than the breaths I've taken.

"Is she in danger?" I ask.

Duncan says nothing.

"If he sees us it'll make it worse."

When I am met with silence I say, "I'm going in."

My hand on the seat belt, his hand on mine. I search his face for some answer. Why wait here if we intend to do nothing? We sit silently in the dark for a long while anyway. I strain to hear sounds from the house and fail. It isn't until the lights are swallowed that we assume the couple has gone to bed and it's safe to leave. But all I can think is that they will hear the engine start up again, see the headlights, know we were lurking out here. It will embarrass Stuart that we were here.

My hands move, signing. *Turn around, go back.*

But Duncan doesn't know this silent language. "What's that?"

"Nothing."

I promised never to do this again, to bite my tongue. To sit still.

Duncan drops me at my car in town. The stench of the rat has started to nauseate me and I'm relieved to climb out.

"I live a little way down the road from you," he tells me. "In fact I'm your only neighbor, in case you need anything."

"Thanks." I can't help thinking it's a creepy way of putting it. "You headed home?"

"I'll pop into work for an hour or two." His gaze has already turned away, his mind on the night ahead.

"What's your work?" I ask.

"Police chief."

My mouth falls open. Then I laugh. "'Course you are."

He smiles. "You wanna report that numpty from this morning?"

I nod. "Tell him there are precious things hiding beneath the snow. It's easy to forget they're there."

He inclines his head. "Aye, I'll do that then."

I'm about to hop in my car when I pause. "So then why didn't you— with Stuart . . . ?"

"Arrest him?"

I nod.

"For what?"

In the morning when I return for the horse, the farmhand is the only one there to greet me because Lainey has had an accident and been taken to hospital.

4

When we were twelve Mum occasionally started taking us to watch the court cases she was called to testify in. When they got bad we would wriggle down onto the floor and have entire silent conversations with each other, dictated usually by the signs Aggie had made up most recently. She was building us a vocabulary, an entire language spoken with our hands. When she made up the sign for "dragonfly" we had silent discussions about how many we could legitimately catch and what colors they would be and how it was likely one day scientists would work out how to grow them to a rideable size. When she made up the sign for "universe" we considered what that contained and after placing just the two of us within it we decided that was enough for one universe. When she made up the sign for "sex," which was a rather crass index finger poking through the hole of her opposite index and thumb, I pointed out that that sign already existed and we both cracked up laughing so much we got scolded by the judge and then in deep shit with Mum when we got home. But honestly—what did she expect? Why did she keep bringing us here to witness the absolute worst in people?

I knew why, actually, if I admitted it. Because she was trying to break me. To make me admit that she was right. That people were, for the most part, irredeemable. And that if I didn't toughen up I would become one of the people in those stands, telling a judge what had been done to me.

But on this I would not be broken. I had a magic power that wasn't magic. I felt what other people felt, and I knew what lived in those touches and how it was mostly sweetness. You didn't touch sweetly unless you were good.

One night on the way home from court we rode in the back seat of her partner's cop car. This was Aggie's favorite thing in the world, pretending to be apprehended criminals and trying to wise-talk her way out of custody. Mum's partner was a guy called Jim Owens who was sort of handsome but also chunky enough to be reasonably called fat and had been obviously in love with her our whole lives. He always bought us ice creams. We liked Jim. I think maybe we even loved Jim. Mum tolerated him. I couldn't imagine what she would look like in love.

But even Jim's dumb jokes couldn't distract me today. "Why'd that woman—Tara—why was she trying to get her kids away from their dad?" I asked.

Don't ask, Aggie signs.

"You'll see that bit tomorrow," Mum said.

"Can't you tell me now?"

She'll just try to scare you, Aggie signs. She rolls her eyes, too, and it catches Mum's gaze in the rearview.

"Words," she warns Aggie. Then to me she says, "Because he's been abusing them."

"His kids?"

Mum nodded.

"No," I said. "I don't believe you."

"Okay."

I shook my head. "Why would he do that?"

"Because he's sick, darlin'," Jim said.

"No he's not," Mum said. "Don't teach her that. He's a cunt, that's why."

The air in the back of the car turned very hot. I went to wind down the window and remembered I couldn't, they were locked shut.

Aggie arranged her hands into a diamond shape. "This can be the sign for cunt."

The rest of us froze. And then dissolved into laughter. Aggie was good at breaking any tension.

"I hope that's the last time I ever hear you say that word, little lady," Jim said, which didn't carry much weight because he was still chuckling.

After a while, though, I couldn't stop wondering. "Why do you hate people so much, Mum?"

"I don't hate them. I'm a realist."

"Dad says caring for each other is the only way to care for ourselves and that kindness will save the world."

Mum snorted with laughter. "You mean the madman who lives out in the wilderness alone and doesn't have contact with other humans? That Dad?" I watched her shake her head and look out the window. "I've cared for more people in a day than that man will in his whole sorry life."

"You don't care much for us," Aggie said.

Mum's body went stiff. Aggie had no filter. I wanted to catch the words and stuff them back in her mouth because I knew that even though Mum acted like nothing mattered to her she still had feelings, she still got hurt. She still spent her whole life trying to help people.

But I couldn't unsay my sister's words, and eventually Mum just said, "Call me when your husband beats you or your children nearly to death."

I drive to the hospital. I don't know why. It's none of my business but here I am and in I go. A receptionist points me in the right direction. At the end of a long hallway stands Duncan MacTavish. He's gazing through a window. I walk to stand beside him. And see.

Stuart is sitting next to the bed, holding his wife's hand. She only has one hand to hold because the other is in a cast and she doesn't even look like Lainey anymore: one entire side of her face is swollen so badly that her eye has disappeared in a pulp of blue and black, and the tissue around my own eye begins to tingle and swell and I lose the vision in it, it slips away, leaving me half shrouded in dark, half still looking at the cut on her scalp, the cut that begins to throb along my hairline, still tender from the six stitches they sewed into my flesh—

I spin away and press my spine to the wall. Here. Here is your body. I re-center myself, I return, let the sensations tingle and fade, slow my gulping lungs. Not your pain. Not your body. A trick.

"Hey," Duncan says.

I open my eyes, vision clear once more.

"You okay?"

I nod. The pain never lingers but the adrenaline does. The vigilance. The exhaustion.

"What did he say happened to her?"

"Thrown from a horse."

"Did she say what really happened?"

"She hasn't woken." He looks at me. "She won't."

"She won't wake?"

"She won't *talk*. She won't say what happened. She never does."

"So then what are you gonna do about it?"

He shrugs, turning back to the hospital room. "She breaks in mustangs for a living," he says. "She does fall. Everyone does sometimes."

"You and I sat there in that car and we didn't do anything. We let this happen."

He meets my eyes and says, "She might have fallen."

I turn on my heel and stride away so I won't put my fist through a window. I need to find someone to ask, to corroborate, except that I don't need that because if I find out he really does beat her up I'm going to want to kill him.

Dad used to tell me that my greatest gift was that I could get inside the skin of another human. That I could feel what nobody else could, the life of another, really feel it and roll around in it. That the body knows a great deal and I have the miraculous ability to know more than one body. The astonishing cleverness of nature. He also taught us that compassion was the most important thing we could learn. If someone hurt us, we needed only empathy, and forgiveness would be easy.

My mother never agreed. She had no kindred ocean of kindness inside her, no forgiveness. She had a different knowledge of what people do to each other. I shied from it. It felt rough and hard and those were not the instincts I was born with. I chose to live by my dad's code, and it was easy until it wasn't.

It's obvious now, and has been for a while. Mum was right, she was so fucking right I am embarrassed, and now I have had enough, I have no more forgiveness left.

⊗

The deer carcass is heavy. It drops from my hands with a meaty thud. The wolves of the southernmost Glenshee Pack don't rush to it, they remain at the far end of their enclosure, huddled against the fence. All but one. Number Ten is not the breeding female of her pack, meaning not their leader, or, in outdated terms, their alpha. That title belongs to her sister, Number Eight. But Ten has something that sets her apart. A restlessness. She is more aggressive, less willing to be caged. She has been trying to dig free, the only wolf to attempt escape. She alone crosses the pen to me and never in all my years working with wolves has one of them done this: she meets my eyes, bares her teeth, and *growls*.

The hairs on my neck prickle because this doesn't happen, it really doesn't. She is sleek and lean. Her coat is shades of browns and whites, a deep orange brown along her flanks, with lighter scruff around her face, almost golden, or Werner's orpiment orange. Her teeth are very sharp; this is what she wants me to know.

My boss at the Denali Wolf Project in Alaska warned me on my first day on the job. *Don't fool yourself into thinking you can predict a wolf. That's dangerous. She will always surprise you.*

A deep thrill electrifies me. I love her ferocity. I can feel it in my throat, tickling there. Adrenaline floods me and she can smell it, I know she can.

The deer carcass is delivered, there's no need for me to stay.

I want to.

I see it now. How I turn to run and she launches for my thigh, tears my femoral, destroys any chance of escape. So I remain facing her and instead she lunges for my throat, for the part of me most vulnerable. The strength in her body lets her fly, the power in her jaws crushes my bones. I am such a simple meal; I have no speed with which to run, no strength to fight her off. My skin is disastrously thin. Does she know this about me? Can she sense it, as the others of her kind don't seem to? They are fooled by the power in our voices and our weapons, by our ability to cage them. But this one seems to see beyond that, to my fragility. Or perhaps she doesn't, maybe she doesn't care that I have a power she doesn't, so immense is her fury, her fighting instinct.

I keep my eyes on her as I back out of the pen. Still she doesn't move, doesn't rush to devour the carcass like the other five wolves in her pack. She continues to watch me.

From behind the chain links I finally see her join her pack. There is still warmth in the carcass, and this fills her mouth, my mouth. Our teeth make easy work of the flesh. I am overwhelmed by the acrid iron of blood. I have been worried that they might not take to the meat because it smells of humans, but clearly hunger has won out. My own hunger has come awake and it disturbs me. I turn away from the feast.

After work I return to the Burns ranch with a hired float and a thousand cash. Nobody comes to meet me so I start loading the horse myself. She is skittish and doesn't want to be bridled. I almost get kicked when I try to lead her by the bit. I just need to get her home and into the front paddock where she can relax and eat and do whatever she wants, but her distress is upsetting me and it's with a measure of relief that I hear a shout from the driveway. Stuart jogs over to grab the reins, pulling the poor beast roughly into the float and closing her in. I stroke her but she jerks at the touch and tries to escape me. *Easy, girl. Easy.*

"Not just her leg that got broken," Stuart says.

"Maybe if you were gentler with her," I say. I look up to where he's parked his car and see Lainey climbing unsteadily out.

"Shouldn't she be in hospital?" I ask.

"Best place to rest is in her own bed," Stuart says. "Follow me in, Miss Flynn, I'll get Lainey settled and we can see to our business."

Inside it's cooler than I expected. I can see down the hallway, through the open bedroom door to where he is easing Lainey into bed. She's woozy and sore, but smiles at him reassuringly. I watch as he perches beside her, strokes her face, kisses the inside of her palm. I clench my hand into a fist so as not to feel his lips.

In the kitchen I fill the kettle.

"Thank you," Stuart says as we wait for the water to boil.

"I left a thousand pounds in her stall."

"I thought we agreed on three."

"We did. I wanted to ask if you could give me some time to scrape together the rest."

"Of course, love." He takes over from me, placing teabags in three mugs and pouring the water on top. He dumps four sugars into his. "To be honest it couldn't come at a better time," he admits.

"Duncan said Lainey was thrown from her horse?"

"She can break the worst of them, my Lainey, but we all get thrown sometimes." Without warning Stuart starts to cry, a choked sort of sound.

I swallow and look away, and then I stop looking away because that's what I did last night. I make myself watch his shoulders jerk and I feel no pity whatsoever. I see myself crossing the space and smashing my mug into the back of his skull while he is turned away and vulnerable. I don't know if this is a desire or just a passing thought. Saliva fills my mouth and I think very loudly, *What is wrong with you, what have you become*.

"I'll take this in to her," I say, and the voice that comes from my mouth is so hard it's the voice of a stranger.

Lainey looks at me with her one good eye as I place her tea on the bed-side table. Probably wondering what the hell I'm doing in her bedroom.

"Do you want some light?"

She nods, so I cross to the window and open the robin-covered curtains. Sunlight falls over half the room.

"You look pretty," I say, which makes her giggle and wince.

"Don't make me laugh. You came for Gealaich?"

I nod. "Say her name again?"

She says a word that sounds like *gee-a-lash*.

"I can't even say that. I might just call her Gall."

This makes her laugh again. I think she might be a bit high. "Sorry he charged you so much," Lainey says.

I shrug.

"We're struggling. These hills die off a little more each year. There isn't much for the herd to graze on."

"How long have you been here?"

"This is my pa's farm. It's been in my family for generations."

"Cattle and horses, right? I haven't seen many horses since I've been here."

"No, it's mostly sheep around here."

"Was Stuart a farmer before he met you?"

"God no. He didn't know a thing about it, but he took to it all right, despite it not being his . . . speed. I'm grateful for that."

"You never thought about a different life?"

"Where would I go?"

"The world's big."

She shakes her head. "I love it here. It's my home."

"It's beautiful country."

"The forest is where I love best," she says, a little dreamy, definitely a little doped. "All that breathing."

I smile. "I used to think I belonged to a forest family and it was raising me."

She laughs, then stops when it hurts her face. "I love that," she says. "I can feel that. Can I tell you a secret?"

"Yes."

"I'm glad you're here to save the trees. Don't tell my husband."

"I'm not saving anything. The wolves will do that."

"You'll never win them over," she says, a sigh. "The others. It's too deep in them."

I sit down on the end of her bed. "When the wolves begin to hunt the deer, the deer will return to what deer are meant to do, they'll start to move again. Everything underfoot will have a chance to grow. Life breathed back into the land. You'll see your hills turn green. The shape of the earth will begin to change." I meet her swollen eye and ignore the tingling of mine. "I've seen wolves change the course of rivers."

She smiles. "Then maybe they've got a chance here after all. Maybe they'll survive."

"Maybe. If you ever need somewhere to stay, you're welcome at my place. It's safe."

She looks confused. "I have a home. You're in it."

I nod.

Her confusion clears and the softness in her that was enjoying this, us, turns brittle. "I need to sleep now."

"Sure, sorry." I stand and head for the door. "Feel better, Lainey."

"Thank you."

Stuart is waiting for me outside the door. "She has everything she needs here," he tells me. "I've taken care of my wife since the day I met her."

I consider replying but find I can't. I walk for the door. Under the sky I can breathe again.

5

There are languages without words and violence is one of them.

As a teenager Aggie was already a language genius. She spoke four fluently and was learning several more. But it was not only spoken languages that she understood; Aggie knew, too, that there were some that did not need voices. By the time we were ten there was the sign language she'd invented so we could communicate privately. She'd built a world for the two of us to live within and we would each be perfectly happy never to leave it. When we were sixteen she started learning the language of violence; she broke a boy's nose, and she did it for me, as most of the things she did were for me.

"'You taught me language, and my profit on't / Is I know how to curse,'" I read aloud one sunny afternoon in the school grounds. "'The red plague rid you / For learning me your language.'" I looked up at Aggie, baffled. "What the hell does that mean?"

She sighed and flopped onto the grass, shielding her face from the sun. Her cheeks were pink; I looked at them and felt the gentle burn on my skin; I looked at her head pressed to the ground and felt the itchy blades of grass on my neck.

"Caliban was wild, and they tried to tame him, and he hates them for it."

I reread the passage and had no idea how she managed to get that. But as I sank back onto my elbows beside her I thought I understood. It took me to Dad's yard and the hooves and the snorts and the knowing those mustangs would rather be free, however much they might have loved my father.

"Maybe if we did something without so many made-up words . . ."

"All words are made up," she said, which was a good point. "Let me be Caliban." Aggie snatched the heavy book from me and jumped to her feet. With a theatrical flourish she called out the passage, loudly and ferociously, not caring that most of the kids in our vicinity turned to stare.

"'The red plague rid you!'" Aggie snarled, like a witch's curse.

I laughed. "Your natural savagery is finally appropriate."

Daniel Mulligan and his friends were under the trees in a cluster, talking in hushed tones, no doubt concocting some prank to humiliate their next victim. I felt their uniforms on their skin, the stiff itchiness, the ever-present desire to rip that fabric off in exchange for their normal clothes. One boy broke away to juggle a soccer ball; I could feel the *thud thud thud* of it against the top of his foot. Behind us girls were playing netball on the court, their tread on the cement quick, skidding, a little jarring on my ankles, while to our left there were girls braiding each other's hair and the slip of this through my fingers was silken. I was lifted away by all this sensation, carried somewhere bright and vivid, and also somehow centered more firmly in my body.

Aggie was watching me. "What does it feel like today?"

"It's like electricity," I offered, even though it wasn't quite right. It was gentler than that. I took her hand, wanting to pass the sensations through me and into her, wanting to share them as we shared everything else. "Here," I said, willing her to feel it. "Take it from me."

She clasped my hand and peered around at the other kids, at the world of sensations. But it didn't work like that, it never had and no amount of yearning for it would help. She sighed in frustration.

My eyes were pulled back to Daniel and his friends gathered beneath the weeping willow, because one of them was staring at us, at me. John Allen, the quiet one, who looked directly at me and, very deliberately, touched himself. I don't have a dick but it rushed through me anyway, as he knew it would, the feeling of being touched between my legs, and I was filled with heat, heat that flushed my body and cheeks, and this was very different, this was not gentle, it was shame.

"Inti? What?" Aggie asked.

I hunched over, wishing the feeling away, sickened by it. I wanted to tear myself from my own body and never return to it. I could hear the boys laughing.

"What did he do?" Aggie demanded, but I wasn't about to say it. So she signed, *Don't look,* and got to her feet and marched over to the boys and without warning she swung the collected works of William Shakespeare into John's face. *Whoomph.*

I knew better, but I looked anyway. I saw the impact of those words— and there were a lot of words—on John's nose, which meant my nose, and then I was boneless, sinking, gone.

Gold and green swelled above, sharp pricks of light and woozy orbs of color. Slowly the leaves of the trees took their shape once more and I returned to myself. Aggie was looking down at me. *You broke my nose,* I signed, and she replied, *I told you not to look,* and then neither of us could stop laughing.

Aggie was expelled from school for the third time in as many years and Mum cracked the shits and sent us to live at Dad's place—which for me was about as far from a punishment as I could imagine. Mum said it was Dad's turn to deal with us but secretly I knew she liked that Aggie was so feisty, so quick to fight. It was me she didn't know how to handle, me who was too soft and vulnerable. It frightened her that I didn't know how to protect myself, because what kind of creature is born without this instinct?

Our arrival in British Columbia wasn't what I expected. It was the tools in his shed that alerted me first. All our lives he had lovingly cleaned and treated and sharpened them, he'd spent hours out there, lost in the meditation of it, because the thought of allowing something to rust when it could be maintained was not only wasteful, but disrespectful to the tool that fed and sustained. That morning in the shed I was hit with the familiar smell of blood and fur and sawdust and grease. The acrid stickiness of it felt like coming home. But when I saw the instruments of Dad's life scattered all over the benches instead of neatly hanging from the wall in their respective spots, when I saw the state of the blades, the blood that had been left to stain and rust the steel, the oil spills that hadn't been cleaned up, the animal carcasses left to rot instead of tenderly treated and stored, I didn't feel at home, I felt scared.

The house, too, was a mess. Aggie plunged into a mountain of washing up so I put on several loads of clothes and started tidying the chaos in the living room. Dad was using it as a kind of recycling center, with wavering pillars of cardboard and paper and empty bottles. He used to take all of his recycling into town to the plants, but when I asked him why he hadn't done it in so long he said he didn't trust that they weren't just throwing it in a landfill. "Well," I said, "I guess that could be true. But you still gotta take it somewhere or you'll drown in it."

"Nowhere to take it. They gotta stop making it."

"Yeah, but . . ." I didn't know what to say.

I spent three days in the shed using steel wool and a can of WD-40 to clean the rust off each and every one of his tools, from the carving knives to the wrenches to the hundreds of tiny screwdriver heads. The pads of my fingers were scraped raw.

While I tended to the shed, Aggie gave all the stabled horses a long ride to stretch their legs. I went with her on the last and we discovered that what had once been forest was now wasteland. The loggers had been. They'd felled in great swathes, right up to the edge of Dad's property, and looking out at the stumps I recalled viscerally the feeling I had when Dad showed us the lone Doug fir. I wondered if this was what he felt all the time now, that hurt, so much that it paralyzed him. Or if it was the memory of the things he himself had torn down.

Aggie and I left the horses to graze and lay with our backs flat on two of the tree stumps. They were wide enough that I could press both my head and feet to the years of rings; if I counted those rings there would be hundreds upon hundreds. It was a giant, this tree. Aggie scared me by letting out a furious yell, a sound flung up to the sky, one filled with all the grief in my chest. That we should be so powerless. That this was the end of our forest family, that it was gone now. For the first time I lifted my voice and yelled with her.

———————

We made spaghetti Bolognese with frozen venison from Dad's storeroom. As I retrieved it I realized it was one of the last packs. The cupboards were pretty bare, too, no pickled or stewed fruits, no fresh vegetables from the garden. It took an enormous amount of work to live a subsistence life and when one thread came loose the rest followed and suddenly the life you'd created unraveled.

"When was the last time you went hunting, Dad?" I asked as we sat down to eat. My finger was throbbing around a splinter I got while chopping firewood, but at least there was a roaring fire to keep us warm.

"Last week. Got a nice big buck."

"Where is it?"

He looked at me like I was mad. "You forgotten everything I taught you already? It's where it always is, drying in the scullery. You can help me butcher it."

"There's nothing there, Dad."

He frowned, pondering this equation, then shrugged. "Must have been more than a week ago then."

Aggie and I shared a look.

"We'll have to go to town," she said. "Do a proper shop, stock up."

"There's plenty of food here," Dad said.

"You've eaten it all, Dad."

"Where do you look for sustenance?" he asked.

Aggie sighed. "In your backyard."

"There's a garden out there full of vegetables. And a forest full of animals."

"It's the end of winter," Aggie said. "The garden's mostly empty."

"And we can't hunt," I added. "We don't even eat meat at home."

"I wouldn't either if it was bought from some sunless metal cage and pumped full of antibiotics," he said. "Look, girls. We have to do our bit to slow the changing of our planet's climate, to halt its degradation. That means reducing our impact as much as we can, living as lightly upon this Earth as we're able. We're not here to consume until everything's gone—we are custodians, not owners. And if others won't do their part in turning the tide then we must do more than our share. You know this."

We nodded because we did know it, and there was comfort in hearing the words he'd raised us on, but that truth didn't stop him from being a changed man. If anything, the fact that he still believed so passionately in the things he always had was an indication that he was unable to keep his subsistence lifestyle going, not that he was unwilling.

A few days later Aggie and I started on the garden.

"What's wrong with him?" she asked as we turned the earth over and buried potato seedlings.

"I dunno. We might have to take him to a doctor."

She scoffed. "How are we gonna do that? Handcuff and blindfold him?"

She was right. When I suggested it he ignored me. And when Aggie drove an hour to town and bought a whole stack of freezable meals, including a mountain of beef mince, jars of pickled vegetables, and long-life milk, he ordered her flatly to take it all back to the shop and get her money back. He wouldn't have her supporting industry, didn't we know how much carbon those purchases alone produced? He wouldn't even touch it, let alone eat it. This is how the world dies, he said, with laziness.

And it seemed to me that what was once the wisdom of a man courageous enough to see another path was now turning slowly toward madness.

He did, however, understand the need for food, despite all his distractions. So he began to teach us how to track and hunt, calling on the lessons we'd had when much younger. He had never expected Aggie to make the kills then, but now he did. I was the better tracker and she the one able to pull the trigger. We made a good team, Dad said. We took the bus forty minutes to school and forty minutes home, and then he would take us into the forest to spend hours waiting and watching, or slinking through the underbrush as silently as we were able. He quizzed us on the signs various animals left, on what their prints and their scat looked like, on their behavioral patterns. He took it more seriously than any teacher we'd ever had. It was like he knew we needed preparing.

On a cold day some months later, I was alone in the woods to collect the fungi that grew at the base of a big red cedar. Its trunk had gnarled roots that made a comfortable nook for sitting, and from here, even though I was in a bit of a hurry, I could lie back and watch the light flicker through the canopy of its needles.

A flurry of blue wings signaled the arrival of a bird on a low-hanging branch.

"Hello," I said, and it gave no sign it noticed me. It had a dark crested head; I would have to ask Dad what its name was.

Something drew my attention. A mark in the dirt, not far from the mushrooms I was picking. A paw print, unlike the tracks made by passing deer. I'd never seen its like, and stood to inspect it. I searched for more, hoping to follow them, but found no others.

At home I dropped the mushrooms into their box and went to find Dad in the garden. He was sitting in a slice of sun, watching his horses in the valley below.

"I have a question, Dad," I said as I sat beside him.

"I hope you have more than one, always."

"I think I found an animal print, but it didn't look like deer."

"How big was it?"

"Too small for a bear, but quite big. About . . ." I made a shape with my fingers. "A paw, I think. And it was the only one, like it just disappeared."

Dad smiled. "You found yourself a wolf print, Inti-loo. About as rare as they come."

"A wolf?" A thrill ran through me. Only twice in my life had I caught a glimpse of a wolf, and both times had been many years ago when I was a child. I'd almost started to believe I'd dreamt those moments. "Can you help me follow it?"

He shook his head. "Can't track wolves, not really."

"Then how do you find them?"

"You don't. You leave them be."

I slumped, disappointed.

He watched me sideways. "All right then, I'll tell you a secret. But you must use it for good. Do you promise?"

"Yes."

"There is no tracking a wolf," Dad said. "They are cleverer than we are. So instead you track its prey."

We grinned at each other.

I couldn't stop thinking about that solitary paw print. "How'd it move with no tracks like that?"

"The infinite mystery of wolves," Dad replied, and I decided then that I would discover the creature's secrets.

6

They don't explode free. They don't run.

The snow is melting; winter has ended. But our wolves don't seem to want to leave their cages.

The Cairngorms Wolf Project was only ever agreed to because we had such a successful precedent. It's what we base some of our decisions on, not all. It's how I know to expect this. The wolves in Yellowstone didn't rush from their cages either. And we were able to learn from them.

So we had gates built on both sides of the pens and we have only ever entered through one of them, leaving the second gate free of our scents. These are the gates we open now, remotely, after having tied deer carcasses to trees beyond the thresholds to draw them out. But still the wolves don't leave.

Be patient, I tell my team. They will.

On day two of the gates being open a single wolf pads from her cage, scents the air, and then runs north. Number Ten, fiercer than the rest.

She is running home, unaware that no home waits for her. Only livestock and those who raise livestock, who may well prove deadly to her. Beyond them, an uncrossable ocean.

I wonder if we will ever see her again.

Days pass and no movement from the others, not from Ten's abandoned Glenshee Pack to the south, or from the Tanar Pack to the east or the northwestern-based Abernethy Pack, made up of newly mated Six and Nine and her yearling daughter, Thirteen. The wolves sit and watch and wait, certainly more patient than we are.

On day five Evan and Niels are in a panic, pacing the base camp and endlessly debating what to do. Have the wolves marked their territories within the pens? Is that why they refuse to leave? This would be a disaster.

Be patient, I say.

On day six the remaining five members of the Glenshee Pack follow their missing sister, Number Ten, who is long gone by now. They are led not by their two alphas, male Number Seven and female Number Eight, but by the old silver wolf, Number Fourteen, who is ten years old and geriatric in wolf lifespans. The world is hard on wolves; if they don't die by illness or starvation, if they are not killed in fights with other packs or in some disastrous accident, they are shot by humans. It seems their lot in life is to die young, for seldom do they reach old age. This silver male is a rare creature. Perhaps he is braver than the rest, his long life lending him more experience. Perhaps he simply knows when to move and when to stay; maybe that's what's kept him alive so long. Either way, something has spoken to him, some call of the forest, and his family trust in it. They trickle out of the pen behind him and go straight past the deer carcass we left for them, flowing into the smattering of trees. It is bleak terrain down there to the south where we have placed them, few trees, but then wolves don't need forests, they grow them. The pack's yearling male pup, Number Twelve, heads off in a different direction. It's possible he will meet up with his pack again, or he may have left them for good, parting ways with his family to find a mate and start a pack of his own.

On the following day, as though it has been arranged between them, the Tanar Pack also make a move. Its alphas, female Number One and male Number Two, our only black wolf, lead their three nearly adult pups out of the pen and into their stretch of forest.

Which leaves only the three wolves of Abernethy, a week after being offered freedom and still refusing to take it.

I walk in the front door of Blue Cottage to find Aggie cooking in the kitchen, and when she smiles at me I almost start crying. She has returned to her body. She is here with me and I can breathe again.

After dinner she signs, *They don't know what's out there. Why would they leave?*

"Because," I tell her, "movement is natural. It's survival."

You moved them. What's natural about that?

I don't have an answer so I give her the finger, which makes her laugh silently. I really miss the sound of her laugh. I think I miss it more than anything. Although Aggie has always been prone to bouts of silence—she didn't say her first word until she was four years old because she didn't need to, I understood exactly what she wanted and asked for it on her behalf—this is the longest. Sometimes I think she will never speak again. Her sign language, at this point, is mostly ASL, but still has some of her own signs peppered throughout, because she likes holding on to our old twin language, likes the thought of returning us to our little universe.

Mum phones, as she does every week. She doesn't know the whole truth of what happened in Alaska. I think it would break her, knowing. And maybe even vindicate her (which is a graceless, cruel thought). She doesn't know why I never put Aggie on the phone, but Mum told me last week that I sound more like my sister each time we speak. Brash, defiant, fierce. I didn't know how to feel about that. Sometimes I think Aggie and I must have switched places and forgotten to switch back.

"How's it going?" Mum asks now.

"Not too bad. Two packs out of three have left their pens."

"Bet the locals love that. They been giving you any trouble?"

"No," I lie. "They've been nice."

"Right. Let's see what they are when their lambs start getting eaten."

"Don't look forward to that too much, Mum."

"Ha. You're funnier than you used to be."

"Thanks," I mutter.

"Where's your sister? I don't have long—I'm on a case."

"What terrible crime are you solving at the moment?"

"You don't want to know, sweet girl."

"Aggie's teaching French to kids in town," I tell her as I watch Aggie do the dishes.

"Fine, *au revoir,* give her a kiss from me." Before we hang up Mum asks, "What about the third pack. Why haven't they left their pen?"

"I don't know."

Mum answers her own question with certainty. "'Course you do. It's 'cause they're sharper than the rest. More awake to the threat of what awaits them."

"There's no threat out there."

Mum just laughs and hangs up.

On day eight Evan, Niels, Amelia, and I hike to the Abernethy Pack. We need eyes on the wolves; they may be unwell. It could be that we need to use our jab sticks to scare them from the pen. We may just need to leave them alone, but we won't know until we see them properly.

Evan and Niels debate the next move while we walk. Their voices grate at me, disturbing the peace of the spring forest. Wildflowers have begun to poke through the frost. Leaves are returning to branches. Trees shake off the winter and turn toward the sun.

I stop.

The scent, maybe. Is my nose sharp enough for that? Or is it my instincts that sense it?

The others stop behind me, falling quiet.

I look up to the crest of a ridge. Beyond it lies the pen. But atop it is the striking figure of a creature in profile: Number Nine, surveying the landscape of which he is now king.

"Fuck," Evan whispers, reverent. Amelia gasps. It's one thing to touch an unconscious wolf, another to see one in a pen, another thing entirely to see one in the wild, and this close, this in charge of his dominion. It is a deep punch to the gut, a tugging on that primal part of us all. He is at once still and full of movement; the wind in his fur makes it glint. I wish Aggie were here with me; it feels wrong to experience this without her.

We retreat, leaving Nine to explore the forest his Abernethy Pack was named after. As of today the wolves have all walked free into the Cairngorms. They've been given a home in Scotland once more but time will tell if that home intends to nurture or destroy them.

To celebrate, the pub.

I met both Evan and Niels when the three of us worked with the Alaskan wolves in Denali National Park. Back then we and the other biologists socialized a lot; it was part and parcel of the job to go for a few beers each night. There's a remoteness to that land that encourages a seeking of each other, and it was the first time I'd really spent with other wolf biologists. We are a particular breed, it's true. Restless and physical, we like to be outdoors instead of behind desks or in labs. I was enamored with the group of us, with the animals and the work and the world. So it had been an easy call for me to recruit both Evan and Niels when I took on the Cairngorms Project: it makes sense to work with people you know, whose attitudes and philosophies align.

Now I would give anything to have hired strangers. Evan and Niels expect the beers after work each night and don't understand why I can't, they don't understand why I am so at odds with the woman I once was.

Alas, tonight there's no excuse.

The Snow Goose is dark and earthy, and as my eyes adjust, I am met with animals. A stag head gazing sightlessly at me from above the bar. Beside it, an array of smaller deer, on another wall a badger, an eagle, a fox. The air hangs thick with their musk, although I may be imagining that. They are everywhere, pulling my focus from the big stone fireplaces, the crooked wooden tables and cast-iron chandeliers. Off the main space sprout secret rooms and corners with low leather couches, all of them full of people. The watering hole, I'm told, for the entire region. I force my gaze from the taxidermy, unnerved.

In a far corner booth sit Red McRae, Mayor Oakes and Stuart Burns. Stuart looks more robust and friendly than ever. We head to a booth on the opposite side of the pub, but I sit so I can watch him. Ways to kill a person: slipping something in his drink, tampering with his brakes, driving him off an icy road, following him into the night and bludgeoning him . . .

"Inti?"

I blink and look at Zoe. "What?"

"What do you want to drink?" she repeats slowly.

"Anything."

I spot Duncan sitting at the bar with Amelia and her wife Holly. He is wearing a thick red jumper, clearly hand-knitted and sporting several holes. I wonder who knitted it for him, a partner, maybe. He laughs at whatever Holly is saying and my eyes slide swiftly away from him, hoping he doesn't spot me. Red McRae shows up at our table with a jug of beer. He places it roughly enough to slop onto the sticky wood. "Congratulations are in order, I hear."

There's an awkward silence.

"Thanks," Evan says.

Stuart is right behind Red, placing a calming hand on his shoulder.

"Drink this now, while there's anything left to drink to," Red says, sounding a little drunk. "'Cause soon enough it'll be murder and mayhem that rule this place."

"At least we're not being melodramatic about it," I say.

"I hope you think it's funny when retribution comes knocking on your door," he tells me.

"You're *threatening* us?" Zoe asks.

Red laughs.

"No threats here," Stuart says, and he is so friendly, so appeasing that it makes my skin crawl.

"No point threatening animals," Red agrees. "Not how nature works. You got a problem with one of them," and here he looks straight at me, "only thing to do is to show your animal who's stronger."

I smile; I can't help it. Because he amuses me, and he makes me nervous. I lift the entire jug of beer to my lips and take a long gulp to calm myself. "Cheers," I say. Then I slide from the booth and stand because I can't put up with them towering over me like this, I need to at least be on my feet. "If it's a conversation about strength you wanna have, we can do that." With this I look at Stuart. His neck turns splotchy and I know

I have unsettled him. In this moment I am so angry with him that it can no longer be contained in my body. The remembered feel of his wife's injuries, and the knowing deep in my body of how frightened she feels, all the time. For better or worse, I must speak. "Anyone here," I ask, holding his eyes, "think it's a strong man who beats his wife?"

A hush sucks the air from the space. I have broken the code, given voice to what they don't speak of.

Stuart looks abruptly apoplectic. "What did you say?"

"You've got a lot of nerve showing up here after what you did today," Red says, trying to steer the conversation back to his own anger, which I daresay is less dangerous. "I'd salute that if it wasn't so disrespectful."

"Look, we're not trying to cause any disrespect," Evan tries.

"That's true," I agree, "but I'm quickly losing what little respect I did have."

"Shut your mouth," Stuart says softly, "and keep it shut," and if I had any doubt about the kind of man he is, it vanishes as I see the shift in him. I think this is what I've been needing to see. To be sure.

I look over at Duncan, who is watching us from the bar, but he sends no help.

"Back up," I tell Stuart, who is standing too close and towering over me. He doesn't, but Red pulls him away and I unclench my stiff fists, remember to breathe.

"All right then, all right, that'll do now," Red says, and Stuart allows himself to be guided back to their table. He doesn't sit, but takes his hat and strides for the door, and have I just earned Lainey another punishment? I can't let that happen, but it doesn't take long for Duncan to follow Stuart from the pub, off, hopefully, to watch from the shadows, and if he's going to watch he'd best watch all damn night this time.

"I've lost my appetite for celebrating," Zoe says.

"Really? I'd take that as a win," I say, gulping more beer to calm myself.

"How come they don't bother you?" she asks me. "That was scary."

It was scary. But, "If you let them intimidate you they've won."

We finish up, the night soured.

Outside Duncan is leaning against his truck. I bid my team goodnight and walk over to him.

"You've been drinking," he says, then opens the door for me.

He drives me home, windows down. The smell, I lose my breath from it.

"Did you follow him home?" I ask. "Is she gonna be okay?"

Duncan doesn't reply.

"He was really angry tonight, Duncan."

"Yeah. Perhaps consider the wisdom of antagonizing him."

My mouth opens but the words dissolve. He's right, and it's easier to see that with my anger cooled. He's right, and also not. A man's anger, his violence, is no one's responsibility but his own. "When does it end?" I ask. "If no one ever says anything, for fear of him, then when does it end."

Duncan is silent a long while, then admits, "I've got someone out there."

Relief swells.

"I want him to know I can see him."

We reach the turnoff to our road. "I'll walk from your place," I say. Because I need the cold air on my burning cheeks. He pulls down his driveway and parks outside his house. It's like mine, but its stone is gray not blue, and has a dog bounding from the steps to meet us in the dark. As Duncan greets the black-and-white collie I turn for the road.

"Night."

"Wolves out there," Duncan warns.

I nod.

He considers me. "Piece of advice, from a local to a visitor."

"I'm not a visitor."

"You'll be leaving again, one of these days, when your animals are dead."

The casual way he says it, a slap.

"This is remote country," Duncan tells me. "You're gonna need people. We all do, out here. You can go mad being too alone in a place this big."

"That why you rushed over to help us tonight?" I ask. "Civic responsibility?"

"In my experience, cops can make a problem where there wasn't one."

I find his eyes. "There was a problem, Duncan."

After a long moment he says, "My apologies. I misread." Then, "You don't seem like the kind of woman who couldn't handle a pair of drunken eejits."

"Why should I have to?"

He tilts his head to acknowledge this. "You're not in any danger here, Inti. I'm watching."

The words prickle my neck. Some place deep, there is a thrill.

"It's out there I'd be more worried about," Duncan adds, nodding to the trees, the hills, the mountains and moors. "You must know monsters well, wolf girl."

"I've never met one in the wild. They don't live there."

Something shifts in the space between us. Or maybe this prickling thing always lived here. I don't know but there is something in his regard and I am filled with frustration, with the need to make him see what I see, to make him understand, and I think I want those things because what I actually want is him.

It's been a long time since I've wanted anyone. It takes me by surprise.

I make a decision, and say, "Can I show you something?"

"Where?"

"Inside."

He doesn't answer, considering. Will he let the wolf in? He leads the way into the warmth. The back door opens straight into the stone-and-timber kitchen. I stand by the windowsill and turn up the volume on my phone.

Duncan waits warily by the door and doesn't reach for the light, leaving us to stand in the red glow of the stove coals.

"Come here," I say.

Slowly, with a pained kind of shuffle, he does, he stands close, each of us near to the phone.

"Close your eyes."

I'm not sure he wants to, but he surrenders, lids falling shut. I press Play on the audio file and the sound slowly swells to envelop us.

At first, birdsong. A call passed back and forth between two birds.

The cries of ravens flying overhead and the air *swooshing* by their wings. The chirps of smaller birds, crickets in the grass, leaves rustling. All the tiniest sounds of a forest, an ecosystem in balance and so calming I see Duncan's entire demeanor change, the muscles in his face and shoulders relax. And then comes something else, raising the hairs on my neck.

It sounds like a distant ocean.

Or the first stirrings of a storm.

Wind in the canopy of trees.

"That's the sound of wolves whispering."

Duncan opens his eyes.

"Two separate packs, speaking to each other as they draw near."

It is eerie and so beautiful.

"Nobody knew they did this until they were recorded," I say. "An accident."

I want him to see them the way I do. I knew playing him this would swallow us and it has.

Duncan lifts my hand to his lips. "You're frozen," he murmurs, and leads me to his bedroom.

I know this dark. I have lost myself in it before. His hands are mine, and his lips and his tongue, and I am inside him, carried deep, far from air. There is no light, only his skin and what it feels, his touch alongside mine and too much and enough to drown in.

I wake to gentle fingers along my hairline.

Full afternoon sun lights his face. "You're alive."

I barely feel that way.

He is sitting beside me on the bed, and the collie is asleep in the crook of my knees. I stay where I am, anchored by both. "How long did I sleep?"

"It's two P.M."

"Oh my god." I struggle to sit up. "Sorry."

He shakes his head a fraction, studying me.

My skin feels raw to the touch; the soft sheets have become rough.

Aggie calls when I get this way "sensation-fatigued" and I have only known it a small handful of times. A kind of dulling of my mirror-touch.

"You okay?"

I nod. "I have to go."

"I'll drive you home."

"I'll walk. I need the walk."

"I don't like you wandering around out there alone."

"Didn't you learn anything last night?"

This makes him smile.

At the door I pat the dog for a few long moments; he gazes lovingly up at me and makes me want to stay. "What's his name?"

"Fingal."

"Hello, Fingal."

The dog greets me silently.

Duncan's expression isn't as transparent, but even so, if I spend too much time lingering here I really will stay: as exhausted as I am I still want more of him, and more. I turn for the trees.

7

At home I chop firewood because Aggie has let the fire go out. My breath makes clouds of the crisp air. Gall watches me from the paddock, ravens dotting the grass around her. I pause and peer back.

"What do you think of all this?" I ask her.

She tosses her head.

"Would you like to stay?"

No movement this time. She is undecided.

I gather an armful of wood and carry it inside, kneeling before the fireplace. Twigs and newspaper for tinder. Small slices of wood to form a teepee. Aggie is curled inside a blanket on the window seat, reading.

"What happened?" I ask her, of the fire. She knows not to let it go out.

You didn't come home, she signs.

"Did your legs stop working?"

The woodpile is outside.

It stalls me. The match I forgot burns my fingertips. "Shit." I light another and lift it to the paper, watching it blacken and curl and smoke. The flame passes its way through the rest of the material, sputtering into life. I rented this place over the phone without having seen it so we'd have somewhere to move straight into. It is smaller and more run-down than I expected, its furnishings and decorations belonging to another time, but we don't need much. Aggie went outside for the first few days, short walks and wanderings to discover the area, and then it was less often and then one day she stopped altogether and now the very thought of leaving these walls terrifies her. I didn't think about the heating, about the woodpile beyond her reach. "I'm sorry," I tell my sister. "I'm really sorry. I'll make sure I bring more in for you." And I'll buy her an electric heater, for emergencies. And I won't stay out overnight again. I should never have left her so long.

I sit opposite her in the window seat, our raised knees touching. She shares her blanket with me.

"The wolves are free."

Aggie smiles. *Bravo. Were you out celebrating?*

I nod.

Then you've made friends?

"I don't need friends."

She considers this and between us hangs the question. Where were you, then? But she doesn't ask it and I don't answer it, and I could cry right now just to end this silence. Instead she passes me the book and I read it to her, my voice wobbly but growing stronger, and as she listens she rests her cheek against the glass and it is so cold on my face. But for my trip to the grocery store and some bread baking, this is how we spend the rest of our weekend, reading and entwined.

On Monday I am the first to work and so I'm alone when I realize why it took the Abernethy Pack so long to abandon their pen—it was because they didn't want to leave their daughter, pretty Number Thirteen, who is curled beneath tree roots in the back corner of the cage where we couldn't see her. But leave her they did.

Evan arrives with a handful of yellow wildflowers. "Marsh marigolds for you, my dear, to brighten your morning," he says. "*Caltha palustris*. I found them on my walk, poking their way up through the frost. They're some of the first of the season." He places them in a glass of water and puts them on the desk beside me. Before I can thank him he is taken by the sight of Thirteen alone in her cage. "Oh no. What are you doing in there, sweetheart? I'm surprised they left her."

"They stayed as long as they could," I say.

I head out, on the hunt for an answer. It's unlikely I'll ever discover why her pack left her there, and why she alone decided to stay, but I'm going to try.

In a landscape this big you need height to find wolves. They wear GPS collars but first we have to be able to locate them and get close enough to download the data stored in these collars, and we do that by tuning in to their individual radio frequencies, most easily done by air.

Our pilot is called Fergus Monroe, and he stinks of booze.

"You okay to fly?" I ask him, making no secret of my skepticism.

Fergus laughs. "Aye, of course. Night on the drink's never stopped me before." He is wiry and orange haired, and has a boyish smile despite his hangover. I'd be more worried about the fact that he's clearly still inebriated if we had any other option, but since he's the only pilot in the area with his own plane and a mind to help us, I'm going up in the air with him today, and there's no point dwelling on it.

I strap myself into the little plane and Fergus starts the engine with a cheerful whoop. I wonder if he makes that sound every time he starts his plane, or if it's for my benefit. Either way I laugh. The propellers whir and we bounce along the grass of the tiny airstrip, and then up we go, stuttering woozily into the air, seemingly defying the rules of physics. My stomach bottoms out and I have to breathe through the sudden nausea.

"How long have you had her?" I call over the sound of the engine. We have headpieces on to talk, but it's still an intense roar of noise.

"Coming on twenty years now. And she's a hell of a lot older than that!"

I must look alarmed at this, because he glances back and chuckles. "Don't worry, she just keeps on going, the old lassie. Never failed me yet."

"There's a first time for everything," I reply, which makes him laugh like he's escaped from the local sanatorium.

I have a map on my tablet that I mark off as we do wide circles, and my radio tracker is ready at hand. Fergus knows the area well, and where the herd animals go for water and grazing—the most recent GPS pings we have came from these hot spots, so we start from them and work our way out in wide circles. I keep my eyes peeled on the ground, trying to learn the land, but it's so different from above. Shapes and colors that need making sense of. Patches of forest, long sloping mountains, bleak moors, and sheep everywhere you look. Unfenced, unpenned. I wonder if these people are trying to get their livestock eaten.

It takes hours to spot a wolf. We've been following a herd of red deer, tracking them north along a river. We fly low, gliding between undulating green and brown mountains that rear up on either side of us. We are high above sea level here, and the mountains further in the distance, those monoliths of the Cairngorms range, are still snow covered. We seem tiny in this giant place, as small as the red dots of deer grazing below.

My eyes seize on something. "There!" I shout. Fergus circles around to give us a better view.

It's the Glenshee Pack, minus Number Ten. They're on the trail of the herd, some distance behind but gaining quickly, loping over long stretches of yellow grass. When they hear the hum of the plane they look up, and as we soar overhead they scatter quickly into a copse of pine-woods where we can no longer see them. I grin, giving a whoop of my own.

"They're a sight, aren't they?" Fergus cries.

"A bloody beautiful sight!"

There is always lingering fear that they're sick or injured or dead, so to see this pack intact, each of its members healthy and on the hunt, is electrifying, it is joy.

Close enough now, I connect to the GPS collars the wolves wear and download their most recent data. Each collar takes about three minutes, so by the time I've done the first couple of wolves the rest have scattered too far for me to catch. But getting two from a pack is a good start. We can look at every location they've been to in the last week and start to log patterns. With enough data Zoe can create a map of their movements, and we can begin to see the packs' territories emerge.

"Let's move on and find the others, I don't want to disturb them too much while they're hunting."

"You got it, boss." Fergus steers the aircraft around in a big eastern arc, while I mark on the map where I saw the Glenshee Pack—heading through the Mounth Hills on the south side of the park. I wonder at the size of the territory they seem to be carving out for themselves.

As we fly over long stretches of peat bog and marshland, Fergus asks, "Do you know how it used to be here?"

"Forest?"

"Aye, that's right. All of the woodland that once covered this area was burned down so as to smoke out the wolves and give them nowhere to hide, so they say."

I am startled, and turn in my seat to look at him.

"A purge, of sorts," he says, seeming unbothered by my interest, lost in the story. "Three wolf hunts a year were required by the old kings, and men being punished were made to pay for their crimes in wolf tongues. Even Mary, Queen of Scots came up here to hunt wolves for sport. An entire nation out for their blood. The beasts had no chance. But they did survive here longer than down in England and Wales. They gave it a good shot." He fiddles with something on the dash, and then, as though I have asked him a question, says, "There's all kinds of stories about the last wolf of Scotland. Every district has its own claim, and all of them violent. But probably the last wolf was hiding out somewhere, and died alone. My guess, anyway."

I close my eyes, overcome.

We don't find the Tanar Pack, but as dusk is nearing and we decide to head home, we loop around to the western edge of the national park and happen upon the Abernethy Pack.

Or one of its members, at least: breeding male Number Nine.

He is in a forest clearing when I shout for Fergus to circle around and get lower. It is a stroke of exquisite luck to spot him here like this. He's come a long way from his cage, which means he's on the hunt. This is no easy feat on his own, which makes it stranger still that he left his stepdaughter behind—wolves hunt best in packs, the more members the better. His new mate, Number Six, should be here with him, too. And so it occurs to me. Number Six must be pregnant. Only the need to build herself a den for the impending litter could explain why she isn't part of this hunt, and why she left her daughter behind.

The thought fills me with excitement but I keep my eyes on the huge gray wolf, the creature I have begun to equate with the health of this project, the strongest of them all. He has always been a mighty creature, larger than any wolf I've seen, but more than that, there is a stillness in him, a calm certainty in his eyes. As we circle lower he looks up and spots the plane. We are close enough that I can see his handsome face clearly, his golden eyes. He is more at peace, free in his habitat, than he was in the cage.

Instead of running to take cover like most wolves do, he stands his ground and gazes up at us, watching. Daring us to land and come for him, daring us to try.

It sends a shiver inside me of great, overwhelming awe.

"My god," I hear Fergus say distantly.

I've no breath to reply.

Nine waits for us to move on, and as we fly away from him my stomach bottoms out because I can see very clearly how close he has traveled to the edge of the forest, to where there is farmland just over the stream.

Some part of me must know, because I begin to tune in to Nine's radio collar frequency far more often over the next days than I tune in to any other wolf's. A week passes uneventfully; I am beginning to relax when on the tenth day I switch to his frequency and hear the mortality code.

The collar might have been lost or damaged. The wolves chew free of them sometimes. It could be lying on the grass somewhere.

But when Duncan calls and says my name I can hear it in his voice and I know, of course I know. I knew before it happened.

The word is cut free of me without my permission. "*No.*"

"One of the wolves has been shot dead. I'm sorry, Inti."

I know whose farm it will be even before I'm told.

Red McRae's land is in the northwestern corner of the park and borders the Abernethy Forest, where we set Number Nine's pack free. He owns an enormous expanse of land, rolling hills dotted with hundreds of black and white sheep. Red and Duncan are waiting for us at the sheep yards. Niels and I climb out of the car. I opted not to bring Evan—this will upset him too much.

"We'll show you to the carcass and you can get the damn thing off my property," Red says by way of greeting.

Duncan meets my eyes and there is pity there, and I must look away from it or scream. I want to shake that pity out of him so hard it hurts.

We start the long walk together, the silent four of us.

I see his body long before we reach it. Gray fur nestled into the earth. Cradled by it. He is lying beside a stream that borders the farm, and he is on the forest side of the stream, and as I make sense of this I realize he has been shot without having crossed over onto McRae's land.

Wild, floundering despair and a rage so hot I think I *will* scream, or vomit, or turn and strangle Red by the throat. Instead I sink to the ground beside Nine and place my trembling hands in his fur as I never would have done when he was alive.

"This is illegal," I hear Niels say. "He's not on your land."

"I thought it was a wild dog," Red replies, unworried.

They fade into the background and all I am is this wolf, all I see is the beauty of him, and the power even now, even so reduced. Why didn't I come to him when I knew he was straying too close to danger? Why didn't I come and move him along somehow? The strongest of them. The mightiest. The most at home here. Snuffed out.

There is blood in Nine's fur. I can't yet see where he was shot. But his eyes are open and glassy and his tongue is lolling out, and the sight is so upsetting that I feel a shift come upon me. This feeling is why we don't give them names. Why we don't get too near to them. Because they are so fragile.

Now it seems cruel that all he was to us was a number among others.

I look up at Red and he recoils from whatever he sees in my face. There is a kind of embarrassment in him that I should be so openly vulnerable, so wounded. So blazing.

I close Nine's eyes and mouth and stroke his fur over and over again, wanting to sit here and stroke it forever. When I can't put it off any longer I ask Niels to carry him back to the car, but when he is too heavy for Niels, it is Duncan who lifts the wolf into his arms and limps his way back over the hills.

An old man sits outside Red McRae's house. The spitting image of Red, plus a few decades. His father, I'd put money on it. He watches us load the wolf into our truck, and he lowers his hat to his chest in a sign of respect I could do without.

We take Nine to Amelia's veterinary clinic to perform the autopsy. We know how he died, but there is more information we can gather from his body, including the contents of his stomach and digestive system to determine what he's been feeding on, and his overall health before the gunshot. When we have worked the carcass we will bury him. I've buried wolves before and I will do it again. I never make peace with it.

Duncan is in the waiting room to hear our findings.

"I want McRae charged," I say.

"He said—"

"I know what he said. Do your job."

I arrive home as night is beginning to fall. The days are growing longer and twilight brings an unearthly glow to the light.

I'm unlocking my front door when I hear it.

The howl of a wolf.

The first in these lands for hundreds of years.

My hands drop and I turn to the forest. A gust of wind rustles through the leaves of the trees and carries the sound to me. It raises the hairs on my arms and neck. It is filled with a desperate aching question. And as it continues on through the night without answer, growing less hopeful by the hour, I know which wolf the eerie sound belongs to. Snowy Number Six, calling her lost mate home.

8

Number Six, alpha female of her dwindling pack, has not stopped howling for two weeks, from dusk until dawn. It's driving everyone in earshot mad. I've had daily phone calls from properties and houses spanning kilometers telling me in no uncertain terms to shut her up. As if she is my dog, and I have merely to discipline her better. I try to explain that she's a wild creature in mourning. But the thought of a beast grieving her mate in such a confronting, almost *human* way is too much for most folk. None of us can help carrying her voice within us.

I wake before dawn and go walking.

Up the driveway and over the fence. Cutting across the paddock to the looming shadow of the spruce forest. Through trees so tall and thick that even were there sunlight it would be dark as night within. I touch flaky bark as I pass trunks, reach my fingertips to the prickly edges of the needle-like leaves. Silently I tell them I hope they are left alone and in peace but I know this won't be. The track leads me up and around, over a stream that trickles invisibly; I only know I'm crossing it because my feet come away wet. I have a destination. Through this man-made forest, its carefully measured Sitka spruces planted only to be cut down, to a wilder place, a much older one. As I leave the heavy, dense trees I emerge into a sloping landscape dotted with thousands of silver birch, glowing in the moonlight. I take a breath; the forest takes it with me. Wind is a distant ocean, calming as it reaches me until it's no more than a kiss to my cheeks, my eyelids, my lips. I recognize this kiss; I have felt it before.

A year passed in Dad's forest. He came and went, but mostly he went. Aggie and I kept going to school, at seventeen it was our last year. We worked the garden to make sure we had food, tended the horses and the house and went hunting for meat we could sell for some cash. We were lonely but we had each other, and really we were too tired to be lonely.

When Dad stayed gone for longer and longer and finally seemed to be that way permanently, when he stopped being able to recognize us, I felt a great defiance in my soul and knew I had to do something, *try* something. So on a Tuesday morning I loaded my little family into our rattling old car and set off on a very long drive. First to the west coast of BC, not far really from where we lived, to the tide pools where a strange and fey-like breed of wolf was rumored to live, the sea wolves who fed on salmon and seals and swam the waves they were born to. Most of these wolves had never seen a mountain or a deer, and on this remote stretch of First Nations land they had not yet learned to fear humans. We parked our car and walked through the conifers and down onto the rocky stretch of beach. The mighty Pacific blew a salty wind onto our faces and we sat, binoculars at the ready, waiting for a sighting. None came. The wolves were off in the land of driftwood and ocean.

Next, south into America. Across Washington and into Idaho, Montana, and Wyoming. Big-sky country and god, it was big. To the Lamar Valley. A river valley wide and famed for its wildlife. The road here curved and then turned straight as a knife through wide flat plains and distant snowcapped mountains. There were dozens of people lined up beside their parked cars, quietly awaiting a wolf or bear sighting through their long-lens cameras.

I pulled the car over at the end of the line of spectators, disappointed not to be alone. Aggie sat on the car bonnet and closed her eyes to the sun. For some reason Dad set himself to the task of weaving grass into a basket and when I asked him what it was for he said, as though I were an idiot, that it was to carry things. We saw no wolves in the Lamar Valley, though I'd read at length about the famous pack who lived there and was named after it. But we did see bison suckling calves and bucking heads and swimming across rivers. I saw birds of prey hovering, watching. And a young man parked beside us admitted to having seen a black bear and her cub amble past only the day before.

Wolves were here somewhere, breathing and sleeping and hunting and playing, and whether we saw them or not they made this place richer and more alive just by existing. I could feel them, and I was glad as the Wyoming sun set purple, pink, and gold over the prairie that the wolves had remained hidden, that their lives were their own, their mystery remained.

Aggie didn't understand. She was bored and wanted to leave but she also wanted me to see what we'd come here for. The wolves were the point of the trip, after all. Except that they weren't, not really. I wanted our dad back, our all-knowing, large as a Doug fir father. I wanted his passion back, his love of nature that I might show him I had cultivated the same. I wanted to share this awakening in me, share what I had learned, what I now knew my life was to be, and for him to be proud of me. That hope trailed behind us like a rattling tin can for a while until I cut it loose for good.

As I drove the rusting old Chevy van out of Utah, Dad fell asleep and Aggie woke.

It wasn't far now.

"When we get back we have to start talking about some kind of help," my sister said from the back seat.

I didn't reply.

"I found a couple of places."

"He needs to stay in his home," I said.

"It's gonna get worse and we don't know how to look after him."

"We can learn."

"Are you gonna feed him and wipe his ass? Because I'm not."

I winced. "Those places would kill him." Being stuck indoors, without his horses, eating microwave meals in front of a TV. It would kill him.

"Maybe a quicker death would be kind," Aggie muttered.

I looked at her in the rearview. "I know you did not just say that."

She sighed, meeting my eyes. "No. But it is gonna get worse."

I nodded, and started thinking of ways to set my sister free. Trouble was, even if I could she wouldn't go.

Left onto Highway 25. Into Fishlake National Forest.

I pulled over. Dad woke and we all climbed out of the van to go the last part on foot. "Where are we?" he asked.

"Fishlake," I said. Then added, "America."

He peered around at the trees, confused. They were not trees he recognized. But he said once that forests are all of our homes, no matter where in the world, and that's what I was hoping for, that this knowledge lived somewhere too deep to misplace.

"Come on," I said. "Follow me, I want to show you something."

The air was warm, gentle.

We three crested a rise and saw a forest of quaking aspen. Thousands of slender white trunks and a canopy of electric yellow mist above.

Our fingers trailed the smooth bark and I said, "It's one tree."

"What do you mean?" Aggie asked.

"It's not a forest. It's one tree. One huge organism. It's called the trembling giant and it's the oldest living thing on this planet, and the largest. Some think it could be a million years old. And it's dying. We're killing it."

I turned to see my father crouch to the earth's floor and place a large hand on it. Over the web of connected roots, from which shot thousands of genetically identical trunks, clones of each other. I watched as he closed his eyes and listened to the giant tremble beneath us. When he opened them once more they held tears and the trees had returned him to us.

"My girls," he said. "You've grown up."

Aggie held him. I pressed my cheek to one of the tender, elegant trunks. Wind whispered through its naked branches and against my eyelids, my lips. A kiss. I could almost hear it breathing, could feel its heartbeat beneath and around and above me, the oldest language of all.

Now, in a different forest, a highlands place as dawn breaks, I hear a bird sing nearby; I imagine it a nightingale. I wish I knew what it was saying. I come to a small loch and sit at its edge to watch the dawn light paint its color, gray to blue to silver. A mist carries in over the water. The water birds are waking, calling to each other.

I want never to leave this place. I want never to see another human again, I want it more than I've ever wanted anything. The aloneness is exquisite; it is calm. Until Number Nine slips back into my thoughts, the way he's been doing since he was killed, and the man who killed him is there too and some savage whim lifts my voice in a bellow, the very same that used to compel my sister to break the quiet. It feels good but only for a moment. When the sound fades I see that the birds have been frightened away.

I don't walk straight home. I take a longer route, my feet leading me to the hill that overlooks the back of his cottage. From here I can see his kitchen window. I can see him moving around, even through the shroud of morning mist. I watch him, wanting to walk down the hill to his door but unsure if it's to confront him—to ask if he has charged Red, to give voice to my anger—or for something gentler and growing.

The dog starts barking and I turn home before Duncan spots me.

My phone rings while I'm driving to work. It's Evan. "Don't get angry," he starts.

I sigh.

"Niels went out and found the den."

"*What?* Fuck!" I hang up so hard it hurts my finger, before pulling into the parking space of the base camp. I burst through the front door, eyes swiveling to land on Niels, who looks sheepish in the kitchen. Zoe and Evan take cover by the computers.

"I must have misheard on the phone just now because I'm sure you did not go out to that den after I specifically told you not to."

Niels holds his hands up to stall me. "We needed to locate it."

"She's going to have those pups any day now, she needs her den."

"She wasn't even there when I found it."

"That's *worse*!"

"Let's tone down the temper," Evan suggests, eyes pointedly shifting behind me.

I glance over my shoulder to see Duncan standing in the doorway, watching this exchange, but don't have space to worry about what he's doing here right now. I turn back to Niels. "What were you thinking?"

"You've been hands-off this whole time, since we got here," he says calmly; he's always so goddamn calm. "I don't know what's making you so timid this time around but you know as well as the rest of us that sometimes we have to get involved."

Heat floods my cheeks. "If you've displaced her from her den," I say, "I may actually kill you. The cop's here—he can be my witness." Instead of waiting for a response, I stride back outside to cool off. I lean against the twisted trunk of a juniper, my favorite tree in the area, and watch the gentle movement of the forest. Sunlight in shafts through the canopy. A rustling in one of the hip-high ferns. I've been non-interventionist, but I didn't think that was the same as hands-off.

It's not long before I hear the door and Evan is beside me. He's quiet a while, then murmurs, "We did need to locate the den."

"Not by going there in person, not this close to the birth." If Six left to find food, and she returns to smell human at her den site, she won't go back there. Even if she'd had the pups she'd be likely to abandon them, so great is their fear of humans. Niels knows this, we talked about it yesterday when I decided we couldn't risk going out there, not yet.

"We might have to bring her in," I say.

"Then we'll make that work."

I glance sideways at him. "Have I been timid?"

Evan tilts his head. "Just . . . unwilling to get too involved."

"I want them to be free."

"Aye, but we brought them here, and we put them in danger. They may yet need our help."

I nod slowly. My father used to say the world turned wrong when we started separating ourselves from the wild, when we stopped being one with the rest of nature, and sat apart. He said we might survive this mistake if we found a way to rewild ourselves. But I don't know how to do that when our existence frightens the creatures we must reconnect with.

I would give anything not to frighten them; it makes me so sad. And yet the truth is that their fear of us keeps them safe from us.

Inside the cabin there is an awkward silence as they wait to see if my temper still reigns. I meet Niels's eyes. "Can you make me a map to the den?"

"Of course." He jumps to the task, while I start readying a travel pack.

"Can I've a word?" Duncan asks me.

"I can't right now, Chief. I've gotta get out to that den." It occurs to me that he might have seen me this morning, watching him from the hill, and if that's the case I might die of embarrassment.

"I'll tag along then, shall I?"

I laugh. "No."

"Why not?"

"I'm going alone. The fewer bodies traipsing around out there the better."

"Tell you what. I'll step where you step and make no noise. I can be subtle when I need to be."

"Is that right." He's watching me. Trying to figure me out. Circling. I don't need to make it easy for him, so I glance pointedly at his leg. "You'd be wasting a day following me out there and I don't need to be slowed down."

I take the map from Niels and shoulder my pack, then head out to the stables to ready a horse. As Duncan follows me and starts to do the same I stare at him in irritation. He's audacious, I'll afford him that.

I give in, my mind already darting ahead to worry about the wolf. "You do what I say, okay?"

"Yes, ma'am."

"The female who's been howling at night?" I say as our horses walk through the dappled morning sun.

"Aye," Duncan says. "I've had complaints. She's scaring people. What's wrong with her?"

"Her mate was the male Red shot. She's calling for him, hoping he'll come home."

"Oh," he says. "I didn't know they did that."

We duck beneath the long, twisted branches of the Scots pines. It's easier traveling now than in winter, when snow turns the ground perilous. Still, there's no path, and the underbrush is thick. We go slowly so the horses don't lose their footing.

"The breeding wolves—you'd call them alphas—mate for life," I say. "We think this female alpha—Number Six—is pregnant. Either that or it's a pseudopregnancy. We might have to bring her in."

"Why's that?" Duncan asks. His leg made it difficult for him to mount the horse, but now that he's up, he looks okay in the saddle, a bit tense. I gather he's not much of a rider.

"Raising pups is a family thing for wolves. Every wolf in a pack takes on a role. They rely heavily on each other for survival. Six will have to do it alone. It'd be hard on her to hunt while suckling. Even harder if we've displaced her from her den."

"Could it make her more aggressive? More likely to make the easy kill?"

"Livestock?" I think about his question. It's been keeping me up at night. Eventually I say, "That's why we might have to bring her in."

Something compels me to continue, "Wolves get lonely, same as us. Difference is that for wolves being alone makes them vulnerable, while for humans it keeps us safe."

Duncan scratches his salt-and-pepper beard. "I'd have to disagree with you there, Inti Flynn."

The white trunks of the birches seem to glow. Their tiny leaves shimmer green, maybe nearest to Werner's siskin green, the color of ripe Colmar pears, Irish pitcher apples, and the glittering mineral called uran-mica. They give the world a spring haze; even the bluebells are coming out, carpeting the ground in purple and turning this forest from the stark, dangerous place it felt in winter to someplace warm, pretty, welcoming. All around us the birds sing a joyous racket.

"Inti Flynn," Duncan repeats. "What kind of a name is that?"

"Honestly, who knows."

"Meaning?"

"I've got a Canadian father with an Irish name, and an Australian mother with an English name, I've got grandparents from Scotland and Ireland and France, and none of us has a clue where my first name is from."

He smiles.

I clear my throat. "What about you then? A sturdy Scottish name for a sturdy Scottish laddie?"

"My family are as Scottish as they come and that's what they've been for more generations than we can count."

"That must be nice."

Duncan shrugs.

"Do your parents live in town?"

"They did," he says. "They're dead now."

It startles me, and I wish I hadn't asked. "Why'd you want to talk to me?"

He shifts in his saddle. "I wanted to let you know we won't be charging Red McRae."

My mouth opens but no words spill free.

"We've got no evidence to contradict his word that he thought the animal was a stray dog, which is within his rights to shoot."

Duncan replies to my silence. "I can't prove anything different, Inti. If you've got some physical evidence you haven't mentioned then please, come forward." He pauses again, then adds, "I've got a community to think about. Charging Red for a mistake so soon after the wolves have been freed is just gonna disrupt my people further. I have to show them solidarity."

I stare at Duncan, who will not look back at me. Some part of me must have thought this was a man with integrity, who would do his job without prejudice. More fool me: we're alone out here.

"You could have told me back at base," I say, flat. "Saved yourself a trip."

"It's occurred to me that it might serve me better to know a little more about what you're doing out here."

Like he did in the auditorium that night, he is surveying his land for threats. What it might serve me better to know is if he thinks the threat is the wolves, or if he believes it's me.

According to Niels the den is twenty feet down the side of a steep forest gully. God knows how he managed to find it down there—he must have clambered all over this spot for days. We dismount and creep to the edge of the drop, searching for some sign of an opening. Six has done an excellent job of disguising her den. I can't see anything among the underbrush, rocks, and fallen tree branches making a latticework of protection.

I uncoil a rope from the saddle of my horse and start looping it around a tree.

"What are you doing?"

"I have to see if she's there or not before I make any decisions."

"And if she is?"

Strapped to my back is the first tranquilizer rifle I brought, and I hand Duncan the second.

"The fuck's this for?" he asks, and I realize he's nervous. He is glancing back and forth, left and right.

"It's not for anything, it's just in case. I don't think she'll be here."

This clearly doesn't comfort him. I turn away so he doesn't see me smile.

With the rope fastened around my waist I climb down over the lip of the gully, facing Duncan. Our eyes meet and then the ground divides us. It takes me some time and a lot of scratches to find the opening to the den. I am assuming I'll find it empty. But this is stupid of me. *Never assume anything with a wolf, she will always surprise you.*

I catch sight of a dark crevice and there she is, two reflective golden eyes gazing out at me. I go still, watching her. *Hello, girl. You came back.*

I don't want to tranq this wolf. Not after everything she's been through. The stress could cause all kinds of problems for her; waking up back in her pen could be damaging. But I hate the thought of leaving her out here to die. That's not a thing I could live with, not after Nine's death, a death that maybe I could have prevented if I'd found a way to move him from the edge of Red's farm. I knew he was in danger and I left him, and Niels is right to think me timid. If I tranq Six now, I can take her in, give her a shot of penicillin and vitamins, figure out if she's actually pregnant or if it's phantom, and then we can support her while she gives birth, feed her as she suckles her pups, let them free once more when the pups have grown enough to start learning the hunt. The shape of this plan takes place in my mind and I start to feel better about it.

I swing the lightweight air rifle off my back and carefully load one of the long cylindrical tranquilizer darts into its chamber. The dart has a furry red tip so we can find it easily, and because the Telazole drug we fill it with is highly dangerous for humans, there's an antidote in my pack in case I accidentally prick myself and go into a coma.

"Can you throw me a torch?" I call to Duncan. "And the radio."

Instead of throwing them down, he uses my rope to slide down the incline, awkward on his bad leg.

I radio Evan and tell him to get a transport crate out here as quickly as he can, and to bring Amelia so she can monitor Six's vitals while we move her.

Duncan floods the crevice with a beam of light. I can make her out properly now, blinking against the brightness. She doesn't move, except to lower her face a little. There is the line of her pale body, the dark of her eyes and muzzle. I move back to make space, and take aim at her front haunch. I need to hit a muscular, insensitive area so it doesn't cause her pain. The lack of light makes it harder but being at close range helps; more often than not when you shoot from a distance the feathered dart moves so slowly—like a shuttlecock—that the animal is gone by the time it lands. I draw a deep breath, let my eyes fall shut, and squeeze the trigger. I don't see the dart landing but I hear the faint *fzzt* sound.

We wait on high alert for the drug to take effect. There's a chance it might have agitated her, and I don't tell Duncan that she's even more unpredictable in these long minutes. But she stays where she is to sleep, and I'm able to gently drag her free. A quick flash of the torch determines the cave to be empty. She is unconscious, she is her dead mate, the lolling of his head as we lifted him, the sack of bones he became. It is so visceral my hands recoil from her body.

"Inti?"

"Sorry."

I check her pulse and find it strong, before turning my thoughts to getting her out of here. Clouds have begun to creep in; the sky turns darker. A storm is on the way. I'm about to climb back up for more ropes when I hear a sound, so faint it barely touches me. I go still, listening, but it doesn't come again.

"Put your fingers here," I instruct Duncan. "Time her pulse and if it starts to slow yell out to me."

"I'm not touching that," he says.

"She's unconscious, Duncan."

He shakes his head, but sighs as he edges closer and feels gingerly for the pulse.

I start climbing. And stop. It's worrying at me, an uneasy feeling like I should check, just to be certain. That sound I'm sure I heard.

A fat drop of water splatters my cheek.

I slide back to crouch before the den. It's dark within, and very small, so small I can't believe Six fit in here. Unless the dark is deceptive. The torch reveals nothing; the cave looks empty. I'm not sure what I'm look-ing for except that the sound was . . . lost, almost, and animal, and—

There. Something shifts. Sighs.

I reach in as far as I can, scraping my arm until my fingertips brush soft. I know suddenly why she came back, even with Niels's scent all over everything. As I pull free the tiny creature it gives an adorable mewling yelp. It gazes up at me, sweet and curious. A male, his downy fur an arctic shade of gray like his father's, his eyes the darkest shade of cocoa. The inside of me gives way.

"Shit," Duncan says. "What do we do now?"

The pup squirms in my arms, gives another squeaky yelp, and then settles. It's cold out here with the rain beginning to fall, and I try to keep him sheltered against my body. I laugh in astonishment. He can only be a few weeks old—Six and Nine must have conceived fast for their pups to be here already.

My mind races with the implications of this, trying to work out what to do. Niels's comment is loud in my head. *You've been timid.* "There are more," I say. "We'll take them too."

I pass the pup to Duncan, who holds him straight out like a football. "Cradle him."

Duncan reluctantly holds the pup to his chest, while I pull the rest of the pups free, passing them to him one by one. "Hang on," he splutters, but I need my hands yet. The last is so deep in the den that I have to tear at rocks around its edges and just about dislocate my shoulder to reach it. She is the runt of the pack, smaller than the others, a female, and more white than gray, like her mother. She nuzzles into me and I am filled with tenderness.

"Six pups," I say, turning back to Duncan, who is managing five squirming creatures in his lap and looking harangued. I laugh again. "They suit you."

He gives me a sour look. "How do we get them back?"

"Transport's coming. We just need to get them up to the horses."

But again I pause. I watch Number Six, lying still beside us, and these little creatures, doing their best to squirm their way to their mother's side.

The others on my team like to feel involved, they like to feel as though they're helping, always. But everything inside me is saying this is a strong wolf. Give her a chance. And at some point, I have to trust my instincts.

"We're gonna leave them," I say.

"What?"

"She can do this. She came back, and she stayed. She can't flourish if we don't let her."

I look at the pup in my arms and allow myself a weak moment, pressing her against my cheek, breathing in her scent. She nuzzles into my neck and oh god, my heart. Then I place her back in the den, where she's safe and warm. Once the others are returned and we've left Six sleeping at the mouth of the den, the restless pups nestle into her body, content. Duncan and I climb out of the gully.

I rest my hands on my head and close my eyes.

"What's wrong?" Duncan asks.

"I fucked up. I shouldn't have sedated her. If I'd known she'd had the pups already I wouldn't have. I'd have known to leave them be."

"What difference does it make?"

"You don't sedate an animal unless you absolutely have to. It's dangerous to them."

Duncan shrugs. "You thought you had to. Let it go."

My hands fall to my sides. Tough but true.

We wait some time for Evan, Niels, and Amelia to arrive with the transport crate. "Change of plan," I tell them. "She's had the pups. I'm leaving them here."

"Then why's she sedated?" Evan asks at the same time as Niels says, "That's unwise. We should bring them all in and feed her in the pen as she suckles."

"And then the pups are raised in a cage instead of the wild," I say, shaking my head. "That's not what we're trying to do here. Amelia, I need you to give her a shot of penicillin and anything else she needs and watch her vitals until she starts to rouse. Do not let that wolf die."

"Got it," Amelia says and Evan starts helping her descend into the ravine. More human scent to stain the area. Regrettable, but I'm sure now that Six is braver than most—she came back for her pups despite knowing a human had been here. And at least now we can make sure she and her pups are as healthy as possible before leaving today, and this won't have been a complete waste.

I pull Niels aside for a private word. "You messed with my head this morning, and I made a rushed decision. It's my fault, I know that, but please, let me do my job."

He is hard to read, always, but he nods and doesn't argue further.

"What will she eat?" Duncan asks me. "I can't leave here without knowing she won't go straight to the nearest farm."

A kind of dread fills me. Excitement for something long forgotten. I know what I have to do, the payment for my decision to leave her here, but how will I end this hunt without my sister?

"I'll find her something to eat," I say.

"What do you mean?"

"I've got more tranq darts. And a knife."

"Do you have a hunting license?"

"Yes," I lie.

"Oh hell," he mutters. "I'm gonna pretend I believe you and hope to god you know what you're doing."

I help him into his saddle, then swing onto my own horse. The big gelding snorts and dances a little and for a moment I think he might rear, but I tighten my knees and keep a firm hold of him, calming him with a hand to his neck. He can smell the wolves, and the storm, too.

We leave the others to mind the wolves and set off, just as the sky ruptures, letting loose a downpour. The gelding's hooves slip in the mud. Duncan by his own admission is no hunter but he does know the general grazing spots of the herds because it behooves him to know where the hunters gather, so we explore the closest. I am secretly relieved he is coming with me; I'm not sure I could do this on my own. The clearing is empty of deer, but I circle the tracks, looking for scat and noting how fresh it is. When I think I know which direction the herd has moved, we follow it east.

"How'd you learn to track?" Duncan asks.

"My dad."

"In Canada?"

I nod.

"I've always wanted to go to Canada. Good forests."

"You like trees?"

"I like timber."

My face creases in disappointment.

"Timber's beautiful," he says defensively.

"Sure, carcass chic."

He laughs. "God help me. You ever cut into the trunk of a tree and opened it up, and seen what's inside?"

I nod. I've never cut one myself, but I've seen.

"The patterns are like sound waves, and none of them alike. Hundreds of years old, sometimes, and no one has ever laid eyes on them before. You're the first person to see the tree's heart."

"But then you've killed it," I murmur, defeated.

Duncan shakes his head. "You can cut a tree to help it grow. You can cut it so it grows back stronger."

We follow the tracks of the herd to a small escarpment. At its base lies a grassy clearing, beyond that a hillside scattered with pines. Taking shelter among them is a herd of red deer. Duncan points further along to where there's an incline we can descend, and we take it, slipping and sliding.

The rain makes it harder for the deer to smell our approach. It makes them more likely to hold still. We circle behind them and dismount. I put two darts in my pocket and one in the chamber.

"This was fast," I tell him softly. "We were lucky. It can take days."

I feel him watching me, taking the measure of me.

"When wolves do this," I say, "they do it slowly. They're patient. They spend days following a herd and watching its deer. They pick the weaker animals. The slower ones. They watch those in particular, and they learn their traits, their personalities. They will know a deer so well by the time they attack that they can predict what will happen. They won't waste energy. They'll wait until they know without doubt that they can kill."

Duncan doesn't speak. He is so close behind me I can feel his warmth. I remember how it feels to be good at this. To be as wolf-like as I'm ever going to be. As animal. And yet I have never been able to pull the trigger. I have always needed my sister for that part.

We crouch behind trees and shrubs, staying low, and now we are too close for words, but I have my deer in sight, a smaller male sitting slightly apart. I take aim. If I miss and spook them, they'll run and we'll have to start again, and they'll be skittish, knowing they're being hunted. So I'd best not miss.

This time the dart is soundless. All I hear when my eyelids fall shut is the rain. I vanish inside it, dissolve beneath it. My body is gone and I can no longer be touched.

When I open my eyes Duncan is above, swimming. The rain co-coons us.

"You fainted," he says.

I didn't faint. I was too slow; I was shot by a dart.

A rivulet of water runs down the center of his nose and off the tip of it, straight onto my lips.

I follow the rivulet from my lips to his nose. I lick the drops from him. From his mouth. He clutches at me, takes my mouth with his. We kiss as though consuming each other. Trembling. My body was gone and now it becomes me. It's all I am, this need.

And memory.

Stop, I said.

"Stop," I say.

Duncan retreats. The distance between our bodies a forest.

I sit up, feeling as dazed as he looks. I don't want this. I came here to be away from the rest of the world, to be safe from it.

"The deer," I say.

"You got it."

Under the curtain of rain lies a shape. My feet lead me to it and I think, not for the first time, that I'm glad I must endure a little of what I inflict. This poor creature. I remove the dart from its hindquarters. Take the knife from my pack.

Can I? *Will* I?

I have so much pity, so much love for this soft warm breathing animal, I can't imagine how I could physically harm it, I can't imagine how I could survive that, but there isn't really a choice, is there? I'm for the wolves, and the wolves need to eat.

"Let me," Duncan says, sensing my distress.

"I can do it." They're my wolves, this is my burden.

And still. I pass him the knife and turn away.

We lay the lifeless body not far from sleeping Number Six, whose vitals I am assured are still strong. There is a chance she won't want this, the carcass being rich with our smell, but I am hoping her survival instinct kicks in, the practicality of motherhood. The pups raise their heads and peer out at us.

The little white runt is most curious. She ventures out of the den to sniff at the dead creature, still warm. And she looks straight at me as though I am the explanation for its sudden appearance, and in fact she's right, I am.

"Back inside with you," I tell her softly over the rain.

She cocks her head, watching me. Places a possessive paw on the deer.

"Funny little thing." Duncan grins.

She returns to the den to await instruction from her mother. She is one of the most important wolves in this country. Born here, she and her siblings have a true chance of making this land their home, and a home for their children to come.

"You don't like them, do you?"

"I mind the wee ones a little less after today, I suppose."

"But why? Why don't you like them?"

"The people here are good people, and they work hard. I don't like to see them scared. Fear makes for danger, whether it was there to begin with or not."

9

I must be expecting Duncan because I quicken, and I don't like how eager I feel, but it's Stuart Burns knocking at my door. Aggie is in bed and I wasn't far from it, cleaning the kitchen after dinner and desperate for my pillow. When she is well she does a lot of the cooking and cleaning while I'm at work, but when she isn't, when she's too tired, I do it all in the hours before bed.

"I'd like a word, Miss Flynn," Stuart says. Instead of risking waking my sister, I step outside and close the door. Stuart towers over me and my skin prickles, here alone with him.

"You owe me two thousand pounds." His tone is neither the friendly one I first met nor the seething fury of the pub; it is neutral, controlled.

"I know, Stuart. I need time to save it up. The job doesn't pay much."

"Call your parents, I'm sure they could help."

I frown. "You don't know a thing about what my parents could do."

"Look, just figure it out, 'cause I'm losing patience." He moves closer, enjoying his size, and I fucking loathe this thing men do so I don't step back like he wants me to, I raise my chin.

"Get off my property."

"Get the money you owe me. And don't bring it to the house, I don't want you bothering my wife. I'll come calling on you each night until you have it, make it easy for you."

He gets in his car and drives away.

I don't have a conscious thought as such, but my feet start moving and when I reach Duncan's house my hands are so cold it hurts to knock on his door.

He doesn't say anything when he sees me.

Then, "You blow mighty hot and cold, wolf girl."

He's right, I do, I am rudderless. "I'm sorry," I say. "I'll go."

He takes my hand to stay me.

We don't sleep, but lie naked at opposite ends of his bed, lamp lit and warm from the fireplace in his room. It smells of wood smoke and a scent that powerfully calls to mind my father's workshop, a scent I can't name but makes me feel at home. Fingal sleeps on the rug before the fire, his tail twitching every so often to the shape of his dreams.

In this soft light I could look at Duncan's face for hours, forever.

"Is this how you keep your lovers?" he asks me. "Waiting for scraps?"

I hide my smile. "Don't say lovers." Then, "What about yours."

"What about them?"

"How did you love them?"

He considers, holding my foot in his palm. "Not as well as I should have."

I wait.

"The few women I've known always seemed to want something I wasn't able to give, and that was my fault, probably, not being clear enough about that. Masquerading as a whole man, as one of them told me."

I am taken aback. I want to ask what he means, what makes him less than whole.

"They all . . . we skated the surface. I don't think I knew who they were, nor them me, and that's as I wanted it. And then it would come, like clockwork, to the same moment. I'd tell them I don't want children and they wouldn't believe me, they thought I needed time and maybe that's the right way for a lot of men, maybe they don't know themselves and that's certainly true of me, but it's also true that I can't reconcile myself as a father, I think maybe I'd be too much like mine and that'd be unforgivable."

I know what he's talking about. I know it intimately. When I turned thirty, almost to the day, I started thinking about a child. Something in my body said *Now, now, this is why you're here, this is the meaning.* An urgent clock I hadn't believed was real until I felt its chiming. The cells of me wanted to nurture, they wanted to love and protect. Aggie didn't share this call of the body, she didn't feel the panic I did. As it turned out, she would be robbed of the ability to have children and that same event would vanish the need in me, disappear it so thoroughly it was like it had never existed at all. All things good, taken.

Duncan lifts my foot to his lips and kisses it; I close my eyes.

"What about your mother?" I ask. "What was she like?"

"She was kind," he says. "That's what I remember best. You couldn't offend her. She cared about everyone, even if they didn't behave well. In the face of anything, she had compassion to offer. It's a kind of strength I think women know better than men, maybe."

"Not all women."

There is a silence and then he asks, "What whim brought you tonight?"

"Stuart Burns was on my doorstep."

Duncan tenses. "Why was that?"

"To collect his money, which I didn't have."

"Did he threaten you?"

"He's not a good man, Duncan."

"Next time he comes round you call me. I can be there in minutes."

"I didn't come here because I was frightened, that's not what I meant. I can look after myself."

I don't know if this is true, actually, in fact I strongly suspect it's not, but he says, "I know you can," and sounds like he means it.

I crawl to his end of the bed so my face is near to his. His fingers trail my spine. He has large, thick hands, rough fingers, and yet his touch is light. "Did you care about those women who left you?"

His hand reaches my neck, my jaw, my lips. "'Course. I just wasn't enough for them."

I cannot imagine in this moment how that could be possible.

"Why then. If not Stuart," he asks.

Why did I come here.

My lips brush the corner of his mouth. *Why.*

This will have to be the last time my feet find their way to his door.

After the trembling giant, Dad was lucid for the longest stretch of time since we'd moved to BC, and I began to hope. Maybe he had been returned to us permanently. Underneath I knew this was foolish and that we were biding time here. At nearly eighteen Aggie and I had finished school and so we spent our time on the work of survival, the three of us, pretending life was normal.

It first happened on a night in the cellar, bottling preserved peaches. Aggie was making Dad repeat words in Spanish and laughing at his pronunciation. I was inspecting a scrape on my calf—given to me by a rusty bit of metal and now growing steadily infected—and scheming how I could go to town for antibiotics without Dad knowing. And so I wasn't looking. But something smashed and there was a short scream.

I looked up. Made sense of it. One of the bottles had slipped between my sister's fingers and shattered into a thousand pieces. And my father had hit Aggie across the face hard enough to leave a red mark on her cheek. They were staring at each other in shock, in disbelief because this had never happened, not ever, not my gentle father who laughed when we made mistakes, smiled kindly when we broke things.

A shadow moved in the cellar. A pall coming over us.

Dad left. Aggie touched her cheek once, as though to imprint the feel of it to her palm, and then she started cleaning up the glass.

I said nothing, didn't move, too aware of my sister's pain and how this time of all times I hadn't shared it with her.

It became a pattern. Something broke in my father's mind. The essence of who he was changed. Mum might have called it his animal but in truth it was all too human. Frustrated. Frightened. Shamed. And violent. Something would feel wrong to him, something was forgotten or remembered suddenly, his vulnerability became too much for him and he took it out on Aggie. A slap or a shove. It was so strange as to be like a dream we floated through, colored mostly by disbelief. I didn't know why it was only directed at Aggie, perhaps because she had always been tougher, but I made sure to watch every small act of violence so I might share it with her, and at first this felt like solidarity, my support of her, but after a fortnight and a blow so hard it split her lip I knew that what I should be doing instead of watching was *protecting* her.

"It's time for a home," I said in the dawn of the third week.

Aggie rolled over to face me; we still slept in our shared room on the single beds we grew up in. "You said you didn't want him in one of those."

"Doesn't matter what I said. And maybe we should call Mum, too."

"God no. She'd just turn this into something it's not."

It was something, it was all things. We couldn't trust him anymore, and that was the worst betrayal of all.

We rose and padded, both of us barefoot, to the hallway outside Dad's room. *Are you sure?* Aggie signed to me.

I nodded.

But when we opened the door his bed was empty.

It took us nearly a week of searching the surrounding land before we could admit he was gone. On that first morning it was plain to see that his favorite horse had been taken from the stables and for a day or two we were able to follow his trail, but soon it disappeared, whether by bad luck or by his design, and it became painfully clear that wherever he went was not a place he intended us to follow. Still we searched, in wide, arcing circles.

In the deep parts of our bodies we knew that he had taken himself off to die quietly and without fuss, like an animal. Maybe to put an end to whatever he was becoming, to exert what little control he had left. Or maybe to protect us in the only way he knew how.

I did not think we would see him again, and we didn't. Our father.

10

I am filling Aggie's sertraline script when Lainey Burns steps into the pharmacy. I take some pamphlets off the counter for counseling services in nearby Aviemore; Aggie is going to need a new doctor soon, and maybe I can arrange for someone to do a house call. Then I walk to where Lainey stands in the painkiller aisle.

"Hi."

She sees me and smiles a real smile. "Hi."

All the swelling around her eye has gone down and the black bruises have been covered as well as they can be by makeup. "Nice artwork," I say, with a nod to her arm cast. It's adorned with colorful doodles of flowers and animals.

Lainey laughs a little. "Stuart's handiwork."

I must look surprised because her smile disappears. "People aren't always what they first seem."

Well she's certainly right about that.

"How's Gealaich?"

"She's okay. Still skittish. She won't let me go near her."

"Give her time. She got a fright."

My mouth opens but I can't find the right words. So I just ask, "Are you okay, Lainey?"

She doesn't get angry. She meets my eyes. "I am. Are you, Inti?"

I don't say her husband's been scaring the living shit out of me each time he sits in his car outside my house at night, because I'd be willing to bet Lainey's dealing with worse. "I am. Thanks."

I see her glance at the pamphlets in my hand and look at me a touch differently. I don't explain they're for my sister, or that I don't expect they'll help her. The bell over the door rings and then Stuart is here.

"Came to see what was taking so long," he says, eyeing me.

"Sorry," Lainey says. "I'm ready."

"I told you to stay away from my wife," he addresses me.

"What is it you think I'm gonna do—corrupt her?"

"We ran into each other," Lainey says. "Inti just said hello, that's all."

"All right, all's well, then." Stuart puts the aspirin his wife was holding back on the shelf and then steers her toward the door. "Goodnight, Mrs. Doyle, you have a braw night now," he calls to the old woman at the counter. Polite as pie.

I follow them.

The pharmacy is opposite the Snow Goose. Outside it stand Red McRae and Mayor Oakes, smoking a cigarette with their pints in hand. The streetlight above us is out so when I say Stuart's name and he stops to face me we are in shadow. Lainey hangs back warily.

I have only one thought. If she won't report him then I will provoke him until I have something *I* can report. I will turn the direction of his anger from Lainey to me.

"What do you do out there?" I ask. "When you lurk outside my house at night, just beyond the fence so you won't get in trouble. What are you thinking about? Do you get pleasure from the thought of intimidating me like that? Does it get you off?"

"Shut your filthy mouth," he says. "I'm just after what I'm owed."

"It must be what turns you on, huh? The thought of scaring women. Only we're not scared. I'm not scared of you, Stuart. I think you're pathetic. I stand by my window and watch you out there and I fucking laugh."

Several things happen at once. He steps toward me and this is it, I brace myself with a thrill of victory and a flash of hot fear, and from the corner of my eye I can see Red and Andy crossing the street and Lainey reaching for her husband's arm, but they're not going to stop him and we both know it. It's a voice sliding into the space between the lamplights, that's what stops him.

"How come I wasn't invited to the party?"

Stuart releases his clenched fist.

We both turn to look at Duncan.

"No party here," Stuart says. "Just a little girl making trouble."

Duncan is between us. To me he says, "Go and wait for me in the pub."

"No, I—"

"*Inti.*"

Goddamn it.

I cross the street, vibrating with adrenaline. That was so close. I cast a look back at the small group, but I can no longer hear what Duncan is saying to them, can only make out their shapes. Lainey is leaving now too, walking quickly down the street, and it occurs to me that Duncan is there alone now, outnumbered, and I wonder if I should go back, and then I remind myself not to be silly. He's a cop, and they're—for the most part—normal people. His friends, probably. I go inside.

Warm air blasts my cheeks. The wash of voices. I get myself a glass of wine from the bar and sink onto the peeling leather cushion of a booth. I'm so hot I must wrench my scarf and coat off before I can breathe again. Painful minutes pass by as I wait for him, imagining what could be taking place outside. If he is simply sending them home then why is he taking so long, and why did he separate Lainey from her husband, and the longer he takes the more certain I am that I will go back out there; I am grabbing my scarf and coat once more when Duncan slides into the booth opposite me.

He has a bruise on his cheek, a split lip. "What the hell are you doing?" he asks.

"I wasn't—"

"Bullshit. I can see you."

I close my mouth. My face is so hot.

"I tell you to mind him and you go aggravating him in the street at night? I'll say it again. You *stay away from Stuart Burns,* do you understand?" I have never heard his voice like this, I think under that anger he is afraid.

"Who did that to you?" I ask.

A waitress brings him a beer; I don't know if he ordered it when he came in or if she just knew what he'd want. He nods his thanks but keeps his eyes on me until she's left. "Have you got a bone to pick with me?"

"I do."

"Go on then, let's have it. Say your piece."

I take a mouthful of wine and it warms me. I live in his hands on his glass, his back on the cushion, his thin T-shirt against my collarbones, his bruise and his blood and his mouth as it touches his beer. I thought I had control but this is what he does to me. Despite my vow, and the guilt that leaving Aggie brings me, I have been slipping through the woods to his house too often.

"What are you so frightened of, Duncan?" I ask.

He doesn't answer.

"I think you must be frightened. Being who you are. And not doing anything about what you know."

"What should I do?"

"Anything."

"What if I've done it?"

I lift fingers to my cheek, feeling the ache. "What have you done?"

He doesn't answer.

"You must be frightened," I repeat.

"We're all frightened."

"Is that the excuse you make for him?"

"Just a fact."

"He's a monster," I say.

"You're giving him too much credit. He's just a man," Duncan says.

"That's dangerous. That's how you let people do terrible things."

He doesn't take to this. "I'm not minimizing. It's just that if you paint a picture of him as a monster then you make him mythical, but men who hurt women are just men. They're all of us. Too fucking many of us and all too human. And the women they hurt aren't passive victims, or Freud's masochists who like to be punished either. They're all women, and all they're doing, minute by minute, is strategizing how best to survive the man they loved, and that's not a thing anyone should have to do."

It's not what I expected to come from his mouth. I keep underestimating him.

Duncan probes his bruise and I flinch. "Don't."

He may understand some things but he doesn't know what it feels like to live in that fear. "Have you ever hurt a woman who loved you?"

He drains of color. "We're not all of us Stuart Burns," he says. "But we are all fallible, and that doesn't make us bad and it's not the same thing."

We watch each other.

"All any of us do is hurt each other," I say.

He reaches for my hand. "You and I have shared something other than that."

"Have we? I'm drowning."

"Inti."

"I don't want it. I came here to get away."

"And die slowly of loneliness."

"What would be so wrong with that?" I shake my head. "You're being dramatic. I have the wolves. I'm here to work."

"They're more dangerous than we are."

"Are they?" I ask. "They are wilder, certainly."

"Isn't it the same?"

"I don't think so. I think it's civilization makes us violent. We infect each other."

"So you'd live like your animals, then. Off in the woods and free of people, but you told me yourself what they need most is each other."

I don't say anything because for a moment I hate him.

"What happened to you?" Duncan asks.

"Nothing."

Then he says, but not like a question, "What kind of thing must you be."

What kind of thing.

"Somebody has to protect her," I say. "If you won't do your job then I will."

Suddenly it's dark behind his eyes. "You pull your head in, Miss Flynn. Do you hear me?"

His anger stirs mine. I imagine baring my teeth, showing him how sharp they are.

"I used to think people were good, too," I say. "I used to think we were mostly kind, all of us forgivable."

"And now?"

"Now I know better."

Duncan's living room is small and cluttered and warm. We've come here without words, only an instinct, as it always is with us. The sparking nature of desire, the combat of it. And something else, something quiet. I sit on the old leather couch and watch him lay the fire. Red bricks. Gray stone. A rough maroon rug beneath his bare feet, beneath mine. Furniture swims in and out of focus in the dim light, all pieces made of timber and broken somehow, crooked or bent or upside down, more and more pieces taking shape as though appearing from nowhere. I feel in a dream. Electric, perilous. I am aware that I have no control left, and deep within there is a surrendering. When he moves he does it uncomfortably. I could look away but I don't. I want to ask him how he got hurt. There are so many things I haven't asked, that I haven't wanted to know until now. He doesn't offer me a drink and I don't want one; I am drunk on the rest.

Duncan sits beside me and we look at each other.

"Your face hurts," I murmur.

"What kind of thing are you?" he asks against my mouth and this time it is a question.

Later in his bed he holds me, his body so hot it's as though he has laid the fireplace within himself. I realize how cold I have been, for so long.

I wake from a dream of a blow to my face. It is so vivid I can almost feel it. But when I open my eyes it's deep night and I'm alone in his bed.

11

My phone's dead. It's colder now, in these earliest hours of morning. The fire has burned down to its coals. I dress quickly and with his dog following on my heels I wander around his little house in case he's here somewhere. Where does a man go at 3 A.M.? I feel embarrassed, and foolish for having fallen asleep.

"He'll be home soon, darling," I tell Fingal, stroking the dog's worried face before I close him inside the house. My car's still parked outside the pharmacy, so I have no choice but to walk home. I'm grateful for the air. My head's pounding, and I wish I'd rooted around in his cupboard for some aspirin.

There is a path but it isn't visible in this light. All the earth seems dark beneath my boots. I let the trees guide me. *Hush,* they say, *be easy.* Thick fog creeps in and I am sure to lose my way. The moon vanishes. I don't understand why he left, and maybe it's nothing, but it also feels like something because last night was different.

Go gently, whisper the trees.

I keep walking but more slowly, touching trunks as I pass them. My feet lift over brush and branches. One of them slips as it lands, and I come down on my butt on the spongey green moss. Beside me lies a body, eyes staring into the fog.

A scream rips from me. I scramble backward.

His guts are open and spilling. Mine are tumbling out of me. I slam my eyes closed.

The first thundering thought: *What if teeth did that?*

I become nothing more than the throb of my too-quick pulse. I have to look. I am so afraid as I look. Not at the wounds of him, the mess of him, but at his face, still intact.

It's Stuart Burns. Eyes open and glassy; the meat of him left empty.

I lean over and vomit onto the earth.

As my body heaves it rushes through me, what this will mean. I can see it laid out so clearly, the fate of every wolf. This will kill them. I don't know enough to recognize the forensic difference between a serrated weapon and the tearing of an animal's teeth, and I can't look for long enough to make a guess, but I know how this will appear. I know what everyone will believe, and it will send them into the forests to hunt the wolves for having killed a man. And then the ancient forest will go too, all the trees we are trying to save, every effort to rewild Scotland, everything will go. This future comes to me in an instant, and I could weep right here, but not for this man. Once I would have pitied him regardless of what he's done, because this is a bad end for anyone. But I feel only fury at him for being here, only terror for my wolves.

It looks like they killed him. It looks very much like that. This is how they attack, either at throat or guts, the two most vulnerable spots.

But I know they didn't do this, they wouldn't, they don't attack people. Someone has murdered Stuart Burns and left him here. And that someone either wanted Stuart dead, or they wanted the wolves dead.

I make a very dark choice. Or it makes me.

I bury his body.

12

My shovel barely makes an impact in the hard ground. It takes all the strength I have to dig enough of a hole, and far too much time. As the dirt scatters back over him in heavy dumping loads, he is slowly disappeared, covered over, slowly given back to the earth and the roots and the world beneath the surface. But as I begin to cover his face it stops being his face and becomes mine, my face that is being buried, my throat choked by the cold ground, my body swallowed whole.

I wash an avalanche of dirt down the shower. I scrub beneath my finger-nails and I do it quickly, and I don't think about anything else. The sun has well and truly risen by the time I am clean. Aggie should be up by now, so I go in to check on her, only to find her awake in bed and staring and when I draw back her blankets I see that she has bled onto the sheets. *No.* Please, not today. Not this morning. I don't have it in me to look after her. Except that I must, so I do.

Back into the shower. I wash her under a stream of water. It might be intimate if she were here, instead I am alone with her body and this is a terrible loneliness. Water slides over her and I see that she's changing, getting softer, thicker, and for the first time we are not physically the same. I hold her in an embrace and press my lips to her shoulder and I grieve for the sameness that is leaving us, stolen from us. I miss her so much and I think I am holding her too tightly, and then I think maybe if I hurt her she will wake.

My grip loosens. She allows herself to be guided out of the shower and this is what disturbs me most, I think, that there should be some level of consciousness, that something of her remains, if only in her muscle memory. I dry my sister and place a pad in her undies before I draw them up over her legs; she steps into them malleably but when I try to meet her eyes there is no awareness there. She is just too tired for it. I hope she is somewhere better. I wish I were somewhere better because here fucking sucks. Here is a waking nightmare.

How long before he's reported missing? How long before the weather or animals or both dig him up? I covered tracks and marks and it's true that I am good at this because I have been a tracker all my life, and in looking at that spot *I* wouldn't notice anything amiss, but could a better hunter than I see through my attempts? Could a detective? How long before I go insane and tell Duncan exactly what I've done?

Honestly, what the fuck was I thinking?

Maybe it's not too late to come clean. If I tell Duncan now, will he investigate? Or will he put Stuart's death down to a wolf attack and think nothing more of it? Red McRae will be joyously reaching for his rifle. And what if Duncan thinks *I* killed Stuart? I buried him, didn't I? What sane person would do that?

I have to leave it. I'm in it now, it's done. All I can hope is that he never gets found, and that if he does, I didn't leave a whole lot of my DNA on his body to frame myself with.

What if a wolf really did kill him? whispers a soft voice within. But I know the answer. If a wolf really did kill Stuart then I did the right thing in covering it up.

I am at work alone when a knock sounds on the cabin door. Evan and Niels are out collecting data from the Tanar Pack and I've sent Zoe to grab us some lunch from town, although when I see who's standing at the door I wish I hadn't sent her anywhere.

Duncan's hat is in his hands. "You must have got away early."

My insides lurch, wondering if he's come to arrest me.

"So must you," I say, and usher him in. "Cuppa?"

"I can't stay, I've got business in town."

We stand awkwardly and it's strange that there's awkwardness, there never has been before and does this mean he knows something?

"I went for a walk," he says.

"I didn't ask," I say, then frown. "At three in the morning? Why?"

"I always walk when I'm sorting things through."

I don't ask what he means.

"I thought I'd get back and you'd still be asleep," he adds.

I shrug. "It doesn't matter."

Everything is different now. I don't have space. There was a body and I buried it and this is the man who is going to have to search for that body.

"It's better this way," I tell him gently, and find that it hurts, far more than I was expecting it to.

He doesn't ask what I mean. Instead, "Would you come to dinner on the weekend? I have some friends round every now and then. You'd enjoy it. *I'd* enjoy having you there." There's something about his quiet vulnerability that makes my chest ache. He knows something has changed.

"I can't, Duncan," I say. "I don't have anything to give you."

"Then take from me. I have more than enough."

My eyes prickle and I look away from him. That way lies danger.

Duncan inclines his head politely, taking my silence as answer enough. "Give me a shout if you need anything, Miss Flynn, or if trouble finds you out here. I'm not far away."

His boots on the wooden floor echo after he's gone.

I feel the exhaustion in my throat, in my eyes and my teeth. Everything aches. The day has ticked by so slowly I thought it would never end. But there is still dinner to be made, and Aggie needs help in the bathroom again, and I forgot to change her bedsheets so there's also that.

A thought like a wisp of smoke in my mind, leaving behind something new. Our cycles have always been in sync. My period should have started too.

I'm no longer tired as I take my second trip to the pharmacy in as many days. Mrs. Doyle at the counter places the test in a paper bag for me and says, "Courage, dear," and I think she must be able to see the fear on my face. Home once more. It's cold in the bathroom. I unpack the test and wee on the stick, waiting in pieces for the minutes to pass, but it hasn't worked, I must not have aimed well enough. I unpack a second test and this time, after gulping down a liter of water, I wee into a cup and place the stick upside down within it.

I don't need to look, not truly. I have known all day, I think, even before the thought formed. But, the proof. Not a double line or anything as vague, a little blue word that reads *pregnant,* so there can be no confusion.

13

"As you know, Miss Flynn, we're speaking to anyone who had contact with him during the twenty-four hours before his disappearance."

The meeting room is small, with a window overlooking a copse of pine trees and no one-way mirror like in the movies. There's a camera and voice recorder but they're off. Duncan is across the table from me. A policewoman introduced to me as Bonnie Patel was beside him, but she left to get us tea and hasn't returned. I guess he's starting without her.

"Can you run me through Saturday?" Duncan asks me. I must look surprised because he adds, "This is completely informal, we're just collecting as much information as we can to piece Stuart's movements together."

I shift uncomfortably. He sounds formal and distant, like this is our first meeting.

"I went to work."

"On the weekend?"

"Wolves don't have weekends."

"All right, and after work?"

"I went to town, to the pharmacy."

"What did you go to the pharmacy for?"

I shoot him a look of disbelief.

"Okay, then what happened?" he asks.

"I saw Lainey there. Stuart came in all pissed that we were talking."

"Why was he pissed about that?"

"Because he's a dickhead."

He glances up at me. Perhaps readjusting to my attitude. I remind myself to be polite and get this over and done with as quickly as possible.

He's only doing his job and yet I feel a prick of hurt that he has brought me here at all.

"What time do you put this at?"

"The pharmacy was closing for the night, so whatever time that is."

"Seven. Then what?"

"I followed Stuart and Lainey outside and spoke a few more words with him. And then you showed up."

"And what were the nature of the words?"

"Provocative, probably."

Duncan's eyebrows arch as he waits. Is he really going to make me say it?

"I was trying to get under his skin," I admit. "I wanted to see what he'd do if he was pushed."

"What did you suspect he'd do?"

"Lash out. Hurt me. Like he hurts his wife."

"Why would you want that?"

"So I could file charges against him."

Duncan sits back and folds his arms. Sighs. "How do you know he was harming her?"

"You told me."

"Did I?"

"Not with words."

"What else is there?"

"Plenty."

He considers this, studying me. "Would it be fair to say there was animosity between the two of you?"

"Yes."

"You owed him money, right?"

"Two thousand pounds, for the horse I bought off him."

"Did he threaten you for that money?"

I consider admitting the truth but I'd rather not create even more motive for myself. "Not really. He just asked for it."

"Did he ever admit to harming Lainey?"

I sit forward, frowning. "Are you seriously trying to imply he wasn't doing anything to her?"

Duncan doesn't reply.

"That's weak," I say. "You're cowering now because he's missing."

"But how do you *know* that's what was happening, Inti?" he asks again.

"I *know*," I snap. "I've seen it before. It's fucking obvious. You know it too."

"What happened next?" he asks.

I grapple with my rampaging thoughts. Saturday night. "I told you. You got there and made me go into the pub. So you'd know better than I would what happened next."

"Was that the last time you saw Stuart?"

I nod.

"Did you see him in any altercations with anyone else that night?"

Just you. And your face was broken. Except I didn't actually see that, did I? I have no real idea what happened outside. I shake my head no.

"You know anyone else who was as crabbit as you?"

"What the hell is crabbit?"

"Angry."

A breath of laughter escapes me.

"There's no one you can point to being a potential suspect in his disappearance?" Duncan rephrases.

"No. Only people I know around here are my colleagues and I'd be surprised if they even know who Stuart is."

Duncan leans back in his chair, idly playing with his pen. "What brought you to Scotland, Inti?"

"I'm head of the Cairngorms Wolf Project. It would make more sense you asking me all these questions you know the answers to if there was a tape recorder on. As it is, I can't really work out who this little charade is for."

"No charade. I just like to be clear. You were trying to get a different project underway, weren't you?" He's done his research.

"In Utah. To reintroduce wolves to save Pando, the trembling giant."

"So why didn't you go there?"

"There was too much pushback from the locals. You think it's been bad here, but in Utah we didn't even get close."

"But didn't they already do it in Yellowstone?"

"Yeah, and it was an uphill battle the whole way. They care more about farming and hunting than saving trees."

"Why shouldn't they?"

"Because this planet doesn't belong to them," I snap. "We aren't entitled to it, we aren't *owed*."

He is quiet a moment, studying me. "Working the land is as tough a job as they come."

"I didn't say it wasn't."

"You ever wondered why conservationists tend to come from higher socioeconomic backgrounds? They've got money. They don't have to rely on the land to survive, they aren't scraping by, one day to the next."

"I understand that the impact of conservation has not fallen equally on rural and urban shoulders, and that we need to share the burden of change equitably," I say. "I do get that, Duncan. Everyone here seems to think I have some vendetta, but the only thing I have against farmers is that they seem to have something against me."

"Your project threatens their livelihood."

"It doesn't, actually. They just don't want to share." I think of my father. "You can rely on the land and you can work it, and you can feed it and care for it at the same time. You can reduce your impact. That's got nothing to do with money. We have a responsibility to reduce our impact. Rewilding is how we fight climate change, and everyone seems to have forgotten that that's the only thing that matters anymore. *We* certainly don't matter." I pause and then add, "Maybe we ought to just wipe out the human race and show some mercy to the poor trampled Earth."

"That's just ecofascism."

I'm surprised, and laugh.

"It must be frustrating," he says, and I wait for him to elaborate. "Being smarter than everyone and not being listened to."

I roll my eyes.

"I'm serious," he says. "You're here to help and all you get is animosity." Duncan sits forward again. "You have a right to be angry. I would be." His fingers lace together and it feels like he's holding my hand. "The question is how angry."

"Angry enough to kill someone?" I clarify for him.

"Nobody said anyone was dead."

"We're both thinking it. And we both know the guy was scum."

"That's a pretty strong opinion to have of someone you barely knew."

"Yes," I agree.

"I've known that man all my life," Duncan tells me. "There's demons that get into a head out here, in a place like this."

I stare at him in disbelief. "You justify his behavior all you want, Chief, but men beat their wives all over the world and it has nothing to do with where they live, and actually it doesn't matter why they do it."

"If we don't know why they do it we got no hope of helping them stop."

I fold my arms. "Seems to me he's been stopped."

Duncan meets my eyes, doesn't say anything.

"You've got plenty of motive without bringing me and my wolves into this," I say.

"That's just it, though. Nobody died out here until you and your wolves showed up."

"I thought nobody said anyone was dead."

He smiles that rare, crooked smile of his. "My mistake." He lets a moment pass and I'm hoping this is over, that he's going to wind it up, but instead he says, "Have you been married, Inti?"

"No."

"Any serious relationships?"

I almost fidget but hold myself still. "No."

"Did your parents share an abusive relationship?"

"My parents lived on opposite sides of the world and barely knew each other."

"I'm trying to work out why you're so protective of a woman you hardly know."

"Because someone ought to be." I spread my hands on the table; they're shaking. "Shouldn't we all be? How many women have to get killed before we get angry?" My voice breaks. "Why aren't we all angry? Why aren't we furious, Duncan?"

He searches my face, giving me nothing.

I take a deep breath.

"I didn't kill Stuart," I say evenly. "I have no idea what happened to him, but the guy's probably pissed off to somewhere sunny where he doesn't have to worry about a failing farm and his own shame staring back at him from the other side of the bed every morning."

"Maybe. Or maybe he's lying dead somewhere."

"Maybe."

"I can't account for your whereabouts after two thirty on Sunday morning."

I'm getting really over this now, I want to get the fuck out of here. I take a breath and tell him the thing I couldn't tell him in tenderness, I fling it at him like a weapon. "I didn't kill Stuart because I can't do someone physical harm."

"How's that?"

"I have a condition called mirror-touch synesthesia. My brain causes my body to feel the sensations I see."

He frowns, bewildered.

"I'll forward you my medical records." There are a lot of them: it took some time to diagnose, given mirror-touch is so rare and understood by so few specialists. Even then it didn't make much difference, having the diagnosis, as it was never a disease to be treated or a problem to be solved, but simply a different way of existing. It was only ever Mum who cared enough to help me find ways of living with the condition. Oddly, I have almost no memories of that time with the doctors.

Duncan takes this in, watching me, turning it over in his mind. Maybe thinking back to our nights together, his wounded face, my reaction to it . . . He holds up his pen, taps his finger against the plastic. "All sensation?"

I nod, not in the mood to go through the whole demonstration.

"You can feel that? Where?"

"On my fingers, as if the pen were in my hand."

His eyes widen a little. "Shit. Whatever you see, you feel?"

"Yep."

"Everything, Inti?"

"Everything."

There's a long silence. I wait for him to test it further, to touch his body somewhere so he can watch me feel it and when he does I will hate him.

Instead he says, "So it's not exactly impossible."

"What?"

"It would be difficult, but not impossible, right? To do someone harm? To end their life. It wouldn't kill you."

I stare at him. Is it possible I haven't been taking this seriously? Does he actually want me for Stuart's murder?

"You really think I'm capable of that?" I ask, trying to keep the hurt from my voice.

"The only thing I know with any certainty," Duncan replies, "is that we are all capable of it. Let's wrap it up now, Inti, I've got what I needed. Thanks for coming in."

Aggie has the fire blazing. It's warm in the little cottage, and she's reading a book with her back to the flames. I sink onto the old carpet beside her; it's seen better days, marked here and there by coal specks from the fire. There is a red stain in the corner that I hope was wine. The whole place needs a good freshen up, and I wouldn't mind furnishing it ourselves (everything is floral) but still, I'm growing fond of our little home. Aggie reaches to give my hand a quick squeeze without looking up. It's one of her good days and I'm grateful for it, so weary I slump to the floor, back flat, eyes on the low ceiling. Tendrils of smoke escape the fireplace and snake their way up. My vision wavers a little, watching them. My hands rest idly on my stomach; I become aware and move them away. For a moment I imagine how Duncan might have reacted if I'd blurted it out during that interview.

"A man disappeared," I tell Aggie.

From the corner of my eye I see her lower the book.

"They're searching the forest for him tomorrow. They've called for volunteers."

Will you go? she signs.

I nod, and something twists within me. It's disgusting to pretend to want to find him. This feels like a worse crime than burying him, some-how.

Do you want me to come?

I tilt my head to look at my sister's face. "Would you?"

She doesn't answer and I know she wants to, she wants to be with me, just as I'd give anything to have her by my side, but there are chains about this little stone cottage, keeping her trapped within, and there are chains about her body, keeping her trapped within. It's too dark for her to face, anyway. I can't ask her to come. What if we found him?

"No," I say. "It's okay."

Do you think he's dead?

I open my mouth but nothing comes out. Instead I give a stiff nod. All the muscles in my body seem to have seized up; I feel a thousand years old.

Why?

I want to admit everything. Before Alaska, I would have. What I knew, Aggie knew. But now there is a world I want to protect her from, there is violence to be kept at bay.

"Because men like him," I say, "don't just leave. That's like giving up all the things that belong to him. If he's gone it's because he's dead."

Something passes through Aggie, a shudder of memory. She is swal-lowed by it and I reach for her, wanting to catch her before she is gone again but knowing too late that I've made a mistake. "Hey," I say. "It's okay."

Is he coming? she asks, and like each time she asks this she takes on a childlike quality that unnerves me.

No, I sign, because this is the language she trusts.

We meet at the Burns stud at dawn. About sixty people have turned up to help, along with a host of local police and several sniffer dogs. Even though wolf Number Thirteen is still in the pen and we're all worried about her, about why, my team is here—Niels, Evan, and Zoe showed up without being asked. I can see Amelia and Holly standing nearby, and clustered around a blank-faced Lainey are a few young men who must be her brothers from out of town, plus Red McRae and Mayor Oakes. Duncan and his team of cops stand out in front to give us our orders—we're to leave no more than a couple of feet between us at all times, and we keep our eyes trained on the ground ahead of us, scanning for anything at all that could be a sign of human presence. Footprints, items of clothing, personal belongings. Anything unusual is worth pointing out. He doesn't say that we're looking for a body, too, but we all know it.

We move into the forest as one, this forest that is meant to be a quiet place but quickly becomes punctured by the noise of shouting voices. Our feet trample the undergrowth without care, our hands tear at low-hanging branches to rip them from our paths. Any animals in these parts will hear us and flee as best they can. Warrens and nests will be destroyed underfoot.

I pray the wolves are far from here.

By nightfall we are cold and exhausted, and we've found no body. Stuart Burns is south of the land we have covered. I want to ask how long we will keep doing this, how much ground Duncan means for us to search. But I don't. Somehow I must pretend to myself that I know nothing more than the rest of these locals; I must bury that body much deeper within myself than I buried it in the ground.

14

After Dad disappeared Aggie and I went home to Sydney, and a mother who hadn't changed at all in the two years we were gone, except that her thick dark hair had gone silver. We blinked and life was returned to how it had been, only I felt a wild creature stuffed into the body of a human. I felt called back. Only alive within the forest.

I studied hard and fast and earned two science degrees before I turned twenty-five. Aggie turned her mind to the adolescence she had missed out on. By the time I graduated she'd dated half the men in Sydney. I didn't admit that I wanted her life instead of mine, that I wanted to be the one who lived in the body, for touch and taste and desire. I didn't need to admit it; she already knew.

On a hot night after I'd started my PhD I went to see Mum in our old place. Aggie and I had moved out by then, into a little terrace near my uni. But I tried to visit Mum as often as possible because she spent her nights alone scrutinizing photos of criminals or victims and both seemed grim company.

Tonight she was sitting in front of two fans that did nothing but push the hot air around. She was alternating between mouthfuls of red wine and ice cubes, and had one of her current cases open in front of her on the floor. I helped myself to a glass of wine and sat beside her, spraying my arms and legs in bug spray because she still hadn't got flyscreens to stop the mozzies.

"What's this one?" I asked her.

She glanced at me, perhaps only now becoming aware of my presence.

"Missing person." She slid a photo around so I could see the face of the teenage girl.

"Could she have run away?" I asked, studying the smiling young face.

"She didn't run away."

"Then what happened," I asked, because I wanted to know but I also didn't. I always wanted to know and also didn't. A kind of dance my mother and I did together, or perhaps a contest I always hoped to win but never did.

"Someone killed her," Mum said.

"How do you know?"

"Because it's always what happened, when someone vanishes. Any cop knows it."

"But maybe not," I said softly. Maybe she went on an adventure.

"I'd like to visit that world you live in, my girl," Mum said. "It sounds kinder than this one." Then, "How are the wolves?"

"A long way from here."

"What's keeping you then?"

"I'll have better job prospects if I do the PhD."

"You're stalling because you don't want to leave Aggie."

"What are you talking about?" Leaving Aggie wasn't even an option. Could it be possible Mum *still* didn't understand that?

She shrugged, running a piece of ice over her forehead. "One of you will have to leave the other eventually."

"Why?"

"Because she doesn't belong in the forest, and you do," Mum said simply.

Abruptly there were tears in my eyes. "But I don't want that without her."

Mum studied my face. Hers blurred. "Toughen up."

Some weeks later, I was sitting on the grass of the Sydney University campus and enjoying the evening sun. My eyes had started to droop shut when a shadow fell across the pages of my book. I looked up at the silhouette.

"Hello," it said.

"Hello," I replied.

The man shifted so I could see him, a stranger's shape and features. Tall, square in the face, clean cut and shaved. His cologne wafted freshly down to me and conjured something familiar. "Are you pre or post class?" he asked.

"Post."

"Shall I buy you a drink and you can tell me how it was?"

Curious.

I glanced at the time. Aggie wouldn't be finished teaching her language students for hours. It wasn't like me to befriend strangers unless I was with my sister, but then they didn't tend to approach me out of the blue and make it this easy.

"Why not," I said, gathering my books into my pack. He offered a hand to help me stand and I took it, noticing its sweatiness.

At the university bar we sat outside in the sun among the gaggles of students. I loved these long summer nights, when it didn't get dark until late.

"What was your class today?" the man asked. He seemed older than me, but not by too much. I wondered if he was a student or a lecturer.

"It was just a meeting with my supervisor."

"Supervisor of . . . ?"

"My PhD."

"Huh. Look at that. You're surprising me already."

I frowned, unsure if I should be offended.

"What's your topic?"

"Wolves."

He laughed. "Of course it is. Classic academic bullshit, studying something in a country about as far from any real wolves as possible, meaning you never have to get out from behind your computer."

I stared at him.

"So tell me what you're learning about wolves from a book," he said.

I looked away, across the lawns to the pond where the ducks swam. Fat white geese waddled along the bank, honking happily. A breeze lifted the hair off my forehead. I could ask him his name, but somehow I knew this was part of the game. I wouldn't ask until he did.

"Come on, kid," he said, "I'm interested, I admit it."

When I looked at him again he was leaning closer. A big man, big like a linebacker, and in this light he had the look of an old-fashioned movie star, all those sharp angles, the *cleanness* of him. It occurred to me how handsome he was and suddenly I didn't just viscerally dislike him, I also wanted him, and much to my horror, wanted to impress him.

"I'm studying the cognitive maps wolves make of their territories. They pass these geographic and temporal maps down through generations, and know their land so intimately that they go nowhere unless it's deliberate. Wolves don't wander. They move with purpose, and they teach their pups how to do the same. They can share the mental images with each other."

"How do they do that?"

"By howling. Their voices paint pictures."

Now he was really looking at me, and I didn't think anyone had looked at me like that before, with such appetite.

"Okay, that's pretty cool," he afforded. "So why that?"

I shrugged. "It's interesting to me that some creatures can pass on memories, and that some memories are so deep they can live in the body instead of only in the mind."

"Nothing lives in the body, not really, that's just a trick of your brain." He traced a finger along my hand, the one holding my gin and tonic. It startled me. "It was your brain that felt that, not your hand."

"And when the brain can't be relied upon?" Sometimes the function of my mind made life very difficult. Of course sometimes it made it wonderful, too. I wasn't about to admit this: a peril I learned long ago to guard against. Men took it as an invitation to test me, to touch me. "What are you studying?" I asked to change the subject.

"Neurosurgery."

"You're a brain surgeon? Fuck."

"Guilty. Or I will be."

"Now I feel stupid for going on about brains."

"Nah. I'm just a butcher. Come on, let's go for a walk."

I blinked. "What about our drinks?"

"I'm not thirsty anymore."

He led us around the park and into the city's streets. I sent a quick text to Aggie telling her I'd meet her at home later, and felt a surge of excitement at the thought of how approving she would be of this unexpected rendezvous. I almost told her to come and meet us because doing anything interesting without her was unnatural to me, but I reminded myself that there would have to be *some* things I did alone. Mum's words flashed unbidden into my mind. *One of you will have to leave the other eventually.*

We walked for a long time and the stranger was mostly easy to talk to, except a moment here or there when he changed the subject so abruptly I almost got whiplash. In these moments there was a streak of something in his eyes, a flash maybe of boredom? And then he launched us elsewhere and I was left scrabbling to get my bearings.

Soon he changed direction as sharply as he changed the subject, and we were in front of an apartment block, and without asking he went inside and waited for me to follow him.

I hesitated. Told myself this was too much, way too much of an assumption, and dangerous besides, but if I'm being honest it was only for a split second. The flare of adrenaline felt like fear but also a yearning for something, anything, and always there was my unyielding curiosity to outweigh the rest. This body of mine that sought and knew things I did not. So I followed him inside and let the elevator carry us to the top floor and then I followed him into his apartment. To have something of my own. To feel something I had not simply watched.

In the morning he drove me home. I still didn't know his name. He still didn't know mine. I was flushed with the heady tactile memories of the night, with the feel of the silk ties around my wrists, holding me to the bed, the feel of his mouth on my body, the rush of excitement this brought, the sense of inhabiting a different life.

As he pulled over in front of our house I was struck by the realization that I hadn't told him where I lived.

Something went cold inside.

But a tiny quiet piece, the darkest of me, it already suspected, didn't it? Didn't I know in that first moment?

He seemed relaxed, a little impatient. He had to get to work. So when he kissed me it was with none of the slow, lingering passion of the previous night, but there was a different kind of familiarity, something that spoke of having done this before.

"Bye, kid," he said. "Do me a favor and think of me today, okay? Think of me when you're in the shower."

I climbed out, dazed, and walked inside.

Aggie shouted to me from the kitchen. "Come. Now. Spill."

I sat at the kitchen bench. Aggie poured the coffee from the percolator on the stove. "You look weird," she said.

"I don't actually know what to say," I admitted. "It was . . . unexpected."

Maybe I did tell him my address. I must have. I was distracted that morning. As the thought took hold I sank back into the thrill of it. "I don't even know his name."

"No fucking way." Aggie threw her head back and howled like a wolf.

"Shhh," I laughed.

Without warning the door to our little terrace opened and a person strode inside. It startled me, but then I saw it was him, the man, and a surprised smile filled me and things happened all at the same time, he said, "You left your phone in my car, kid," and I said, "Oh," and Aggie said, "Hello, handsome," and for some reason we were both walking toward him and then he stopped and we stopped and we all just stared at each other as mutual horror dawned.

"Shit," he said. He threw me a swift look, one that seemed to plead for something, for mercy, maybe. And then his eyes shifted, permanently, to Aggie. "I didn't know," he said clearly. "I didn't know, Aggie. I thought it was you."

Aggie looked at me, and I looked at her.

"He did," I said. "He did think it was you. He never asked my name."

We waited in agony for her response.

And she said, breaking my heart with her generosity, "Should we laugh? Or kill him?"

His name was Gus Holloway. He was Aggie's new boyfriend, the one I hadn't yet met because of his crazy work hours. He was thirty years old and played rugby every Tuesday night, and he was doing his residency at RPA Hospital. He liked six sugars in his coffee in the morning and drank Fireballs religiously, and he met Aggie because she taught his nephew Japanese. He broke rules. He was confidence personified. He could make her come with a look. He had seven sets of French linen bedsheets and changed them every day.

Those were the things I knew before I met Gus.

What I knew after that night were things I had no right to know.

And what I didn't know. The things I didn't yet know about him belonged deep in the ugliest recesses of his soul, in a place my mother had seen and tried to warn us about, only I didn't listen to her, I never listened.

It was late when he finally left. I hid in my room, unsure how I'd ever face him again. They talked out there for hours, and then they did the other thing they apparently do all the time, the thing that probably meant they'd made up. How small and unworthy I must have been last night, compared to the passionate creature he normally had. How could he not have known?

Aggie came into my room and slid onto the bed beside me.

"He says he thought we were playing our game," she told me. "Where we pretend to be characters." She shook her head, then admitted, "We do play it sometimes. It started as a way to help me rehearse." The amateur theater company she joined. That play she only got cast in because she could speak German.

I nodded, and didn't know what to say.

Maybe he didn't know. Maybe I didn't either. I didn't, not really. Not consciously.

I thought of the look on his face when he saw us standing next to each other this morning. There was no surprise in his eyes, only guilt.

"I'm sorry," I say. "Aggie. I fucked up."

"We'll share him."

"I beg your pardon?"

"I can't imagine he'd say no." She took my hand and squeezed; there was something feverish about her and she was really not joking, something had come loose in her head. "I don't do anything without you. That's not what we are. We share."

I tucked her hair behind her ear. "Oh man. You have got to be the most generous and unhinged person on the planet."

She laughed into my shoulder and I couldn't tell if maybe she was crying.

"I can't be with someone knowing you like him," she said. "I won't. I'll dump him."

"I don't like him," I said. "He got bored when I talked."

She laughed through her tears. "He does that. He's a bit of a dickhead, actually."

15

She still howls, some nights. Number Six. Evan wanted to call her Ash, didn't he? She howls for her mate, but now also for her strength, to define her territory, to stake a claim to it and ward off enemies. She teaches her babies to howl, defiant in the dark, growing stronger by the day. Soon she will teach them the hunt. They'll have to learn early, for there is no pack to kill for them.

A town meeting in the school auditorium is called about the search for Stuart. Nobody is on the stage this time. Duncan is in his spot by the door, watching the crowd. This isn't a cop-run meeting, it's been called by Lainey's brothers, who are huddled at the front of the audience. One of them, at least a decade younger than Lainey, goes to the microphone. "Thank you for coming," he says. He can only be a teenager, but he speaks with clear and resounding confidence. "My brother-in-law has been missing now for two weeks. The police don't have any reason to suspect that he's taken off—they look for things like phone records and any debits from bank accounts, and there haven't been any, and they have his phone too which was left at home, meaning it's looking more and more like something's happened to him. Whether it was an accident or not, somebody knows something, and we intend to find out. We're offering a cash reward for any information you might have that could direct the police to Stuart's whereabouts."

Somebody in the crowd stands up. A woman. "You're not going to get anyone coming forward, son. Not unless wolves can start confessing their sins."

Oh fuck.

Evan is sitting beside me. He grabs my hand and squeezes it hard, less to comfort me than himself, I think. We've been hoping this day wouldn't come.

"We all know what's happened," she goes on. "We need to put that poor man to rest but we'll have to do so knowing his body's lost."

"Not lost," someone else says.

"This is exactly what we knew would happen," another voice says.

I get to my feet and stride to the microphone on the stage. "Do you mind," I say to the boy, and he seems like he might argue, but shrugs and moves aside. "Before this gets out of hand," I say clearly, "I would like to explain that if a wolf had killed a person, we would know. We would have found remains. Wolves don't eat the stomachs of their kills. They crush bones but only to get to the marrow inside, which leaves shards. I can assure you, there would be something left for us to find. At the very least, blood, and a great deal of it."

There is a heavy silence and I realize I have done nothing but disturb them further.

The meeting ends. But I've seen in their faces what I dreaded. They don't believe me. They don't care what I say. Something approaches, much like a storm. I will try to hold it back, but sooner or later their fear will surge. If no culprit is found, they'll take to the forest with weapons.

Outside I call to Lainey, but she's being jostled into a car by her brothers. There are five of them, and one of the older ones, not the kid who spoke, steps into my path. "Not now," he says. "She's tired."

"I just want to see if she's okay. My name's Inti, I'm her friend." The word comes easily, but is it true?

"We know who you are. She doesn't need any more visions of wolves crushing bones, all right?"

I deflate. Lainey is staring resolutely ahead, and clearly doesn't want to speak to me. I didn't want friends when I got here, and now I wish I could be there for her but it doesn't work that way. I made myself a force for conflict in her life. I made things worse. "I'm sorry," I tell her brother.

"I didn't mean to conjure that. But you guys know that's not what happened, right? Or else you wouldn't be posting a reward."

"We're just covering our bases," he says flatly. "None of us expects to have to pay that money."

The wolf pups are about two months old, and have emerged from the den, scrawny and scruffy, with paws and ears too big for their bodies. They wrestle and play unceasingly, tripping over themselves and yapping with excitement. They've moved to a rendezvous point—where they'd hang out with the rest of their pack if they had one—not far from their den site, and luckily for me, it's a visible grassy stretch amid sparse trees. I visit them most days, staying at a distance to watch without disturbing them. They know I am here. They can smell me from nearly three kilometers away. The more I come, the more used to me they will grow, which is exactly what I should be guarding against, and yet I keep coming, transfixed by them and also getting more frightened by the day that some hunter will step out of the trees and gun them all down.

Despite my own rules I have taken to thinking of Number Six as *Ash*. She watches over her pups until she is forced to leave them to hunt. Normally there would be other wolves here to babysit them, so I tend to stay during these times, hunkered down in a sleeping bag, though what I could do if hunters arrived I have no idea. Put myself between them, I guess—though at this point I'm not sure that would be much of a deterrent.

Human hunters are not the only threat the unprotected pups face. The Tanar Pack, strong with five grown wolves, isn't far from here. They've been roaming, widening their territory. If they have a mind to stake this land they could turn up determined to kill the pups before they mature into wolves old enough to present threats. But no other wolves come, and the pups spend their time playing and sleeping, or practicing how to stalk and pounce on their siblings.

I've watched Ash return a couple of times, her belly swollen from gorging as much as she can because waiting for her are six hungry mouths. She is surrounded by her pups, who lick her muzzle to let her know they're famished. She regurgitates the meat from her stomach and they gobble it up, fighting each other to get the larger shares. If they keep licking her mouth she sometimes growls to curb their greediness, and in the flash of dominance there can be no mistaking that this is a breeding female, a leader. Her pups back down immediately.

If they're to survive, this young pack, Ash will need to recruit new members—wolves who can hunt with her, help her raise the pups, and help her fight off rival packs.

I can't seem to leave them. It's becoming a problem.

At home Aggie has made a vegetable lasagna, forced to use mainly mush-rooms once I'd explained that it was beyond my powers to get a hold of eggplants in rural Scotland.

"You must have been cooking all day!" I say as she removes the foil and a heavenly smell hits me. She still hasn't gone out to meet Gall. Prob-ably a greater indication of her mental health than just about anything. She loves horses as much as Dad did.

Has Thirteen left the cage yet? Aggie asks.

"She goes in and out to find food. But no, not really, and Twelve—the young male from the Glenshee Pack—he's been sniffing around."

Is she in danger from him?

I hesitate, then nod. No use lying to her.

Close the cage.

"Lock her back in? No way, I can't do that."

I watch my sister cutting the lasagna and serving it onto plates. She's mad at me. I try to explain. "She won't survive if she can't look after her-self. If she fears him, she can run, or she can fight. But it's no life being locked in a cage. Better she's free to die."

Aggie looks up at me. *She's stayed in there for a reason.*

I shake my head and start eating. Around a mouthful I mutter, "Fear. It's just fear and that's weakness."

I am not looking at her as she tries to sign something, so she shoves me hard to get me to watch her hands. *You're all clenched.*

"What?" I snap, thinking I've misread some sign, but she makes the same words again. "What do you want me to say?"

Let it go.

"That's rich." I finish shoveling the lasagna into my mouth but I can no longer taste it. "I need to go out for a bit tonight."

Boyfriend? she signs.

"I don't have a boyfriend."

Her eyebrows arch.

"I've been with the wolves."

She glances at me skeptically. Then signs, *It's a blueberry.*

"Huh?"

Aggie tilts her head. *Your baby is the size of a blueberry.*

Heat fills my cheeks. Any irritation I felt leaks away and I take her hand because of course she knows. "It doesn't matter. I'm telling him tonight. That I'm not keeping it."

You don't have to tell anyone anything.

She's right, that's true. There is no real need to burden Duncan with this—I know he will agree with my decision, because he's never wanted a child and explicitly told me so. Besides which, it's not his decision to make. And yet I can feel myself being drawn through the woods to his cottage, and I know I need to tell him, only I'm not willing to dig into *why* I need to.

Whose is it? Aggie asks.

"No one's. It was a mistake."

Did he hurt you? she asks, and the question is what hurts, that this is what she has come to expect, and really, why wouldn't she?

"No."

Aggie considers me. *Don't do it for me. Because of me.*

"It's for me," I tell her. "It's you and me, remember?"

Aggie hugs me fiercely.

"You and me," I say again. A mantra to hold her pieces together, to hold mine.

There is still a mound, but if you didn't know it was man-made you wouldn't be able to tell. I pause by it, wondering what secrets the body down there holds. Living in the moment I found him, in the openness of his flesh, the emptiness of his eyes. I imagine crouching to press my hands to the insides of him, pushing them back where they belong and sealing him up, I imagine fusing his skin back together until his eyes open. I'd give anything to have dreamt that morning in the fog. I fantasized about him being dead but his death has brought only more trouble.

I sink to a crouch and think back, despite the nausea this brings. I try to conjure the memory of his body, try to notice something I might have missed, a wound unlike the others, something that could give me a clue, a push in the right direction, anything. If I could by some miracle work out who actually killed him, then I could absolve the wolves of blame. They'd be safe. I might not be, but that's a different issue.

In any case, if Stuart had such a wound I didn't see it. All I saw was blood and the insides of things I shouldn't have been able to see.

I carry on through the dark forest. Returning along the path I took that morning, and so many instances before. Sound laps gently from Duncan's little house. I hear it before I see its rosy light. I wasn't expecting to socialize, but I steel myself and knock on the door anyway. "I'll get it," I hear a woman's voice say and the insides of me drop out and I'm about to turn and run when the door swings open and I see Amelia.

"You look relieved," she laughs.

"I . . . yeah," I say. "Hi."

"Hi." She kisses my cheek and pulls me inside. "I didn't know you were coming. This is a lovely surprise."

"I just came to talk to Duncan, but I can come back."

"Don't be stupid."

I forgot about Duncan's dinner parties. The small living room is at capacity. Holly is here, and so is Fergus Monroe, our pilot, which surprises me because I didn't realize he and Duncan were friends, and the policewoman, Bonnie. They're all squeezed in, doing what seems to be woodwork on a huge piece of calico that's been put out to protect the floors. Duncan himself is in the kitchen cooking, and when he looks up to see me he frowns.

Who will I be tonight—suspect in a disappearance, or woman who recently ended things with him? Either way, I guess, he doesn't have much reason to welcome me here. He pours me a glass of wine and when he hands it to me our fingers touch and I think it might be on purpose. He's playing a game then, one that marries the two women together and could get him in trouble. I wonder if I have the stomach to play it right back. I think, in fact, that I do.

"What are you doing?" I ask the group.

They all chuckle, except Duncan who turns away to hide his smile. "Duncan's decided the mission of his life is to become a carpenter, only he's truly, inarguably rubbish at it," Amelia explains, "so we get together every now and then to help him fix the crap he's made, and he cooks for us in return, which he's actually not rubbish at."

At least now I understand why his place is so full of poorly made furniture.

"How are you with sanding?" Bonnie asks me.

I sink down next to her on the floor. She's sanding down the leg of what looks like a small, crooked coffee table. "It's my middle name," I say.

She grins. "Best get started, then."

I listen to the others chat as we work. Their voices drift over me as I concentrate on my task. I don't want to become too overwhelmed with the feel of what they're doing. I'm tired tonight, and my own sensations are enough.

Duncan finishes cooking and brings us each a bowl of shepherd's pie. "No thanks," I say.

"Did you eat already?"

"I don't eat meat I haven't hunted myself."

He bursts out laughing. "You're too much, Inti Flynn."

I can't help laughing, too. He has on another hand-knitted woolen jumper, this one cream-colored and diamond-patterned. It darkens his eyes.

"So have Duncan and Bonnie interrogated you yet, Inti?" Amelia asks me with no small measure of mirth.

"We interviewed everyone," Bonnie says, like she's said it before. "Had to."

"Actually I had Duncan all to myself for that one," I say, glancing at him, and for a moment we are back there in that room together.

"How'd she come off then?" Amelia asks him. "Do we have a killer in our midst?"

"I haven't decided yet," he says, and then he smiles that crooked smile, and I'm not altogether sure he's joking.

"She had an alibi, actually," Bonnie says.

"What was it?"

Bonnie seems to be finding it funny too. "Not my place to say."

So Duncan told her then. I suppose he was my alibi and I was his. "You never asked me," I say.

"What?" Bonnie says.

"You never asked me for my alibi. Don't you think you should have?"

"We got it from someone else."

"And you didn't think to follow up, confirm it with me?"

She has the grace to look embarrassed.

I turn my eyes to Duncan.

"I didn't want to make you uncomfortable," he says.

"What are you on about?" Amelia demands.

"I was here that night," I say, because I want to see how Duncan reacts.

"Duncan's your alibi?" Fergus says, then erupts into giggles. "That's gotta be some kind of conflict of interest."

Amelia and Holly seem to find this amusing too, while Bonnie fidgets uncomfortably.

"And I'm his," I say. "Not that I was asked."

"An oversight," Duncan says. "I'll have you back into the station at your convenience. I have some follow-up questions I've been wanting to ask you anyway."

"Goodie."

"It's all a great waste of time, isn't it?" Holly asks. "When we know the bastard must have taken off. In debt up to his eyeballs."

My ears prick up at that. "Who was he in debt to? The bank?"

"Among others," Holly says.

"We don't need to be talking about the man's finances," Fergus says.

"No, but it's a good reason to duck out of your life," she says.

"Could have been Lainey," Amelia says.

"Meels," Bonnie admonishes.

"I'm just saying! If it'd been me he was slapping round like that I'd have buried him years ago. You can't tell me she's not your number-one suspect."

"He hasn't been ruled dead," Bonnie says.

"It was more than slapping round," Holly says.

"My point," Amelia says. "He was a nasty thug."

"Wasn't always," Fergus mutters.

"And should we give a shit?" Amelia says, her perpetual humor evaporated now. There is a sense of betrayal in her, and I think she must have known Stuart a long time, like they all did.

"What changed him?" I ask.

Nobody has an answer, they just shrug, shake their heads.

It's Duncan who says, "Men get taught to expect control but a modern society no longer supports that, so some men feel it slipping and it humiliates them. The humiliation makes them angry, and then violent."

"Topple the patriarchy!" Amelia roars.

"Jesus," Fergus mutters, clutching his chest.

"I don't blame her for looking elsewhere," Holly says.

"Holl," Amelia warns quickly.

"Sorry."

There's a silence at that. My mind darts ahead to make sense of it—was Lainey having an affair? I try to imagine who it might have been with. Seems to me like he'd be the prime suspect in Stuart's death.

Fingal pads over to curl up on the floor beside me, resting his head in my lap. I set aside my sanding duties in favor of stroking him. He has fallen asleep by the time the wolf howl cuts starkly through the cottage.

"God help us," Fergus sighs. "There she goes again."

Fingal lifts his head to listen, bristling with tension, ears peaked. He looks at me questioningly, then at his master for instruction. Should he be protecting us? Is this a call to him, a warning or an invitation? Does it stir some primordial heart of him?

I think it must, for he lifts his snout and lets out a long, excited howl of his own. It sets my skin alight.

"Jesus!" Fergus exclaims, louder this time.

The howls echo outside and in.

"See what you've done to me?" Duncan asks, and I realize he's talking to me. "He does this every damn night."

I can't help it—I smile. Something about the dog's response thrills me.

"I love them," Holly says. "Could I get a pup, do you think?"

"A wolf pup?" Amelia asks, laughing.

Holly is looking at me and she seems serious. I shake my head.

"Why not?" she asks. "If it was ours from a young age, if it didn't know any differently . . . That's how dogs came to be, isn't it? Someone did it, way back."

"Forty thousand years back," Fergus says. Then adds, "During the Mesolithic era."

I grin. "You're a history buff, huh, Fergus?"

He shrugs. "I try to know a little about a lot of things."

"But not a lot about anything," the others chorus, a well-worn tease.

I stroke Fingal to calm him. He's fallen quiet for the moment, intent on listening to the howls from the forest. They aren't for him; Ash has bigger creatures to warn off.

"The pup would come to know you," I tell Holly, "and you might train him. They're intelligent and they learn quickly, and they're very loyal."

"See!" Holly says.

"But why would you want to?" I ask. They're all watching me now; I can feel their eyes, because this is the thing, isn't it? This is the fear they live with now. The children in us long for monsters to take forms we understand. They want to fear the wolves because they don't want to fear each other. "Wolves don't understand or socialize with humans the way dogs do, even when raised from birth," I say. "Domestication is a product of breeding. It takes *many* generations to breed the wild from a creature. This dog and the wolf outside aren't even the same species anymore. No matter how much you loved a wolf pup, it would grow into the predator its nature dictates, and keeping something like that chained up or bound to a house is about as cruel as I could imagine."

Fingal lets out another mighty howl and we all jump.

Duncan gets awkwardly to the floor beside me and pulls his dog into his lap. "Easy, boy. She's not crying for you."

Fingal wags his tail and licks Duncan's hand.

"I can't take this tonight," Fergus announces, and gets up to put on some loud music. As the others go back to their chatter and woodwork, I glance at Duncan. He is lost in thought. Maybe now is the moment to tell him, quickly and be done with it. But the words don't come.

"Do you think it can ever be?" he asks me softly. "Bred out of a creature?"

"The wild?" I reach to pat the dog and my fingers come very close to his. I want to touch him so badly I could combust. "It happened to us, I think," I murmur. "Most days I think we couldn't be farther from it, that it was slowly bred from us until we became more like machines than animals."

"And the other days?" he asks.

"On the other days," I say slowly, "I think I will go mad with the wildness."

Several hours have passed when a second knock comes at the door.

"It's like Grand Central fuckin' Station around here tonight!" Fergus says. He has become steadily drunker by the minute, his accent growing concurrently thicker. I can barely understand him. He sways where he sits, still pretending to work but having long since lost the ability to wield tools.

Amelia has remained sprawled closest to the door so she rises to answer it a second time. "Hello, love," she says, but there is no response, only Lainey Burns pushing past her into the living room. Her eyes dart in search of Duncan.

"What the hell are you doing?" she asks him. "I *told* you—" Lainey sees me and falls silent.

Duncan struggles to get up off the floor, and I can see his leg is really hurting him so I reach a hand for him to push off from. He glances at me in thanks, then goes to Lainey and guides her down the hallway.

"I need to bury him, Duncan," we can hear her saying. "I need for this to be over."

They disappear into Duncan's bedroom and the door closes, shutting off the sound of their voices. I guess it wasn't Lainey who killed him then, unless she's one hell of an actress.

I take a gulp of my previously forgotten wine.

"Poor girl," Fergus says.

"She's better off," Amelia says.

"Hey," Fergus says. "A little respect for an old friend."

"He was no friend of mine."

"And that may be true but no one deserves to get eaten alive."

An awkward silence descends. They're all careful to avoid my eyes.

"It's what we're all thinking, isn't it?" Bonnie pipes up. "There's been no answers to find because the man was eaten by the damned wolves we're all pretending we can't hear. You said so yourself, Inti. They're predators and nothing can change that."

I get to my feet.

"Inti—" Amelia tries.

"I just need the loo," I say, which is true, and head down the hallway. But when I reach the bedroom door I pause to listen. I can hear them from here, the lilt and cadence of their words, and there is something that strikes me about them, about the way those words have become hushed, intimate. I see again the way he took her arm to lead her down the hallway, the way she went straight into his bedroom. They're friends, of course, they've known each other a long time, but some instinct in me recognizes something more. When their voices drop away completely the knowing in me is even louder; there is far more intimacy in a silence this long.

I return to the living room without having used the toilet. I sit on the couch beside Fergus and say, soft enough that no one will overhear, "It's Duncan, isn't it. The one she's seeing?"

"Nah, 'course not," he says, but he's so drunk I can see through him with ease. "Look, we don't know, who's to say?" he tries. "They had a thing, way back in high school before she ever got with Stuart. They were sweethearts and everyone thought they'd get married but it didn't work out, what with him going through that bad time. These days there are rumors but you know how rumors are."

I grab my jacket and head for the door. I don't want to be here anymore. I bid a quick farewell to everyone, ignore the cries for me to stay longer, and head out. The night air is fresh on my hot cheeks. I've only made it to the tree line when I hear the door open and a deep voice. "Inti?"

I don't need to stop. I'm beyond the sphere of light thrown by the house, I could be gone before he's seen me. But something is surging up within, an all too familiar fury, and beneath it something more sinister. A slow, horrifying realization of something I should have seen.

"I'm here," I say, and wait for Duncan to meet me in the dark.

He moves slowly, as he always does. "You wanted to talk to me."

"Why didn't Bonnie follow up with me? Why didn't she ask me to confirm your alibi?"

He takes a moment to adjust. "Because she trusted me when I told her you and I spent the night together. She didn't feel the need to embarrass you."

"Why should I be embarrassed?"

He shrugs.

I look up into his face. "Should she trust you?"

Duncan's eyes are black in this light. I can only just make out the lines of his face, his nose, his mouth.

"We didn't spend the night together, did we? Not the whole night. I woke and you were gone, Duncan."

The silence ignites.

"Where did you go?"

"I told you."

"You went for a walk."

You went for a walk right at the time a man was killed near your house, and you were fucking his wife.

The blood rushes in my ears.

"I'll drive you home," Duncan says.

"I'd rather walk," I reply, because I'm not getting into a car with him. I don't know this man. He said it himself. He told me the truth of what he'd done, and I didn't listen. We are all capable of killing.

16

It was only a year or so after the incident with Gus. I was late to meet Aggie, which she made no small thing of. "Of all the days," she kept saying, as she smeared lipstick on my mouth and tugged me down the street.

"Of all what days?" I asked, but she powered on. She was wearing a T-shirt dress that made her look skinny and leggy, and she'd cut her hair into a chic bob, her bangs reaching her huge sooty eyes. She looked gorgeous, and painfully cool, and light-years from the girls we were in the forest. "Wait, where are we going?" I demanded.

Aggie only smiled. And pulled me into the Births, Deaths and Marriages registry.

Gus's cousin James was there to be the second witness. They weren't brothers, but they could have been—there was a striking similarity to them, though James was the slightly shorter, slightly skinnier, less handsome version of his older cousin. There was a running joke within our little foursome that if he and I happened to fall in love it would make life a lot easier for us all. It would make sense, the last piece in a jigsaw puzzle.

James smiled at me as Aggie and Gus were married. I tried to smile back. I think I did. But the blood had leached from me and I honestly felt like I could throw up.

After, we went for dumplings. The restaurant was more of a bar, with graffitied black walls and dim red lights and intimate velvet booths. Gus and James did shots of Fireball, because that's what they always drank. Aggie and I hated the stuff but she was in such a good mood that she had a couple anyway. The chemistry she and Gus had was astounding; they came alive in each other's company and I could see the spell they cast on each other. He held her hand on the table and, because I looked, he also held mine.

I had to force my eyes from his touch because it wasn't mine, it wasn't for me. I was only a thief.

I went to the toilet to splash cold water on my face. Aggie pushed in and sat on the sink, despite it being wet. "Go on then," she said.

I shook my head.

"You don't have to worry," she said. "I've got him wrapped around my little finger."

"Good for you."

"What's wrong?"

"Nothing."

"Cut the crap, Inti."

I looked at her reflection in the mirror. "What are you doing?"

She folded her arms.

"What is this?" I pressed. "What the fuck is all this?"

"Chill out."

"What are you trying to prove?"

"Nothing! Why are you so pissed off?"

"Because you sprung this on me out of the blue and you didn't invite Mum because you know she'd hate him and you know you're rushing the hell out of this and it's all making me think you're really out of control right now."

"What's wrong with being out of control?"

"You hurt yourself."

She held my eyes. "Did you think one day he'd end up with you?"

The air left me. A reminder that her temper could flare without warning. I crossed to her and held her face. Her cheeks were so hot in my hands. "No, you idiot. You're a force of nature. No one would ever choose me over you."

"Shut up, Inti," she snapped, pushing my hands away. "Stop saying things like that."

"I don't want him," I said, and I really, really meant it. I didn't want him for me and I didn't want him for her. I didn't want him in our lives and here he was, bound to us by law. "You could have told me," I said softly. "I can't believe you didn't tell me."

"I didn't want you to talk me out of it."

"I got the job," I said miserably.

She stared at me. "So we're moving to Alaska?"

"You have a husband now."

"So?" Aggie demanded. She slid off the wet vanity. "So fucking what? He can come if he wants but it's you and me, right?"

Relief, so profound I was embarrassed by it. "Right."

A grin split her face. "It's wolves, baby. Fucking wolves." And then she grabbed me and threw her head back and howled her wolf's howl and a woman who was entering the bathroom took one look at us and turned straight back around and I laughed and laughed and then I joined in.

When we were done, Aggie headed back to the table but I lingered to use the toilet. As I washed my hands I told my reflection to go out there and enjoy herself. My sister knew what she was doing, she always did. This would be okay.

Someone was moving through the dark hallway as I came out of the bathroom. We bumped gently, and I was pushed against the wall and it was Gus, I'd have known the feel of him even were it pitch black.

"I missed you, baby," he said, breath hot on my ear, hands moving to my breasts.

I shoved him away. "Gus, what the fuck."

He blinked, then looked shocked. "Oh shit. Inti?"

"Bullshit," I snapped, my face burning. "My hair and clothes are different, for Christ's sake."

The shock fell away to reveal amusement. "It was a joke, kid. For old times' sake."

I stared at him, stunned. "No more of this, all right? Whatever this little game is that you're playing."

"No game," Gus said. "Friends, okay?"

I gave him a hard stare.

He laughed and put his arm around me, guiding me back to the table. "Actually," he said, "it's family now, *sis*."

Bonnie is sitting at her computer when I enter the tiny police station. There's a receptionist who asks me how he can assist me, but Bonnie spots me and waves me over. There are about six desks in the open-plan room, most seem to be shared by a couple of police officers, while the largest sits in an office separated only by a glass wall on which a plaque reads DUNCAN MACTAVISH, CHIEF SUPERINTENDENT. He's not in his office—I made sure of that before I came in here.

"How are you, Inti?" Bonnie asks.

"Well, thanks. Thought I'd follow up on the alibi."

She nods. "Let's use Duncan's office for some privacy."

I follow her in and she takes a seat behind his desk, while I sink into the chair opposite. It's a small, untidy office, full to the brim with towering stacks of paper. He doesn't have any photos or personal items. "Guess he hasn't embraced the digital era, huh?"

Bonnie glances around at the chaos and smiles. "Yeah. No. But it is actually easier to keep things straight when you have them in front of you. Would you like to make a written statement, Inti?"

"I'll just tell you, if that's easier."

"It's less formal."

"Okay, well I'm guessing you guys don't much care about formal."

She sighs. "I'm sorry I didn't speak to you directly. Duncan's my boss, and I wanted to afford him some discretion because of the nature of his statement, and I figured you'd appreciate that discretion too."

"I just don't really get it. Am I a suspect or not?"

"At this stage you're not. You're a person of interest. Which is why I haven't yet followed up on your initial interview." She pauses and leans back in the chair. "I did think it was strange that he didn't record it. So I asked him, off the record, and he told me he hadn't made it formal because he knew where you were that night, and that was enough for me." Another pause. "You're not a suspect, Inti, not as far as I'm concerned. But if you have anything you'd like to tell me, anything that could help . . ."

"That last time I saw Stuart was outside the pub with Duncan, and when Duncan came inside he'd been punched or something. Did he tell you that?"

Bonnie nods. "We have a solid timeline of Stuart's whereabouts until early in the morning, when he disappears and isn't seen again."

"So where was he?"

"I can't discuss the details of an open investigation with you, I'm afraid. Is there any particular reason you're concerned about this?"

"Sure, he was abusing his wife, and I want to know what happened to him."

"What I can say is that we found no evidence of him having left."

"Meaning . . . ?"

"Meaning we've decided to treat this as a possible homicide."

"Couldn't he have had an accident or something?"

"Of course. Back country out here is pretty perilous. We lose hikers sometimes, to rough terrain. Always find their bodies, though. And now we have animal attacks to consider, too."

"You'd find remains," I assure her.

She nods. "We have your expert advice on that. But you'd be pretty highly motivated to assure us of that, wouldn't you? If the wolves have killed a person they'll need to be destroyed."

"What, all of them?"

"Unless you can identify a single culprit, and then we'd need assurance it acted on its own."

Which, she knows, would be very hard for me to give her.

"Shall I ask the question then?" she asks. "Where were you on the night Stuart Burns was last seen?"

"I was at the pub in town and then I went home with Duncan."

"To his place?"

"Yes."

"What time was that?"

"Best guess, about nine."

"And you were there for the whole night?"

"Yes."

"Thank you, Inti, I'll include that in your file."

She doesn't ask me if *he* was there all night. So I don't say anything. I think it's because revealing his lie could uncover mine. But there is also a voice inside telling me not to speak up yet, not until I have some proof, or at least more of a concrete sense that Duncan really did kill Stuart, more than this terrible gut feeling. I don't want to land him in shit if he hasn't actually done anything.

"How do you narrow down your list of suspects for something like this?" I ask.

She shrugs. "We look at anyone Stuart might have had conflict with, anyone who had a reason to want him gone, to harm him. It's always hard without a body."

"What if it wasn't about Stuart at all?"

"What do you mean?"

"Well . . . getting rid of someone so thoroughly, and leaving no trace—it's a good way to make everyone jump to the conclusion that he must have been eaten by the brand-new wolves they're all so determined to see the end of."

She nods slowly. "I understand. We'll consider that."

"Thanks, Bonnie." I stand up to leave.

"See you at Duncan's for the next one?" she asks brightly.

I pause at the door. "Bonnie, look. He's not coming off too well right now. Sleeping with married women. Sleeping with multiple women at the same time."

Bonnie shifts uncomfortably. "I don't know what to tell you, Inti."

"Tell me if you think he's a good man or not."

"I think he's human."

"Yeah, that's what I suspected."

I sit in my car and type "Duncan MacTavish, Chief Superintendent" into Google. Pages of links come up. Most of them are newspaper articles about Stuart Burns, given Duncan is the officer in charge of the investigation. He's also mentioned in other articles for just about every minor and major crime in the area, dating back years, mostly because he's the one making the statements about them. I start reading through the articles and when I come up for air I realize hours have passed and it's dark outside. I haven't got any real sense of who he is, except that he's a good cop. He gets things done, as far as I can tell, although there are also a few unsolved crimes, from vandalism to farm equipment theft.

He doesn't have any social media that I can stalk. So I call Fergus and take him up on the drink offer.

The pub is quiet this evening. Fergus and I sit at a corner table and share a jug of beer and a bowl of chips. I don't drink the beer but he doesn't notice. We chat idly for a while—meaning Fergus chats idly for a while and I listen—and I get a sense of his restlessness; I think he is a man who longs for the time when everyone still partied into dawn. He paints a picture of his adolescence, a time out of control, when he had only his friends and they all adored each other, they were as restless as he was, as keen for experience, as bored as you become when you grow up in a small town.

"I feel stuck there, to be honest," Fergus admits. "A sixteen-year-old in a forty-year-old body."

"Was Stuart part of this group?" I ask.

"Sure. Lainey too. And Duncan and Amelia. We all went to school together."

"What do you think happened to him?"

Fergus shakes his head. "Maybe he just got done with it all."

"All what?"

"The farm. Such a thankless life. I dunno, it's a strange one."

I get the sense he doesn't feel right talking to me, an outsider. I try to probe gently but I'm not that good at gentle anymore. "Do you think he would have left his wife like that, though? Out of the blue, with no word?"

"Doesn't seem likely, no. No one could have accused Stuart of not loving his wife."

"Sure, he seemed set on loving her to death."

Fergus tenses. "They've been together since we were kids," he says as though this explains everything, and maybe it does. "All the boys round here were a little in love with Lainey. But she found her match with Stuart. Good-looking and kind and all that, and everyone knew they were meant to be together."

"So what changed?"

"Nothing."

I shake my head. This whole fucking place was blind to a woman in danger.

"I mean, I guess . . ." Fergus thinks about it for a while. "The drink's a curse for some men. Makes them not themselves anymore. He kept trying to quit, but I suppose there was a time there when I would have put money on her being the one to disappear, if either of them did."

"Do you mean leave? Or get killed?" I demand.

"Leave!" he exclaims. "Jesus, if I thought she was gonna get killed, I'd have . . ."

"You'd have what?"

Fergus looks back at me. "You're so hard."

I forge on. "Do you think anyone might have hated him? Jealousy or anger, or whatever?"

"Now you sound like Mac, sniffing around."

"Duncan? He questioned you?"

"Sure, he's questioned everyone in town."

We go quiet a while.

Eventually Fergus says, "You ask me, if someone did get rid of him, they'd have to have a gargantuan set of balls on them. He'd be no easy man to take down, that Stuart—and getting away with it, that's another story."

"Why do you say that?"

"'Cause Mac won't stop sniffing. Bloodhound, he is."

And will he sniff his way to a false culprit if it means protecting himself? Has he got his sights on me?

"Has he always been that way?" I ask carefully.

"Yeah. For as long as I can remember. He fixates. And you never know with someone if that's what they were born like or if it comes from the shit that happens to them."

"What happened to him?"

"It was in the papers. It's not a secret or anything."

I wait.

Fergus sighs. "Duncan killed his dad."

Fergus drinks to get drunk. I see that pretty quickly. He speaks of what happened but only a little, enough for me to know that he was there, after, and he saw what had been done and he's never forgotten it. They were all there, Duncan's closest friends. He called them before he called the police. Lainey, his girlfriend. Fergus, Amelia. Duncan didn't cry, Fergus remembers. He never once cried, through all the bits of it that came after.

I drive Fergus home and help him inside. He stumbles and I feel a pang of such pity for him as I put him in bed and get him a glass of water. Then I head home. Aggie's already in bed, so I crawl into mine and sink low under the covers, scrolling on my phone until I find the article from twenty-five years ago.

It was Christmas night. The police arrived to discover two dead bodies.

Duncan's father had been bludgeoned to death. His mother beaten to death. At first the cops couldn't make sense of the terrible crime scene. They thought it must have been a home invasion. But when they found Duncan and his friends huddled together upstairs they were able to piece together what had happened.

Duncan had been trying to protect his mother. He hadn't been able to.

His actions were ruled defense of another. He was sixteen. I stare at the picture of him, his head shaved, shadows beneath his eyes. The boy gazing back at me is broken.

I turn the light off and try to hold my body still, but it won't stop shaking. Trauma can create new patterns. I'm no stranger to this.

There is a party. It moves around me. Soundless. Weightless. My body is alive with them, with these bodies in my house, bodies I don't know but can feel. I walk from the living room. I am looking for Gus. Looking for Aggie. My edges are smudged.

My feet take the stairs slowly. Surely. My spirit is racing ahead. To their bedroom.

The door is closed.

I am inside, somehow. On their bed, a bed that is moving. There is a hand around my throat and I can't breathe, I can't get away.

"Inti!"

I wake with a lurch. My sister sits on my bed, holding my arms, holding my seams. I must have dreamt her voice saying my name, because she doesn't speak, my sister who knows more words than anyone.

You were crying, she signs.

A wave of nausea rocks me and it takes every ounce of energy I have to dash into the bathroom and vomit. Aggie pulls my hair back for me and when I'm done she hands me toilet paper to wipe my mouth and we sit facing each other on the cold tiles.

What a pair we make, Aggie signs.

I nod. Exhausted.

Morning sickness?

"I guess so." It's easier than telling her what I was dreaming about. She knows anyway, of course she does.

"Work with Gall today," I say, voice breaking. "She needs love."

I can't go outside.

"Why not, Aggie?"

He could be out there, she replies simply.

I stare at my sister and think—and it's bizarre that this should be the first time I truly think it—I don't know if I am equal to this madness.

I dream again, but this time not of monsters. Of wolves. Of running with them into the shadow of the mountain.

have known some truly bad days. In one of them I killed a wolf.

It was my first plane-darting. I'd been working out of the Alaskan base in Denali National Park and Preserve for many months and dreading this moment, the moment I'd have to pull a trigger and tranquilize a wolf without knowing what would happen to me in the process, knowing I would have to find out at some point. So we took the plane up. I was strapped in, and shown how to hang out the side, so that when we flew low and close to the ground I would have the best shot, and soon we found her, loping along a stretch of grassy prairie, and I took aim, using all those years of Dad's practice shooting at painted targets to slow my breathing, to calm my hands, to sight my crosshairs and squeeze the trigger. The dart hit her and I let out a gasp as she fell to the ground; I was watching and felt my legs liquify, my chest sting with the impact. It was lucky I was strapped in.

By the time the plane had circled down to land I was myself again. Niels, who'd gone up in the plane with me, led the way to the fallen wolf. We crouched over her but something was wrong. She wasn't breathing.

The dart had collapsed her lung and killed her.

My own lungs stopped working, but I don't know if it was because of my mirror-touch or because I was sobbing so hard. In all that time spent in the forest I had never killed a living thing. The moment was unbearable, sitting there with her fur between my fingers. I had been watching her for months, learning her, caring for her. I began to wonder if what we were doing was right. If our involvement in their lives was too much. We were trying to save them but we killed them sometimes, too. We stomped through the world and crumpled things where we walked, too human, not creature enough.

At home, in the flat I shared with Aggie and Gus, I locked myself in the bathroom and cried in the shower for so long Gus started pounding on the door because he thought I must have collapsed. Aggie slept in my bed with me for days, even though after the first night it pissed Gus off. He shared Mum's attitude, that I needed to toughen up. This was my job, wasn't it? Shit happened when you worked with living things.

After a week Aggie made me take them on a hike I'd been rambling on about for ages. She hadn't wanted to go before, this was a patent attempt to cheer me up, but I went along with it because we weren't spending much time together. Work was a maelstrom, a whole new life. For her part she'd started studying linguistics and our schedules rarely lined up. So we returned to the national park I worked in, and Gus tagged along, as he always did.

As we staggered to the top of an incline I held my breath, knowing the view that waited. A world of autumn color. A feast. One sloping hill covered in deciduous larch, aspen, and black cottonwood trees, all having turned so yellow they hurt to look upon, and some among them a fiery orange. There were paper birches with bright red leaves, and dotted throughout were the evergreen spruces. On the other side of the lake the landscape was more like tundra, treeless hills covered in cherry pink and red shrubs that ran down to embrace the edges of Lake Wonder, shimmering lilac now under the streaky gold and purple sunset. And looming over it all was the snow-covered peak of Mount Denali, crisp and white and staggering in its enormity.

I had never seen a place like this, and would never see another like it.

Aggie reached us, breathless. She managed an "*Oh*," and then she too fell silent.

"Will we see animals?" Gus asked eventually.

"Maybe," I said. "If we're lucky. Let's set up camp."

Later we told stories around a little fire. Aggie told Gus with relish of the times we swapped places as children to see if anyone would notice. No teachers or friends. Only Mum.

"Did you swap a lot?" Gus asked.

"No," I said.

"All the time," Aggie said. "It embarrasses Inti how much she liked it."

I flushed, glad for the dusky light.

"What did you like?" Gus asked me.

I thought about it, remembering those days vividly. The truth was simple: Aggie was the one who lived more, who connected more. When I draped her upon me I felt more alive than I ever did as myself.

To Gus I said, "It was just a challenge. Just fun, I guess."

"How did you do it? 'Cause you guys are pretty different . . ."

"It's called acting, darling," Aggie said.

"She's as familiar to me as I am to myself," I said. "Becoming Aggie is easy."

Gus seemed to be enjoying this topic. "If I had a twin there'd be no end to the shit I'd do to people."

"That's nice to know," Aggie muttered.

"Have you ever swapped with me?" he asked.

We fell quiet because this was a land we didn't approach.

"You know we haven't," Aggie said. "Not intentionally."

"How would I know?"

"You just would."

"I didn't know the first time," he said.

Bullshit.

Something moved in the dark. I shot to my feet.

Scuffling footsteps approaching from the bottom of the hill.

"What the fuck is that?" Gus hissed.

I grabbed my torch and shined it down the incline. "Relax," I said. "It's just people."

"Hi!" Aggie greeted the hikers, who stopped by our fire for a chat.

Two middle-aged men who sounded American. "You're Aussies?" one of them asked.

"True blue," Aggie replied, which was laying it on a bit thick, but she always enjoyed broadening her accent when we traveled.

"We're from Colorado." As it turned out they were on a hunting trip.

I saw the shapes at their backs, the long narrow barrels of hunting rifles. "What are you hunting?"

"Wolves."

"Why?" Aggie demanded.

"'Cause this is the only state it's still legal to hunt them in," the man replied, like it should be obvious.

"But why hunt them at all?" she pressed.

"What's the alternative? Gunning down poor pathetic antelope, who couldn't hurt you if their lives depended on it?"

"It's true sport," his friend agreed. "Hunting a predator. More of a challenge than going after its prey, more of an even playing field."

"If you want an even playing field maybe you should leave those rifles behind and try to kill a wolf with your bare hands," Gus suggested.

They laughed as though he'd made a joke. "Tell you what. We'll use the tech made by man and they can use the tech at their disposal," one of them said.

"You're disgusting," Aggie said clearly, her voice so cold it cut through the night and made everything else fall quiet. An awkward shuffle of feet.

"We'll be on our way," said one of the hunters. "Sorry to disturb."

"What you're actually disturbing is this entire ecosystem," my sister said and I loved her so much.

"Plenty of wolves up here," the other guy said. "They're not endangered."

"And with men like you around, how long do you think that'll last?"

"All right, we're off. You folks enjoy your night." And with that they left, and I hated them for their politeness, hated that they seemed perfectly nice and yet they were out here doing this heinous thing, hunting for the sake of it, not to survive, not to eat, only to feel power over another creature.

I walked down the slope toward the lake.

"Inti?"

"Give me a minute."

It was proper dark now, but the stars were so many, the gibbous moon a dazzling white orb. The sky lit my way over the tangled shrubs, the dips and rises and little burrows of rabbits. I walked all the way down to the edge of the water, stars glittering upon its surface, and I sank to the ground beneath the glowing mountain.

Time passed and a body moved to join mine; I was expecting Aggie but it was Gus.

"They probably won't get any," he offered.

"Some of the wolves out here are ones I raised myself," I said. "We raised them from birth. I held them and fed them and played with them. And then we set them free to be hunted and shot." And not just by hunters but by us. By me.

Gus didn't say anything for a while, then, "Everything dies."

"Not everything gets killed."

Without warning he said, "I killed someone."

"What?"

"In my first year. I was repairing a brain bleed. My hand slipped. I killed a woman."

I didn't know what to say, turning this over in my head.

"I never told Aggie," he admitted.

"Why not?"

"A woman doesn't need to know that about her husband."

I frowned and looked at him in the starlight. "The truth?"

"That he can make mistakes."

"Um. I hate to break it to you but she definitely knows you make mistakes."

"I can at least try to protect her from that."

"Do you think about what happened a lot?" I asked.

"Nope," Gus said. "Never."

"Why not?"

"I can't let myself or I'd never go back into the operating room."

I considered this, knowing what he meant. If I wanted to continue to do my job I would have to compartmentalize what I did. But I didn't know if I could. I thought that might mean forgiving myself.

"It doesn't matter, anyway," Gus said, his voice harder now, as though trying to convince himself. He leaned back on his hands to look up at the mountain looming over us. "It's all meat. All just fuckin' meat."

I winced. "A butcher after all."

"That's right. And you'd better become the same. I don't want to see you bruised by life, Inti. You're my family."

18

The wolves have all begun to howl. They call by night and day, running circuits of their newly established territories, calling to each other to define the boundaries of their pack's land, calling to other wolves a warning to stay away. They truly are making homes here, creating maps they will pass on for generations.

I go out daily, sometimes with Fergus in the plane, other times on horseback with the team. Sometimes alone, able to move faster. I track their movements and collect data from their scat and the remains of their kills.

The pups of Ash's Abernethy Pack are about three months old, and growing quickly. They are juveniles now, their hair thickening like an adult's, eyes having shifted to the striking pale amber. They eat meat, but only the rodents they are capable of catching. They howl with confidence. I would spend every waking minute with them if I could. The little white runt of the pack, Number Twenty, whom I held when she was newly born, remains the smallest and palest of them. But she is also the boldest of her brothers and sisters, having caught more than double what they've managed. I suspect, despite her size, that she might end up leading this pack one day.

The Tanar Pack, to the east, has staked out the largest territory and its three yearlings have grown to full size and sexual maturity, meaning they may also leave to find mates of their own. But for the moment the pack of five wolves is intent on hunting together, and have proven themselves the most harmonious pack in this respect, with no challenges to dominance. They give me hope, the Tanar Pack, because they are hunting and growing strong, meaning the conditions of the Scottish Highlands have been good to them.

And as it has finally turned out, delicate Number Thirteen, left behind in her pen because she was too afraid to leave, might not have been afraid at all. Maybe she was simply waiting. Because yesterday, yearling male Number Twelve, who was circling dangerously close to her pen and worrying us all, moved within its chain-link fence. But he didn't attack Thirteen, he mated with her.

Most days I wake wondering if this will be the day I get a phone call reporting that a young female wolf has strayed onto private property and been shot. Or found entangled in a trap, and died of her wounds. Fierce Number Ten of the Glenshee Pack ran free of her cage in those very first days and has not returned. Every time I go out into the field and am not specifically looking for a different wolf, I turn my radio to her signal in case I happen to pass near her, but I never do. We've lost her completely. But the rest of her pack remain, and have piqued my curiosity.

I am lying flat on a distant hill, binoculars raised and trying to ignore the ghastly bites of the midges. I need to figure out why the five Glenshee wolves keep congregating in a spot on the southern side of a sloping mountain, alongside a river carved through the range. It's also right at the heart of their territory, so there's less chance other wolves will stray close, which makes it the safest spot for them. I hoped, but didn't dare to assume, this is because they are denning, and watching them now I think I was right. Number Eight, the breeding female of the pack, or the female alpha, seems to be digging a den. It takes all my self-control not to give a great shout of elation, but I do laugh, soft, and my hands shake for the relief of it.

Without warning a small ding comes from the radio in my pack. I must have left it tuned to one of the pack's signals, but it dings again, quickly now, to tell me it has locked onto something close. The radio is picking up a signal much closer than the Glenshee wolves on that neighboring mountain.

This is open country. Wide, windswept mountains and hills. Not much cover. Nowhere to hide. But at the base of my hill is a stretch of marshy moorland, its grass long enough to conceal wild creatures within, if they are particularly good at hiding.

I wait, eyes scanning below. Grass sways with the wind, disguising any movement. That's the only way back to the car.

"Where are you?" I murmur.

I think I know. I think it must be her.

I stand up tall and walk with big, loud steps, like you might if you were trying to scare off snakes. If I act like prey, that's what she will think me. As I stomp, I draw the radio from the pack, switch off the beeping monitor, and begin to download the data from the nearby signal.

It is a long, hair-raising walk back to my car. My boots squelch in the smelly peat bog and I think this is a terrible place to be attacked, I will have no hope of escaping, and I also know that trying to run would be the worst possible response and think at least she, too, will have trouble in the mud. But let's not pretend I have anything like her lithe, nimble power. Let's not pretend I am safe. I know from the signal that wherever she is, she's close, and she's not fleeing from me. She is watching me. Bold girl.

We will need a hide out here, if we want to keep watching this pack. Number Ten has returned and she's not likely to allow her family to be vulnerable.

When I reach the car, I don't want to get in. I realize I have loved every second of this terrifying walk.

Back at base, the identity of the wolf is confirmed. Female Number Ten. My team and I watch, stunned, as the data streams in, all her GPS pings over the last few months, the thousands of kilometers she has covered, the places she has run, the world she has explored, only to return in time to protect her sister and her pack as they prepare for the impending litter. As if somehow she knew.

I sit on the front step of the cabin and watch the thunderheads roll in.

The infinite mystery of wolves.

Niels joins me with an offered mug of tea. In his mid-fifties, he still cuts a tall, athletic figure, is almost militaristic about his health regimens. "Congratulations," he says. "Female Number Ten, safe and well. It was a good day."

"It was a good day," I agree.

"You said she would come back."

I shrug. "I figured she'd turn up at some point." Feared she wouldn't. We sip our tea in silence for a while.

"I'm sorry I got so angry about Six and her den."

"There's no need. You were right about her capabilities. I apologize for going against you," he replies. "And for calling you timid. You know I have immense respect for your work. I have never known anyone with a superior instinct for the animals."

I look at him, astonished. I didn't know that. In fact I'd thought he found me frustrating. "Thank you, Niels. Honestly? Maybe I have been timid. I don't know, I just can't reconcile our role in all this and I've started questioning it more and more. How much action is too much, and when is it not enough?"

"The difficulty of working with wild animals," he agrees. "I often ponder how their fear of us is not a natural state for them. They are not born with it, it is a learned habit, taught to them by us. My family had a wildlife park when I was growing up, and in it there was a small pack of three wolves."

He has never told me this. I know he grew up in the very far north of Norway, way up in the Arctic Circle, and he has spoken to me before of his memories of the '80s, when wild wolves returned to Norway. Debate immediately turned to the conservation of these wolves versus the desire to cull them and protect Norway's agricultural industry. It caused a division among the people, and passionate conflict, because wolves, as Niels said, have an unrivaled ability to make humans *feel*.

Now he says, "The wolves we kept were born in our park and acclimated to our presence, our touch. Most wolves I have known in parks remain hidden from visitors but these three would rush over to the fence, and they were just as fascinated with the people as the people were with them. When the visitors left, the wolves would follow them as far as they could and watch for their return. There was no fear, but a mutual curiosity."

I smile.

"And have you not heard the tales of those lucky men and women who have raised wolves and set them free, only to come upon them somewhere in the wild, years later, and be shown affection by the creatures?"

I nod, though I've never been sure if I believe these stories, or suspect them to be made of longing. "Do you believe them?" I ask Niels, expecting his certainty in the unambiguous scientific.

But he says, "Of course. Many animals are capable of this, we see it time and again. I believe they are more inherently loyal than we are and that connections are built deep within, where instinct lives. With the disappearance of that man there is anger brewing here, and there are those who would fight to destroy the wolves, and those whose apathy would see them destroyed. And so we must be the ones who fight *for* them. That will always be the right action to take."

His words stir my protective instinct, my certainty.

All creatures know love, Dad used to say. All creatures.

Summer has begun and the land has turned its face to the sun, blooming under its warmth. The canopy and the earth are green, luminous above and below. The Scottish heather has overrun the fields and hills, turning the ground brilliant lilac and burnt red. But even in summer the sky seems not to notice; still it leans more to gray, to white, still it rains most of the time, still there is an eerie fog that settles over everything. I am reminded of how Duncan sees this place, as big enough to dwarf you, as so beautiful and desolate you can go mad if you aren't built for it. I can feel it getting inside me.

Hunting is harder now, for the deer are healthier, they have more to eat and so they grow strong and fast, challenging not only the speed but the endurance of the wolves.

I hope with each day that Stuart's disappearance fades into memory. I hope the rumors about his death cease. It's been two months now. But with every mention I overhear, with every wary look I am flashed in the supermarket, I know they haven't, and that Niels was right. The concern is only growing.

And always, there is the little one within. *A cherry,* signs Aggie. Then, *A plum.* Time ticks by. My body changes. My organs shift. I feel alien, but I don't make any move toward my initial decision.

Some part of me must be hoping it just goes away.

Mostly I don't think about it. I can't afford to.

What I think of is Duncan. And though I feel a great ache for him at the thought of what he went through, I also understand what violence does to people, what it makes us capable of, and know I need the truth, one way or another.

This evening, as I've been doing for the last few nights, I duck out early from work and wait down the street from the police station to follow Duncan when he leaves his office. He never goes straight home. He picks up food or tools and goes to visit people. Tonight I follow him as he checks in on old Mrs. Doyle who works in the pharmacy and lives by herself. She's seventy-six and has arthritis, but she refuses to give up work. They have tea in the sunroom before he does chores around the house; yesterday he cleaned out her gutters, today he digs the weeds from her garden bed. Next he takes food around to a woman who is raising five kids alone, just some bread and milk, and meat from the butcher. He kicks the soccer ball with her boys in the front yard. Then I follow him to Fergus's house, and from the end of the street I watch the two of them drink beer in the garden while the sun goes down. I've watched him enough days now to know that these are his regulars but there are others he fits in too, people who need help, or perhaps simply some company. He cares deeply; it is the fabric of his life here. I think he must be a good man. But nobody is only one thing.

I follow him home and his taillights in the dark stare back at me. *Why am I doing this. Why spend night after night watching him? What is it that I expect to see?* The only thing I am able to recognize is the instinct to survey I have felt when hunting. You watch to learn.

I expect him to turn down his driveway, expect that I will carry on past to my own little cottage, done for the night. But he doesn't, he drives further, and I think *Shit, is he going to my house?* And does it matter if he's going to my house? It does, somehow. But I see his brake lights and then he is pulling onto the side of the road. Heading into the woods on foot. I park in my driveway and double back along the road until I reach his car and plunge into the trees.

The world flashes, a streak of lightning above. There's no tracking in the dark but I am quiet and still and soon I can hear his footsteps crunching through the underbrush. Then the light of his phone, and I see him searching for something. No, just walking, covering ground.

He's looking for Stuart. I know it. And he's really damn close.

I step into his path and he jumps in fright. "*Fuck*, Inti. What are you doing out here?"

"What are *you* doing out here?"

"You been following me again?" Duncan asks.

My face flushes. That's mortifying. Instead of denying it, I nod.

"Why?"

"Because I'm trying to learn you."

"To what end? I thought you wanted us over."

That's not what I want.

But.

"I suspect you killed Stuart."

He is silent.

"Did you?" I ask.

Lightning, and in it he has seen something of me. "You're bleeding," he says.

"What?"

He shines his phone light at my face and I wince. "Your nose."

I lift my hand and it comes away bloody. I've never had a bleeding nose before. It disorients me. "Did you kill Stuart?"

"You wanted something done, didn't you?"

"For you to arrest him! Or help her get away from him! Not *murder* him, Duncan, Jesus Christ."

"Would it matter?" Duncan asks. "If I did?"

I've asked myself that a million times now. I breathe that question. Because didn't I want to do it myself? Wasn't I fantasizing about it like some kind of psychopath?

The answer I keep coming back to is that there is a difference. Between thinking and doing. I have seen violence and I have seen what it takes and what it leaves behind. There is no coming back from it.

And honestly? I don't care about Stuart. He can rot. What I do care about is how he was killed, and whether whoever killed him meant for it to look the way it does.

"It's being blamed on the wolves," I say, and my voice breaks.

Duncan says nothing and maybe it's because he doesn't care and in this moment he seems callous.

"If they come to harm over this," I tell him clearly, "I will make sure you pay for it."

"I think I'm already paying for it, aren't I?" he asks.

I don't know what to say. I can taste iron.

When I get home my sister is hunched on the cold kitchen floor with a knife in her hand.

"What happened?" I say, forgetting about the need to stop my nosebleed and crossing straight to her. She doesn't let go of the knife until I pry it from her grip, and then her hands shake so much she can barely sign. She has to repeat herself several times before I can see what she's saying.

He's out there.

"What?"

I heard something.

"No, he's not," I say. "Come on. Come with me."

She shakes her head.

"Aggie, come outside and I'll show you." I am trembling with frustration, and without warning Mum's words spew from me. *"Toughen up!"*

Betrayal in her eyes. She knows how painful that instruction was to me growing up. She knows how small it made me feel. She makes for the bedroom but I grab her arm and start pulling her toward the front door. "You need to see there's no one out there!"

Aggie struggles, a freaked animal. I manage to pin her down and then take her foot and start dragging her to the door. She bucks, kicking me in the leg and I grapple with her and we go to the ground, wrestling madly. The blood from my nose is dripping on both of us. "Aggie, stop!" I grunt. "Just—fuck—come outside, I need you to see!" If I can't get her to come outside right now I am going to go as insane as she is.

Let me go, she signs. *Inti, let me go.*

The air goes from my chest, and from hers, too.

"I can't," I say, and then we both sag to the floor, exhausted.

It hits me: what I must tell her. What I should have told her from the start.

"He's not out there," I say, "because he's dead. I killed him."

Aggie stares at me. *But you can't kill.*

I shake my head. "I never wanted to."

She searches my face for the truth and must find it, and then her body slumps against mine with the weight of her relief. She makes one sign, the motion for *thank you,* and then she takes herself to bed. Not realizing, I suppose, that she isn't the only one who needs help. Leaving me here to lie on the kitchen floor, to bleed onto it, and think of what it takes to kill a person. Only the flesh of you, only the soul.

He is lying on their bed when I find him, where she lay not long before, on a bed that moved beneath her, and I climb on top of him now and there is fear in his eyes as I lower my mouth to his neck and tear it open—

I wake in agony. My muscles have stiffened on the tiles and the scent of the dream lingers; blood is smeared beneath me and crusted onto my hands and face. The first morning light hurts my eyelids and through the window drifts the sound of a horse's distress. At first I think I am still dreaming, that I'm a child again and Dad is about to take the beast in hand. But it's no dream, it's my poor horse who is upset by something, whinnying and rearing skittishly. Something has spooked her and for a second I think: wolf.

I am moving for the door when through the kitchen window I see Aggie.

She's outside.

My feet stop.

I watch my sister walk to the horse and reach up to Gall's mane and swing herself onto her back. She presses her body and my body against the horse's spine, laying herself flat and heavy and ardent, calming her with our heartbeat, our firm, gentle hands, our breathing. Gall's hooves fall still on the grass, her whole being falls still, one with the woman on her back. Bewitched by that whispering touch, that knowing my sister was born with. When Aggie places her face against the neck of the creature and smiles, I sit down on the kitchen floor and weep.

I am the first to base camp so I'm the one to discover it. The two mortality codes.

When they arrive, Evan, Niels, and I head out on horseback to find the bodies and work out what happened. The two members of Tanar Pack, wolves Number Four and Number Five, are lying dead well within the boundaries of a territory that doesn't belong to them. Ash's territory.

"There's been a fight," Evan surmises, because the two wolves have been torn at throats and guts and this is clearly the work of a fellow wolf.

No shit, I manage not to say.

I feel deep sadness at the look of them, but there's no anger. It's the nature of things that has brought their lives to an end.

We will bring the bodies in, but first we trace the blood trail back to the center of Ash's territory and discover that she is alive but bleeding from the muzzle, and that her daughter Thirteen and new mate Twelve are with her, both also injured. Instead of creating a new pack of their own, the newly mated pair must have come here to join Ash's. Thirteen has come home to her mother and they've fought a battle together. I don't breathe as I scan the forest for any sign of the pups, because if they are dead then I don't know what I'll be. But a movement catches my eye and I see all six emerge from a thicket, wrestling happily as though nothing has happened, and I know that Ash and her two grown wolves managed to fight off a pack of five to protect them. It would make sense for Twelve and Thirteen to lay claim to her dominance as the new breeding couple of the pack, but I don't think they will do that. I think Ash is the strongest wolf I have ever come across.

Evan, I can tell, is rattled by the dead wolves. He is as sensitive to their deaths as I was when I first started the job. Back then, even when they killed each other or died from an illness, the grief was as profound as discovering one killed needlessly by a human. So I take him for a walk and we pick wildflowers, which he has always loved as much as the animals.

"I never get used to it," he admits.

"That's not a bad thing, not really. Grim thing to get used to."

"But I should be. We see it enough. It's why we don't name them."

I shrug. "Still. There is too much love for it to ever be easy. Forgive yourself for that." I squat to point out little yellow flowers, each with five petals and not unlike a daisy.

"*Ranunculus flammula,*" Evan says. "And some *Filipendula ulmaria.*" He picks a few of each and we walk on. A marshy field stretches before us and we go off the path.

"Are you going to Glasgow this weekend?" I ask. Evan's whole family lives there, and I think he might be seeing someone there too, since he's been ducking down there every chance he gets. This is a family that fully supports his work; he told me once that they love having a cause to rally behind, with as much noise and fuss as possible.

"Not now," Evan says. "There'll be too much to do, with the packs fighting."

"Go," I tell him. "I won't need you over the weekend, but I do need you rested."

"You gonna take your own advice, boss?"

I ignore that.

"Have you been going out to the survey spot?" he asks me.

I nod.

"Me too. I go there all the damn time. Staring at the ground, willing the wee things to pop up, shouting at them sometimes, like a right lunatic."

I laugh. "Maybe they're staying below ground to spite you."

"Aye, maybe. At what point do we decide this hasn't worked?"

"We're a long way from that yet."

"I know, but is there a point?"

I shake my head slowly. Not for me, not really. But there will be for the locals. I say, "Give the wolves time, Evan. They just need a bit of patience."

"Never my strong suit. Ooh, look here. This is a beauty. *Dactylorhiza incarnata*. A marsh orchid."

Sitting alone in the marshy grass, about thirty brilliant spotted pink orchid flowers shoot off the one upright stem. It is more vivid than any of Werner's colors, but in the family, I think, of lake red, the shade of red tulips, *Rosa officinalus*, and the mineral called spinel. No animals are this shade, except perhaps some lucky birds. It is almost strange to see such a vibrant hue out here in this land of browns and grays.

"That'll make a beautiful bouquet," I say.

But Evan straightens without having picked it. "I think we'll leave this solitary sweetie. It has its own role to play here."

❈

I phone Mum and get her early in the morning before she's left for work.

"How are the wolves?" she asks. I can hear her coffee machine in the background.

"Killing each other."

"Sounds about right. How about Aggie?"

"Yeah, she's . . . good." The best she's been in a long while. This morning she was *outside*. "Mum, can I ask you something?"

"I expected you'd like to."

"How's that?"

I can almost hear her shrugging. "Tone of voice."

That gives me pause. "You're really good at reading people, aren't you?"

"Is that what you're asking?"

"No."

She laughs a little, an exhale.

"What's the first thing you do when someone's been murdered?"

There's a pause. "You all right, sweetheart?"

"I'm fine."

"And you'd tell me if you weren't, wouldn't you."

"I'd have thought you'd just want me to toughen up."

She doesn't say anything for a while. Then, "Darlin', you're going to figure this out one day, but we're most fallible when trying to raise our children."

This is, I think, the closest I'm going to get to an acknowledgment of poor choices on her part. About as close to an apology as she'll ever come.

"You were right, you know," I say abruptly. "I did need to toughen up." And I have, I've toughened so far up I'm wrinkly old leather now.

She sighs, but doesn't argue.

"You need a timeline," Mum says, and as she speaks pieces of this float back to me from childhood; these are things she has already taught me, but I'd tried to forget them. "Make a timeline of your victim's movements, their habits, their routines. Make a detailed picture of their life so you can see anything that sticks out. Whatever doesn't fit is your first clue. Look at people you might not have thought of. Look for motive. Look for lies."

"How do I spot the lies?"

"Assume it's all lies, and then prove what's true."

"That sounds like a lot of work."

She laughs. "Yep. Now I'm going to imagine to myself that you've taken up a new career writing crime novels, all right?"

"Yeah, all right. Thanks, Mum."

She waits, but I don't know how to word it.

"What else, Inti?"

"Is there a reason you do this work? Because I know it consumes you. I know you haven't got space for much else. And it must be a pretty dark place to go voluntarily, particularly because you don't think all that highly of most people. So I've just been wondering if something happened to you."

Mum doesn't say anything. I can hear her pouring her coffee, adding the milk and putting the bottle back in the fridge. The sliding door opens and closes and I listen to the sound of her lighting a cigarette. I can picture the concrete balcony she's sitting on, can see in my mind's eye the crashing ocean she must be watching, the sun rising slowly behind, burning everything.

"Your dad didn't beat me up, if that's what you're asking."

"No," I say quickly. I hadn't been asking that, not directly, but a great pressure lifts off my chest.

"You don't have to be a victim to care," she says. "You just have to have empathy in bucket loads."

I breathe out. "Yeah. Thanks. Sorry for asking that." And I mean it genuinely. This is her business. I just wanted to know if she's like Duncan. If her need to protect people exists because she wasn't protected herself.

"My stepdad," she says suddenly, softly, breathing out a long lungful of smoke.

I've never met any grandparents, or stepgrandparents.

"Oh," I say, on a long breath of my own. "I'm sorry. How long, Mum? How long until you got past it?"

"Sweetheart," she says, "I sleep with dead women watching me from the walls."

But I cannot accept that. That hers is the only way. Aggie will be different. There has to be a way to heal, and if she has not the will for it, then I will be strong enough and sure enough for her. She can have my soul in place of hers, if she needs it.

19

Despite the faint, ever-lingering nausea that's been hanging around for the last few weeks, I must try to build this timeline. In a lilac-hued twilight I knock on Red McRae's door. His father answers.

"Sorry to bother you. Red home?"

"He's out with the sheep. Come in. I'll radio him."

I step inside and wait by the door while the old man gets on a walkie-talkie and tells Red the wolf lady is here to speak with him.

"No phone service out here either?" I ask when he returns to me.

"Not a hair. Come in, come in, it's rude to lurk by the door. I'll make us tea. Unless you'd like coffee?"

"Tea's good."

"I won't ask what you're doing here."

"Okay."

The stone house is cozy and well lived in. I'd guess it's been in the family a long time. "I'm Inti," I say. "Let me make the tea."

"Douglas," he replies, then lets me bustle my way around the little kitchen.

"Just the two of you live here?"

"Aye, since Quick passed."

"Who was Quick?"

"Red's wife."

"Oh, I'm sorry." As the kettle boils he points me to the cupboard with the tea bags. "Good name, Quick."

"Aye, and well deserved."

"Why's that?"

"Quick on the draw."

"And from the Wild West?"

"She was witty," he clarifies with a chuckle, "and she could lay down a fatal insult with ease, quicker than you could blink."

I smile. "She sounds great. You been here a long time?"

"All my life and my pa's life before me."

"All sheep farmers?"

"That's right, and even further back than that. We've all of us been sheep men, at least half a dozen generations of us. You ought to come into town more, missy. Be good for you to get to know some folk."

"Oh yeah? Why's that?"

"Not good to spend all your time with animals, and I say that from experience. I go to a thing on Thursday evenings, in the wool shop. You come along."

"The wool shop? What kind of thing?"

"A knitting circle."

I look up at him. "You're in a *knitting circle?*"

"Too right I am. It's relaxing. You come along, all right? We don't bite."

"Neither do the animals. Mostly."

He eyes me as I pour the water into the cups. "Why are you here, wolf girl?"

"I'm a woman," I tell him.

Douglas's face creases into a smile. "Beg your pardon. Wolf woman."

I hand him his mug and lean against the kitchen counter. "I don't really know, Douglas. I don't actually know."

"You're doing a good thing."

My mouth opens in surprise. "You think so?"

Douglas nods.

"Aren't you worried about your sheep? Everyone else is."

"The time for sheep is over," he says simply, and sips his tea.

When Red returns he takes me into a small, messy office and sits me down before his desk as though I am in trouble with the principal. "What do you want?"

I sit back in my chair. "I got a warmer welcome from your dad."

"He's got dementia."

I laugh as I rub my tired eyes. "Right. Look, it's nothing to do with the wolves or your sheep or anything."

"What then. I've got animals to drench."

"That night outside the pub, before Stuart went missing."

His eyebrows arch and he sits back, mirroring me. Relaxed now that he senses he has the upper hand.

"I went inside. Left Duncan out there with you. And when he came in he was all beat up."

"What's your question?"

"What happened?"

Red stares at me. Now that I've seen his dad's, his mustache isn't quite so impressive. "Why are you interested?" Red asks me.

"I'm trying to piece together a timeline."

He grins. "Interning for the police department, are we?"

I don't reply.

"You've been causing a lot of trouble for me, Miss Flynn."

"How's that?"

"Do you know how much it costs to build fences?"

"No, I do not."

"Do you know what it costs a person to stay up all night guarding their flock?"

"The cost of the job, I'd imagine. And I'm sorry we've made that cost higher, I truly am, but what are you getting at, Red?"

"Why exactly would I help you with anything?"

"Because you're a good man who cares about what happened to his friend." I have to hope this is true. There's always the possibility that Red's desire to get rid of the wolves makes him a suspect in this, but I don't know if I can stomach the thought of a man murdering his friend in order to frame the creatures he wants to hunt.

"What will you do for me?" Red asks.

My eyes narrow. "What do you want?"

"Drop the charges for the wolf I killed."

The charges that were never getting laid because Duncan is a coward? I almost smile. Clearly Duncan never informed Red he'd decided to let the kill go. I spend a few seconds pretending to weigh it up, then nod. "Fine."

"Stu was wound tight by what you said to him. He wanted a bit of a scuffle and he picked the wrong man for it. There was bad blood already between him and MacTavish. They were friends once, which is probably why things had gone so sour. It didn't take much to set either of them off. Mac got him in hand and then he beat Stu, he beat that man black and blue and it was old demons in him that did that."

I am breathless. "Had they fought before like that?"

"Not since they were kids, I guess."

"Then why that night?"

"I told you—you stirred Stu up, Inti. Threw a light on something he'd been trying hard to keep buried. That's if we're to believe what you accused him of, anyway. He wanted to fight someone and Duncan was there, and Duncan had some built-up grudges of his own."

I process this. "So then what happened?" I ask. Expecting, maybe, the hospital.

But Red says, "Took him off to the lockup for the night."

"That's it?"

"That's it."

"Do you know for sure he took him to the station?"

"Where else would he have taken him?"

"And that's the last time you saw Stuart?"

Red nods.

I stand to go. "Thanks, then."

"Miss Flynn. I don't have much love left for the chief, not after witnessing his temper. But MacTavish is not a man you want to go up against. And frankly? You trying to throw attention anywhere but your own backyard is pathetic, and it's dangerous. We all know what happened to Stuart. You won't win this fight."

"You think this is a fight?" I smile as I head for the door. "When I start fighting, Red, you'll know."

I park in front of the police station, properly queasy now. I lower the window and let the air cool the sweat on my hot face. One would imagine that if Duncan had marched a bloodied Stuart here that night then he would have been held in a cell until morning, presumably with some record of it, and let free in daylight. Which would mean he couldn't have been in the forest getting killed in the middle of the night. Which seems to imply Duncan took Stuart somewhere else. And then came back to the pub to see me. And then disappeared again, sometime around 2:30 A.M. My timeline isn't getting much clearer.

The motive, though.

I understand full well why Duncan would kill Stuart Burns. The thing I can't reconcile is why he would do it and then just leave the man's body to be discovered.

The only motive for doing that that makes sense to me is to make it look like a wolf kill.

Perhaps Duncan never meant to kill Stuart, but the man died of wounds from their fight, and the chief saw an opportunity to kill two birds with one stone. Save himself from a homicide charge and create a legal reason to get rid of the wolves, easing the tension among his people and setting it all back to normal.

He must be wondering who hid the body.

Or not. It's starting to seem obvious.

I drive out to the Burns farm. I have avoided coming here since my run-in with Lainey and her brothers, it very clear how little she wants to see me. But I'm worried about her. I want to see if she's okay. If, and only if, she's open to talking about that night, then maybe she can shed some light on what happened outside the pub, and whether or not Duncan took her husband to the police station. But my first priority is bringing her the loaf of bread and pot of soup Aggie has made, and a bottle of wine.

I juggle my bounty in order to knock on the door. Her light is on and I see a flash of her face in a window before the curtains are pulled shut. She doesn't answer.

Perhaps she blames me for the conflict that night, the fight that led to his disappearance. Perhaps she blames me for getting involved at all.

Frankly, I too am beginning to think I should have stayed right the hell away. I place the food and drink on her doorstep and leave her in peace.

"Inti Flynn. What can I do for you?"

"I wanted to invite you out to the hide this afternoon."

Duncan doesn't answer for a long moment. I listen to his breathing down the line. "Why's that then?"

"It's rare to get a hide set up with such good visibility of a pack's den site. We can watch them quite easily."

"And why would I want to do that?"

"Because few people in this world get to watch wolves in the wild. It's a very special thing. I'm trying to change your mind about them, Duncan."

I can hear him deliberating. "What time then?"

The hide is made of timber and is only large enough for two to three people to sit inside. It's low to the ground, has a grass roof to blend in more easily with its surrounds, and a narrow viewing window from which to see 360 degrees of undulating brown hills that make up part of the southeastern slopes of the Cairngorms mountain range.

It is truly remote out here. The landscape is enormous in a way I can't make sense of. I feel a million miles from humanity, and so tiny.

I haven't been to base camp in days because from here, with binoculars, I can watch the Glenshee Pack denning for the birth of their new litter. The mother, Number Eight, has disappeared into the crevice she and her mate dug out, and she hasn't come out for a solid six days. Which I think essentially means she's had her pups in there, and will soon emerge. The other four wolves, including Number Ten, the sister returned from her long journey, have remained close. I spend the morning watching two of them play, one with a long white swan feather, which brings her no end of joy, waving it between her teeth and batting at it with her paws, while the other—the male alpha—dances with the shadows of clouds for hours on end. Old male Number Fourteen, our oldest wolf, watches them se-renely, while vigilant Number Ten stalks the riverbank, up and down, mesmerized by something in the water. The more I watch them, the more I understand that I will never know what happens inside a wolf's mind, I won't even come close. I smile at the foolish teenager in me who thought she could discover their secrets.

The door bangs open and I about jump out of my skin. "Jesus, Duncan."

He is hunched over to fit into the little hide, looking completely unsure what he's doing here.

I hope he sees the invitation as a peace offering instead of what it really is: a tactic.

He shuffles awkwardly in so he can close the door. Sits as far from me as he can. As I pass him the second set of binoculars and point him in the right direction, I watch the tiny expressions on his face, the movement of his eyes, the twitch of his lips. I watch how his hands move, how he inhabits a space. Trying to learn him, learn his tics and tells the way the wolves learn their prey. I will have the truth of that night, one way or another. If it takes drawing a little closer then that's what I'll do.

"This is the Glenshee Pack," I say. "They're waiting for the breeding female to have her pups."

He watches them quietly, moving his sightline from wolf to wolf. "Only four?"

"And the mother in the den."

"Which is the alpha?"

"The breeding male is Number Seven, on the far left."

"What's he doing?"

I lift my binoculars to see Seven chomping on a stick and wrestling it between his paws. I shrug. "Playing."

Duncan frowns. "They don't look so scary." He glances sideways at me. "But then neither do you."

I don't know what to say to that. With the two of us wedged into the small space it feels hot and airless. "Who ever told you I was scary?"

"I didn't need to be told."

I am meant to be getting close to him and here I am getting annoyed. "Rich, coming from you." I brush the hair off my sweaty face. "I *knew* you couldn't be as nice as you seemed. No one ever is."

"What happened to you?" he asks.

"Nothing," I say, pissed off and returning fire. "What happened to your leg?"

I don't expect him to answer, but he says, "My father took to it with a cricket bat. Shattered my femur. Mam didn't want to anger him further by taking me to a hospital so she bandaged me up as best she could, and it healed very badly."

My chest deflates. Every ember of anger dies instantly and there are tears in my throat and I want to reach for him, must hold myself very still.

"How old were you?" I ask as evenly as I'm able.

He shrugs. "Dunno. Thirteen?"

It starts to rain, as the clouds have been warning me all day. "This weather's relentless," I mumble, distressed and unsure how to be, what to say. I was wrong again about him.

"'Summer on the high plateau,'" Duncan recites, "'can be delectable as honey; it can also be a roaring scourge.'"

"What kind of cop knows poetry, huh?" I say, swatting a midge away from my face—even with the door closed the little bastards find a way in. I think I am relieved to be taken elsewhere, away from the cricket bat and broken bones, and hate myself for this cowardice.

"Many kinds, I'd guess."

I shake my head. "None of the ones I know."

"Let me guess—your dad a cop?"

"My mum. And not the kind who knows poetry."

"Oh yeah? What kind is she then?"

"The kind who suspects something and follows it through instead of sitting outside in a car all night waiting for bad shit to happen inside."

There is silence at that.

And I realize it might be this, most of all, that I can't forgive: his inaction.

"She tell you much about her work?" Duncan asks.

I shrug.

"'Cause any half-decent detective knows you don't go after the man unless you can keep him locked up, unless you've got him iron tight, or else he goes straight home and hurts his wife a thousand times worse than he would have. Sometimes he kills her."

I look at Duncan. "Is that what happened to your parents?"

He turns back to the wolves. Nods.

"And you tried to protect her."

"No," Duncan says. "I didn't. Not that day. On that day I watched him beat her to death and I just sat there, still as a corpse."

Within me, a painful recognition.

Duncan says, "I killed my father but it wasn't in self-defense, or defense of another, like they said. There was no one to defend. I guess you ought to know that."

"Then what was it?"

His jaw twitches. "Revenge. Hatred. She was dead already when I took that same cricket bat and shattered his skull."

I swallow, my cheeks on fire. The words tumble from me without my permission. "My sister was brutalized by her husband."

Duncan's head whips around to me. "What?"

"My twin."

He lets the air from his lungs. "I'm sorry," he says, a hitch in his voice. "I'm so fucking sorry. Forgive me."

A strangled laugh leaves me. "Why? You didn't do it." I lift a trembling hand to my eyes, fingers pressing my eyelids closed. I am starting to feel nauseous again. "It turned me into something I hadn't been," I admit. "Something I'd never imagined I could be. I wanted to kill him. I wanted it so badly. I was feral. Duncan, I—you have no idea how *gentle* I used to be. I believed there was magic in the space between our bodies, and now I'm just this . . . hard, angry thing."

"You're gentle still," he says. "You pretend not to be but I see it in everything you do."

I am crying after all.

My hand goes to my tummy, where the small bump is forming. I must force it away from there or be undone.

In another life, maybe.

Duncan's palm rests on my back, large and warm, and this is what I should have been able to do for him.

"Where's your sister now?"

I wipe my eyes. "At home."

"In Blue Cottage?" He frowns, confused. "I didn't know you had anyone living there with you."

"She doesn't leave. Except in her mind." I shift, struggling with the words. "I didn't know . . . that that could happen. To a person. That they could just be snuffed out. That we have the power to undo each other."

"Are you getting her help?"

"I tried. I took her to a facility where she could get proper care, you know, therapy and medication and all of that. But she hated it so much. She just wants quiet. And to be alone. It's why I brought her out here. I thought it might be quiet enough to heal her."

There is a long silence and then he asks, "Were you there? When it happened?"

My eyes search for the wolves through the curtain of rain, but they've disappeared. "No," I reply.

A while later, rain still heavy.

"Come on," I say. "I promised you wolf watching and this lot won't give us much more."

"So . . . ?"

"So we'll find another pack, if you're up for it."

We head out into the sideways-lashing rain, lifting our raincoat hoods. It's a fair hike down the side of the mountain, and I can see in the distance where he's parked his truck. "My car's further along," I tell him as we approach. "Follow me."

I lead him back toward home then cut north to Abernethy Forest. By the time we park at the edge it's stopped raining, and Fingal leaps from the truck's cabin to lick my hands excitedly. *Hello, you.* "Will he be able to stay quiet or should we leave him?" I ask.

"He knows to be silent out here. Will his scent disturb them?"

"No more than ours."

The three of us set off, soon enveloped by trees. Moss carpets the ground in lime. There are ferns as high as my shoulders. I touch rough trunks and smooth boughs, run my fingers through soft foliage, over prickly needles. My feet sink a little in the sodden ground. Through the canopy is a gray sky, its light turning the edges of everything crisper, illuminating colors from within. It's cold, still, even in summer. Without the sun to warm us it feels colder. The rain has left its scent behind, a scent like no other, and glittering droplets on the end of every leaf. We move as quickly as Duncan can, while Fingal bounds joyously ahead, chasing rabbits.

"Does he catch any?" I ask.

"Naw," says Duncan. "Wouldn't know what to do if he did."

We emerge through the birch trees to the edge of a silver loch, the dog waiting patiently for us at its edge. We stop to take in the lovely sight, and as we stare quietly at the water a large brown and white bird of prey swoops down and catches something wriggling and scaly in its talons. It flounders within the splashing water and must work hard to lift the heavy trout back up into the air, its magnificent striped wings so powerful even with the extra load.

When it's gone, I remember to breathe. "*Oh my god.*"

"An osprey," he says, smiling.

"I've never seen anything like it."

"Timed just for you, then."

"The fish was half its size!"

"I've heard stories of osprey catching hold of fish so large they're dragged under the water. Their talons lock onto the prey and they can't let go, or they don't, and they're drowned."

My smile drops away. Even so, I won't forget the gift of having seen that. I wish Aggie had been here.

I turn to scanning the ground for prints, scat, broken foliage. The forest climbs an incline and we follow it up.

"Do you know where they are?" Duncan asks at one point, sounding out of breath.

I slow my pace. "No."

"What about the collars they wear—aren't they locators?"

"Only if I turn to the right frequency at the right time, and anyway I don't have my gear." I glance sideways at him. "Wolves are very difficult to find. If you don't know them, know their territories, you've got no hope. I met a group of documentary makers once who spent a decade looking for wolves to film and they only ever saw two glimpses."

"Why's it so hard?"

"Because wolves are shy. They survive by staying hidden and they're just about the best survivors there are."

"So what—we gotta think like wolves?"

"Nope, that's impossible."

"Then how the hell are we gonna find them?"

"Can you keep a secret, Duncan?"

He smiles ruefully. "Perhaps to my detriment."

"You have to promise to only use it for good. Do you promise?"

"I promise."

I return the smile. "You don't hunt wolves. You hunt their prey."

We climb up to a high, rocky crag covered in deep bell heather, named for its purple bell-shaped flowers. The herd is in a clearing below us, grazing idly. A stream lies to their side, cutting through the hills. On our rocky plateau I spot some scat and crouch to look at it.

"Wolf?" he asks, and I nod. "They've been up here then. Is it safe here?"

I shrug, enjoying his unease.

"Why's it white?"

"Probably from eating bones," I say.

"Christ."

I glance at him over my shoulder. "I won't let them hurt you."

He meets my eyes. "That so?"

I straighten. "Do I seem like the sort who'd let your bones get eaten by wolves?"

"That's what I'm trying to figure out," Duncan replies.

We sink onto the edge of the rock, our legs draped down toward the cliff drop. He goes to remove his rain jacket, revealing a brilliant orange jumper, almost neon in hue. Another knitted masterpiece, my favorite so far.

"Wow. That's quite a jumper."

He smiles.

"Who's making these for you?"

"There's a knitting group in town."

"I've heard of this knitting group."

"Well, the members have varying skill levels which means my jumpers have varying quality." He pulls the collar of his raincoat back to reveal the stitching along his shoulder has come loose and gapes open, threads hanging loose.

I smile. "And you wear it anyway."

"Of course."

"Better zip back up, it's bright enough to spook the animals."

He does so quickly.

Fingal lies between us, tongue lolling as he pants, eyes locked on the deer below.

"Why the wolves then?" Duncan asks. "Why this, as your life?"

"If we're talking about conservation, about saving this planet, we have to start with the predators. Because if we can't save the predators, we've got no chance of saving anything else."

He doesn't respond for a moment, and then he says, "Yeah, but why really?"

"I . . ." I stop and try to think of the answer. "I have always loved them, without reason. Have always wanted to know their secrets. And then I learned they could save forests . . ." I glance at Duncan. "Some people need wildness in their life."

He nods slowly. "Did you discover their secrets?"

"Of course not."

We both smile.

"What about you? Why'd you become a cop? Because of what happened with your parents?"

"Aye. But it took me some time to get from that night to the badge. I was ugly inside, all my adolescence. Picking fights. Needing chaos. Thinking it was the rage that was feeding me, but all it was doing was poisoning. I knew if I kept on that path I'd get someone killed. So I made a choice. Peace, at all costs. Kindness. Mine is a drop in the ocean compared to my mam's, but I try every day."

We are quiet a while, and I think about the deceptiveness of that rage he speaks of.

Duncan makes a gesture to encompass the forested hills. "These trees are directly descended from the Ice Age," he says. "The first pines in Scotland arrived here around 7000 BC, and these are what remain, an unbroken evolutionary chain."

I know, I think. *It's why I'm here.*

"But then you'd know that already, wouldn't you?" he asks.

"Was Lainey there when you dropped Stuart home that night, after the pub?"

Duncan takes a second. "This is why I'm here then?"

I don't reply.

He shakes his head. "I sent Lainey to wait for us at the station. I didn't want her there if things went sour. When we were done I took Stuart to find her at the station so she could drive him home."

Ah. "And did she?"

Duncan searches my face. "What are you fishing for?"

"I'm just trying to sort it all out."

"I can't share details of an ongoing—"

"Yeah, I know."

After a long moment he says, "I put him in her car and she took him home."

"Then she's the last person to see him? Shouldn't that make her suspect number one?"

"Yes."

"Oh. What was her story, then?"

He spreads his hands. "Just that she drove him home and they went to bed and she woke that morning to find him gone. She thought he was just out working but he didn't come home."

Shit. If Lainey's telling the truth then that changes things. It means I still have no clue how or when or why Stuart got to that patch of forest.

Of course, she could be lying. And so could Duncan. I guess it's even possible they came up with the story together.

"Are you still sleeping with her?" I ask. Of all the questions I have asked that I don't want an answer to.

I feel his body tense. "No," he says. "Not since before you."

I find myself wanting to believe him and also not, wanting there to be a good solid reason to mistrust him, instead of this yawning pit of uncertainty.

"Do you still love her?" I ask, more softly.

"Inti, what—"

"You did once, right? When you were younger. There must be some love left if you go to the trouble of having an affair with her, otherwise why not fuck someone single?" I am being crass now, and realize I am angry, too.

"I care about her," Duncan says with more maturity than I've displayed. "I worry about her. I hate what he was doing to her. I don't think I've loved her in a long time. I stopped being able to, and it's just as well. She was scared of me after what happened. Everyone was. Death gets under your skin, you carry it with you. People can sense that."

We are about to give up. A cold wind is keening through the trees around us. The deer have been idle for a while now, chewing away, eating all those little tree shoots and buds of plants before they have a chance to grow. No hope of that clearing returning to forest at this rate. I am just thinking the wolves ought to get off their butts and do their jobs here when I see something move. At first it seems like nothing. Then a shift in the quality of the light between trees.

I grab Duncan's arm, alerting him to be still.

From within the shadows melts a pale foreleg. Then a snout, black tipped. The points of her ears. A white wolf.

I direct Duncan's gaze to her.

Then move my hand further upstream. To where the brown wolf watches just as calmly from behind the tree line. Downwind, where they won't be scented.

"They smell us," I murmur, "but they're wounded and hungry. And who knows how long they've been watching this herd."

"Will they attack?"

"Maybe. It's a clever spot."

The two wolves we can see—Ash and her new son-in-law Number Twelve—hold very still, watching. Ash's daughter Number Thirteen will be here somewhere, perhaps streaking silently around to flank the herd. And hiding further back will be the six gangly pups, keen to learn. I brought Duncan here to watch the herd but I can't quite believe our luck at this spotting. True, the deer are within the Abernethy Pack's territory, but for all my earlier bravado, I have rarely come across wolves I wasn't actively tracing via GPS or radio signal.

I wonder what Duncan sees when he looks at them. To me they look subtly powerful, endlessly patient, and more beautiful than anything I've seen. And just as I am thinking so, some silent language is spoken between them and they explode from their cover. Fluid, strong, undeniable. The deer flee. Most head north, for the mountains. Five hundred head of deer running together, shaking the earth with a mighty rumble I can feel through my body, from my hand into Duncan's arm, the ground is vibrating with their power, vibrating through us, the world has been shaken by two wolves.

A splinter group of deer heads for the river. Sometimes it's good cover; the wolves don't move as quickly as the deer in water. But today it's a mistake, because there is Number Thirteen and each of the pups, guarding the far bank so the deer can't cross. They flounder in the water, panicked.

Ash and Number Twelve are cutting between the deer, separating out the one they have already chosen. It's a small doe. They would have been watching her for days. Ash herds her into the water, where she comes up against the rest of her kind, blocking her passage. They are scattering both up and downstream, it's chaos, and within this maelstrom Ash wades almost casually into the river and closes her mouth and mine on the throat of the doe. "My god," Duncan breathes. As the deer tries to run Ash simply holds tight, the force of her jaws like an iron clamp, unassailable. She lets herself be carried a few paces until the doe stumbles to a halt, sinking gently into the water. Both animals go very still and stay that way for some time. A game of patience, and something intimate about it. The rest of the herd have escaped, now that the wolf pack has let them. The wolves watch their leader wait out the final breaths from her prey and then drag the beast onto the grass. Ash, Twelve, and Thirteen set to devouring the doe, blood staining their fur. The younger wolves prowl around the outside, darting in for tastes but knowing they'll get what's left.

Warm saliva has filled my mouth; I am ravenous. Nothing for humans is as simple, as certain.

I blink in the fading light, only now aware that darkness is falling. Soon we won't be able to see the feasting wolves, nor our way back. I realize I am still holding Duncan's arm and let it go.

"We need to leave," I say.

He doesn't answer, and then he says, "That was . . ." Slowly he shakes his head. In the twilight I think there are tears in his eyes.

"Yeah," I say softly. "I know."

Something passes between us, a different kind of understanding. There has been desire since the start, but there is something else now. The quiet he makes me feel. The calm.

But too quickly I realize I was so inside the wolf I didn't feel what the deer did. No tearing at my flesh, no being eaten. Only the taste of blood. I turn away from Duncan.

It's a long way back to the cars. I'm worried about Duncan's leg; his limp is more pronounced and his face has paled. I start to wonder if he will make it back to the cars, start to brainstorm what I will do if he can't. I could make some sort of stretcher and drag him. I could go for help. But he keeps limping along, one dogged step after another. By the time we reach the cars Duncan is trembling and I am dizzy, convinced I've been seeing bodies move around us in the dark.

"Night," Duncan says, and I'm relieved this is it. But then he says, "I understand why you don't. But trust has to be offered before it can be met."

I can see the tops of trees swaying slowly in the wind. I wait for the howl of a wolf but she doesn't lift her voice, not tonight. Busy eating.

"No such thing as trust in the wilderness," I say softly. "It's only people need that word."

20

Five years passed in Alaska. The three of us managed to coexist, for the most part. But I'd noticed a change in my sister. She no longer seemed lit from within, excited by the prospect of waking to a new day. There hadn't been any new signs invented in a long while; in fact I couldn't remember the last time she'd used our sign language. She taught language studies at University of Alaska Anchorage, and she went out a lot at night. She and Gus fought all the time, bright savage screaming fights. Neither of them ever left the other; the fighting seemed to make them cleave more fiercely together, though I couldn't imagine how respect remained, given the nastiness they had no trouble conjuring, or the competition they made of debasing each other. I wanted to end it for them but didn't know how, knew that only they could do that, and yet I hated my position as bystander and wondered if I would regret not taking action.

But this was my place, where it had always been. A silent third party to their intimacy. I told myself Aggie was a force and she knew what she was doing, what she wanted and what she could endure, and it was true—she was very much a force, but what I didn't know then is that any force can be stopped by enough resistance.

I started working longer hours, and sleeping at the base. I couldn't bear the thought of going home to the sound of their raised voices, or to the sight of their lips touching, to the stolen feel of his mouth on mine and the blistering shame that accompanied my desire. I missed my sister terribly and hated Gus for coming between us as nothing else ever had. Maybe a part of me was angry with Aggie, too, for letting him.

It was a Sunday night when I finally dragged myself back to the house after sleeping at work for a week. An ocean tide of weariness threatened to pull me under, but the voices throbbing from the house let me know I wasn't about to sleep anytime soon. There was a group of men gathered in my living room, Gus's gaggle of surgeon mates. They greeted me politely and then turned back to the football game. I found Gus gathering beers from the fridge.

"Hey."

"Hey, kid, give me a hand with these."

I dropped my bag and took the armful of cans.

"I'd give my right nut for a VB," he said wistfully, looking regretfully at the American beer in his hands.

"Where's Aggie?" I asked.

"Out." He said this offhandedly as he returned to the living room, but there was tension through his shoulders.

I followed him, handing out the beers to men who didn't thank me. "Who's she out with?"

"The other teachers."

"Okay. I'm going to bed, so can you keep the noise down."

"Sure thing, princess, we're headed out anyway."

I went upstairs, sat on my bed, and called Aggie.

A man's voice answered. "Hello?"

"Who's this?" I asked.

"Luke."

I breathed a sigh of relief because I had heard of Luke, one of Aggie's colleagues at the university. "Luke, can I talk to Aggie?"

"She's indisposed." I could hear the amusement in his voice and irritation flared.

"What does that mean?"

"Means she had too much to drink and she's currently puking her guts up in my bathroom."

"What's your address, I'll come get her."

"She's all right here."

"No, she's not. Give me your address."

There must have been something in my voice because he told me. I grabbed my keys and pounded down the stairs.

"Where's the fire, kid?" Gus called from among the rowdy crew as I darted for the door.

"I'm getting Aggie."

My feet crunched on the gravel outside. It was cold, my breath made clouds. Soon there was another set of boots crunching, another mouth breathing. "You don't have to come, I'm just picking her up," I said but he got into my car and we drove in silence through the night streets of Anchorage. I still didn't know the city well, having spent so little time in it, but Gus directed me to the house.

As we walked to the front door I said, "Don't . . . do anything weird, okay? They're just mates from work."

"Of course," he replied, and to his credit he definitely did seem relaxed. Luke answered the door and that was when Gus sent a heavy fist into his face, dropping him straight to the ground.

"Fuck!" I sank to one knee, dizzy, my vision gone. Fuck fuck *fuck* it hurt. Eyes streaming, face throbbing with heat. When my thoughts returned I counted through the pain, one breath, two breaths, three four five. The pulse in my nose and eyes and skull began to dull. Blinking the spots from my vision, I got to my feet and followed Gus into the house, pausing beside Luke to check he was okay. He was groaning and holding his bleeding nose and as I saw it I instinctively reached to stem the blood gushing from mine, blood that wasn't there but that I could feel so warm and slippery on my face, between my fingers, in my mouth. "Sorry," I said. "You okay?"

"Just get her out of my house," Luke mumbled.

I found Gus in the doorway of the bathroom. Aggie was sprawled on the tiles, embracing the base of the toilet, her vomit fresh in the bowl. She was barely conscious and seeing her like this made me woozy. Gus was staring at her with a kind of coldness.

I sank to the floor and pulled my sister into my arms, stroking the hair off her face. Gus at least had the wherewithal to flush the toilet.

"Aggie, hey, you okay?"

She opened her eyes and when she saw me she smiled. "Hello, you," she said, then laughed. "Hello, me."

"Can you stand?"

"Of course," she said, which turned out to be at least half true. Gus and I supported her as she stumbled on the legs of a foal to the car.

"Darling," she said to her husband as he tried to bundle her into the back seat. "Wait."

"Get in the car, Aggie," he said.

"Are you angry with me, my love?"

"Have a fucking guess."

She laughed. "That's strange."

"Just shut up," he told her flatly, and something of me came awake, some alertness.

"I didn't want this," she said.

"Bullshit."

"Don't you get it?" Aggie asked. "I'm not your property."

Gus shoved her hard onto the seat. She fell back, almost hitting her head. I stumbled, unbalanced by the sensation.

"Hey!" I said, but Gus was wrestling Aggie into her seat belt, and he was being too rough, which was making her buck against him, and he snarled something and grabbed her by the throat to hold her down and with his fingers squeezing my windpipe I made a fist and punched him awkwardly in the back of the skull, punched myself awkwardly in the back of the skull.

Gus spun around, holding his head and staring at me with feral eyes. "What the fuck? I was just getting her in the car!"

"Don't touch her like that," I managed, dazed.

He laughed. "Jesus fucking Christ. You've got no idea, do you, kid? She fucking loves the drama—she *creates* it. She loves to be roughed up."

"Stop it, Gus."

"And she's not the only one. You liked it rough, too, from memory."

I pushed past him and leaned into the car, my head pounding with adrenaline. Aggie had given up the fight and was now struggling to get her own seat belt clipped. I reached across her and gently clicked it into place, then I gave her hand a squeeze. "You okay?"

"Sure," she said, and she sounded so tired, more tired than any human could safely be. She ran a finger gently from her forehead down her cheek; a loving touch to my face, one of our secret languages. "Are you, Int?"

"I'm fine. Let's go home."

She was asleep by the time we got back. Gus carried her inside. Our fevers had passed. There was no more anger in the air, only weariness, only sadness. I took water and painkillers to Aggie's bedside and then found him sitting on the vacated couch in the living room. His surgery buddies had gone home and he hadn't turned on any of the lights.

I sat next to him, tingling, senses wrung dry. "That was too much," I said. "Way too much."

"I know."

"She didn't do anything wrong."

"She gets pissed at another man's house and you don't think that's wrong?"

"They're friends. She's allowed to have friends, and she's allowed to get pissed."

His stony silence was disagreement enough.

I got to my feet, done with him. "Grow up, Gus."

"I didn't know you had it in you, Inti," he said, pausing me.

"What?"

"That fight. I thought you were too sweet for that."

I turned so he could see my face when I spoke. "When it comes to my sister, I can be anything I need to be. Don't forget that."

After Gus left for work the next morning, I sat on his side of the bed. Aggie was pale and hollow-eyed, but she accepted the coffee with a grateful smile, and sat up to enjoy it.

"You're usually gone by now," she said.

"I'm going in late. We need to talk."

"I already know, Inti."

"I'm going to say it anyway, for my own sake." I licked my lips, glancing out the window at the sun-drenched street. "I should have said it ages ago. I didn't want to . . . I didn't want to be involved, but this has to stop. You need to leave Gus."

"I know."

"He's not a good man."

"Then he's perfect for me. I'm a piece of shit."

I looked at my sister. "It scares me, that you'd say that about yourself."

"What am I, except a pale shadow of you? What do I do but follow you through life? Without you I'm just nothing."

My mouth fell open. "That's how I feel about you."

Aggie laughed a little. "So which of us is right?"

"I don't know."

"I've missed you," I said.

"I've missed you too," she said.

"I'll pack our bags. We can leave today."

She shook her head, and I knew it was going to take something really bad happening before she would consider it. Then she said, startling me, "You should pack just for you. Find somewhere else to live. Closer to work, maybe."

I stared at her. "What do you mean?"

"There's no reason for you to put up with our crap. All the fighting. It's horrible, and I can see how much you hate it."

"I'm not leaving you."

"It's not *leaving*," she said with an eye roll. "Don't be dramatic. You could get a place closer to work. Have your own space."

It wasn't an unreasonable suggestion except that we had never lived apart and never wanted to, and the certainty we had always shared about this set alarm bells ringing in my mind. He was coming between us and she was letting him, and something about it felt very wrong.

And so an idea began to take shape.

21

Thursday night at the wool shop. I stand outside in the cold for a while, trying to drum up the energy to go in. What am I doing. I don't want to socialize so why the hell am I here?

I steel myself and push through the door. The bell rings and several faces look up.

"Here she is," Douglas says. "Come on in, lassie." The old man stands up to offer me his seat and pull another over for himself.

"Thank you," I say, sitting beside Mrs. Doyle, who Duncan visits most days and who I bought a pregnancy test from. In the circle are a few faces I know—Holly and Bonnie are both here, and wave to me—and a few faces I don't recognize, not only women but a couple of men too.

Holly sits on my other side and passes me a cup.

"What's this?"

"Nettle wine," she says. "Douglas makes it."

"Of course he does." I take a sip and let out a long whistle.

"Yeah, it's rocket fuel, but we don't have any choice—he makes us drink it," Holly says.

"Where's your knitting, love?" Mrs. Doyle asks me, only I don't understand her broad accent so she has to repeat it.

"I don't have any. I've never knitted before."

"Good Lord," she says. "Well now, that's all right, I'll show you what to do, love." This she has to repeat too, until she starts laughing and says, "Now I thought I was the one going deaf," which Holly has to translate for me and then we are all laughing.

While Mrs. Doyle teaches me to knit, using enormous needles and thick loops of wool I suspect are normally used to keep the children occupied, Holly chatters away—turns out she and Amelia have twin daughters who are giving them no end of grief. When she finds out I was once a teenage twin who gave her mother no end of grief she squeals with excitement.

"Help me, Inti, *please*. All they do is whisper to each other and laugh at us!"

I shrug as Mrs. Doyle has to untangle the pathetic effort I've made, and it should be known that the seventy-three-year-old woman has arthritis in the hands and can barely move them, but even she is able to knit a few stitches without getting them knotted into a mess.

To Holly I say, "It won't be what you want to hear."

"Lay it on me."

"You will never be as close to them as they are to each other, so just give up on that now."

She slumps back against her seat. "Christ. She packs a punch, huh, Mrs. Doyle?"

"Don't take the Lord's name in vain, love," Mrs. Doyle says without looking up.

"Sorry, Mrs. Doyle."

Next the conversation turns to the Dundreggan estate, west of here near Loch Ness, a flagship rewilding effort by the charity Trees for Life. Mrs. Doyle, as it turns out, is a longtime volunteer and is headed there tomorrow for the next phase of tree planting.

"How long have you been volunteering?" I ask her.

"Years now. Most of us in these parts have planted trees at times. We have to look after our home, now, don't we?"

She tells me, slowly so I can follow her, of the four thousand hectares of the estate's land that are being rewilded, of the millions of trees planted, but also of the trouble they've had. "Birch seeds cover the ground each year, trillions they say, but the deer come along and eat up any of the tree shoots so nothing can grow. Now we've been tackling the deer trouble for many, many years here, love, since before you were alive. And out that way they're not as fortunate as we are here—they don't have any wolves to move the deer along."

"Maybe the wolves will find them," I murmur. "One day when it's safe for them to roam further."

"Och aye, I do hope so. But for now, do you know what we do over there to keep the deer moving?"

"What?"

She points across the circle to Douglas and wheezes with laughter. "Mr. McRae heads over that way with me sometimes and he and some of the younger laddies go out at night and they screech away on the bagpipes. Bless them if it isn't the worst sound on Earth and drives the cheeky pests right away."

I laugh with her as Douglas straightens in his chair. "Now I know you didn't just insult my piping, Mrs. Doyle."

"Not at all, Mr. McRae, I was quite generous, considering."

Douglas holds his belly while he laughs and soon the whole circle is chuckling along with us. I think there's a bit of flirtation going on between the two of them.

"What else is being done to rewild Scotland?" I ask Mrs. Doyle, wanting to keep her talking, thrilled to have found her.

"Oh, many things, love. It started out all wrong, I'd say, when we first realized our forest clearing had brought us down to a few pathetic groves of Caledonian pines. Instead of planting natives our forest management planted groves of non-native conifers! The lunacy! Just terrible for the native wildlife. In any case, we started getting back on track and began to plant the natives and reintroduce the poor lost animals. There were the beavers, to start. I hear now down south the landowners are *paying* to have the critters on their land, they love them so much. And soon enough we'll head up far north to the flow country."

"What's the flow country?"

"The Mhoine, love. The world's largest peat bog. It stores hundreds of millions of tons of carbon. More than any forest, I believe."

"Truly?"

"And they want to put a space station on it! Of all things! The eejits. You know what happens to peat when a spark hits it? It catches on fire and it burns on and on and it releases all that carbon into the air. It's *fragile*. And they want to explode rockets on it! The insanity of the rich, aye?"

I nod, horrified. "Why are you going up there?"

"To protest, of course."

I look at her in awe. "I hope you don't mind me saying but I haven't come across many people your age who are so open to conservation."

"Oh, rubbish. We're here, in among the rest of the noisemakers. We're here."

I feel a stirring of hope in my chest to hear the passion in her voice.

"And you know the secret, love?"

"What's that?"

"Well now, you don't have to rewild on such large scales. You can start small, in your own backyard. I've been growing wildflowers for years and *oh*—all sorts of wee creatures have been coming to visit me."

"How wonderful," I breathe. "Could I come and visit you, too, sometime?"

"Of course, love, I would be honored to have you. It's so much easier than most folk know," Mrs. Doyle adds. "But now, change is frightening to some," she concedes after a little while. "And when you open your heart to rewilding a landscape, the truth is, you're opening your heart to rewilding yourself."

A couple of hours pass and I get to chat with most of the knitters, and Douglas tells a lot of really terrible jokes that have us all giggling, and we eat delicious cheese except when I reach for the soft Brie and Mrs. Doyle says under her breath, "That one's not for you, love," and by the time we're wrapping up it occurs to me that this is a perfect opportunity to ask some questions about Duncan.

"Mrs. Doyle?" I say as I copy her method of coiling up the leftover wool.

"Yes, love."

"I've noticed Duncan visits you a lot . . ."

"Oh, bless him." She smiles such a smile. "We love our Duncan."

I'm not sure what I'm trying to ask, so I end up simply saying, "He seems very kind."

"Oh, aye, he is that. Very kind indeed. That's why we all have him around so much, the poor laddie."

"What do you mean?"

"He just needs some love, that boy. He needs family."

I stare at her. It didn't occur to me that they might be the ones looking after him. That actually, Duncan is the lonely one.

After the knitting, I go to the Snow Goose. In the crowded pub sits Lainey. She's with her brothers and Fergus, drinking white wine. I don't want to corner her, but maybe she'll feel more inclined to talk to me in public. I cross to their table and receive nods from the men, but nothing at all from Lainey. She glares at me, wordless and waiting. She seems weathered. Tired beyond her years. She's the sole owner of a failing farm now. But at least she's not afraid for her life.

"Inti," Fergus greets me. "Come to join us?"

"Can I pinch Lainey for a quick word?" I ask.

She hesitates, then gets up.

"What are you drinking?"

"Chardonnay."

I point her to a quiet corner table beside the fireplace while I go to the bar. I'm about to order two wines before I reconsider and get myself a mineral water.

I sink into the seat, squeezed in behind a stone wall. It's private here. We won't be overheard. "How are you?"

"All right, thanks."

I swallow and admit, "I've been worried about you. I came to see you a couple of times . . ."

"Thank you for the food and wine. What did you want to talk about?"

"First I wanna say I'm sorry for Stuart. For your loss."

"Why? You made your feelings about him clear."

Did I? I thought I'd been pretty damn restrained. "How are his family coping? His parents live in town, right?"

She nods, her hands unclenching slightly. "They keep asking where he is."

"What do you tell them?"

"That I don't know."

I'm about to say something when she adds, "It happens to be a lie."

The words die on my tongue.

She's watching me, searching my face as I am searching hers. My fingers fidget uneasily.

"What happened that night?" I ask. "After you picked him up from the station."

"I took him home and we went to bed. He was gone when I woke up. That's what I've been telling people."

"So what's the truth?"

"Stu was really beat up. Over his ribs and stomach, horrible bruises. When we got home he said Duncan had gone at him, like he was really angry. And it'd got him thinking, on that drive home. He thought it was weird to fight like that unless it was about something. And so he asked me if it was about something." Lainey gulps her drink. Her words are calm, measured, but I think she needs the wine. "I said no," she goes on. "I couldn't imagine what would happen if he knew the truth. I would lie and I'd take that lie to the grave with me. But he knew it anyway, I guess. Maybe he'd been thinking it for a while. He was woozy, still, but he made me change direction. He didn't say where we were going but he was very quiet. That's how I knew something bad was happening, because he hadn't got angry at me—he was just holding on to it all. Letting it build."

Suddenly I am nervous. I don't understand why she's telling me this. I wanted her to, of course, but I didn't think it would be this easy. The danger warning in my brain is triggered.

"We got to the turnoff to Duncan's house," Lainey says. "I pulled over. He told me to keep driving, but I couldn't. So Stu got out of the car and started walking."

"When was this? What time?"

She shakes her head, doesn't know, lost in the memory. The events she describes are like bullet points, moments she must have gone over a thousand times in her head. "I started driving home. I called Duncan. Warned him Stu was heading for his place and he knew about us. I was thinking fuck Stu. Fuck him, let him do what he wants, maybe it would finally get him in trouble if he attacked the chief of police. But he was in such a state . . . It was about as bad as I'd seen him. I couldn't just . . .

I dunno. Something made me turn back. Maybe I thought I could still stop him from doing anything." She drinks more, nearly finishing her glass. "I couldn't find him at the turnoff so I kept driving. Past your place. Through the trees. And that's when I saw you."

My mouth goes dry.

"I saw what you did to him," Lainey tells me. "You were right near the road. Didn't you know you were right near the road?"

I had been. Too fucking close. But then that hadn't really been my choice, had it?

A waiter arrives to take Lainey's glass. She orders another wine.

"Make it two," I say faintly.

When we're alone I push my chair back as far as I can, wedged in against the corner with no space to breathe. "Did you tell Duncan? Is that what you were talking about that night at his house?"

She shakes her head. "I didn't tell him what I saw but I wanted to know why he hadn't looked in that area—he knew Stu was coming to him. So why hadn't he looked there?"

"What did he say?"

"That he had looked. He'd walked all around there and found nothing. Said it didn't make sense, and Stuart must have been going somewhere else."

There is a silence.

Lainey could have told him exactly where I buried Stuart. But she didn't, and I realize it's because she isn't sure that Duncan didn't kill him.

It's the only thing that makes sense to me now. He didn't tell anyone about Lainey's call because he was protecting himself. It placed Stuart near his house, and it placed him out in that forest at the time of the murder.

When Lainey called Duncan to warn him, he was in bed with me. He went out to meet Stuart in the night. Maybe they fought again. Duncan killed him. And then maybe he was interrupted by me stumbling through the dark. So he left. Was he hiding in the shadows, watching me bury Stuart's body as Lainey did from the road? Or did he leave and never know I was there? He must have guessed though, surely, when he got home to find me gone from his bed.

To think the four of us were out there wandering that patch of forest together, passing each other like ghosts in the moonlight.

I feel like I'm going to throw up.

At least—and this is one small consolation—if Duncan does know what I did, I don't think he could arrest me for it without implicating himself in the worse crime. But Lainey had nothing to do with it. She could still come forward and turn us both in.

"What are you gonna do?" I ask.

"I could smash this glass into your face right now," she says, and she is so calm it's chilling. "I think it would feel good."

"Yeah. Probably."

"Who are you?" she asks. "Where did you come from? How did you . . . How does someone make that decision?"

"To be honest, Lainey? That's the question I ask myself every fucking night."

Our wines arrive and we both gulp thirstily. I don't care that I'm not meant to. Right now, I actually could not care less.

"Did you ever imagine hurting him?" I ask her. "When he was hurting you?"

"Of course. I thought about it all the time. Wondering if I could. How I would."

"That's what I thought about too. When I met you both, and I saw what he was doing. It's all I could think about."

Lainey stares at me.

"But there's a difference between imagining something and doing it, and the difference is the size of a goddamn ocean."

She frowns. "What are you talking about?"

"If you want to report me," I tell Lainey, "I won't blame you. If it means you can put him to rest properly. That's what's best for your family, right? So do it, if you need to."

She sits forward, holding my eyes. "You think I need your permission? If I wanted to turn you in, I would have. Fuck you, Inti. Fuck you for making me owe you. I fucking owe you, and that's bullshit, because you shouldn't owe someone for this." Lainey lifts a hand to her eyes and I can see it trembling. Without warning she gets to her feet so explosively the chair crashes to the ground. "We'll talk, all right?" she says. "We'll talk again. I just . . . I'm meant to be having a nice night with my brothers, I can't do this now."

"Of course, whatever you want. I'm really sorry." Then, "Are you . . . Lainey, are you glad he's gone?"

The answer matters too much.

She stares at me. "You're really asking me that?"

I nod.

She passes a hand over her face. Then says, "He was my best friend and I loved him and I've been a ghost for years. Of course I'm glad he's gone."

Outside I feel all my certainties slipping. Her words have dislodged something in my mind.

I climb into my sister's bed. She is awake, and rolls to face me. We gaze at each other in the dark.

"Are you real?" I whisper.

She makes no sound, no movement.

"Or did you die?"

Aggie reaches to trace her own face, her finger probing her cheeks, my cheeks, her forehead, my forehead, her lips, my lips.

"I couldn't let go of you," I press, feeling her touch upon me so viscerally and yet isn't this the trick of my mind? To pretend there is truth where there is none?

"Are you a ghost?" I ask her.

Aggie squeezes my hand so hard it hurts, so hard my bones could be crushed. She must be trying to hurt me. Then she makes a sign. One of the first she ever came up with.

I don't know.

22

There are no new shoots in the mapped quadrants on the hill. I come out to the land Evan showed me when this began, the botanists' survey grounds that are being closely monitored, but there is nothing. Nothing in a valley that has been grazed to dirt. Nothing green among the brown, pushing its way through to reach the sun. It is too early, I know this, and the wrong season now too, we must give the experiment time to work, give the wolves a chance to perform their magic, I know this, but still I walk the land as though to punish myself. In my mind, always, Red and his rifle. He's even less patient than I am.

Aggie leaves me a sketch that is little more than a rough circle and scrawled words beneath. *A grapefruit. And she can hear you now, too.*

This week she is the length of a zucchini. She might not be a she, but she's taken her own form in my mind, without any decision from me. My body makes and I wait. Will this be the day Lainey changes her mind?

Bursts of autumn color set the forest trees alight. Hyacinth red, the color of the spots on the *Lygaeus apterous* fruit fly. Dutch orange, of the crests of golden-crested wrens. The lemon yellows of hornets. Colors so vibrant they caress the air around them, and make of this land a different world. Leaves glitter as crisp winds shake their branches. Most around town say winter will come early and brutal this year. It is only October but we can, all of us, feel it in the air.

Number Eight has long since given birth, and the new Glenshee wolf pups are now fourteen weeks old. They have abandoned their den and begun to eat meat; unlike the Abernethy pups, they have a healthy pack to hunt for them. Their eyes turn golden. They are becoming predators.

And little one is now an eggplant.

The first is a cow, killed on a farm near Glen Tromie. It is bleak country here, in the midwest of the national park. Stark moorlands. Empty of most living things and yet dotted with shaggy cows. Livestock, everywhere. A gray drizzle, somewhere between rain and fog. We have all been waiting for this day. There has been a kind of hush but it will vanish now: there will be noise.

Evan and I drive out to the glen to inspect the carcass and confirm it a wolf kill. Most of the cow has been torn away and there is no doubt that only a large predator with extreme force in its jaws could have done such damage. No chance a fox did this, not to a cow, not in such unforgiving terrain, not with this much power.

The farmers are an older couple, Seamus and Claire. Seamus is inconsolable—the cow in question is one of his best breeders, an older girl he's had for many years. She's left behind a calf that will have to be poddy raised. I get the sense he'd feel as distraught over any of his cows being killed.

"Is this your land?" I ask, gazing out over the windswept grass.

"Our land ends a way back to the west," Seamus admits.

"Are there fences anywhere here?"

"'Course not, it's unowned land."

I look at him. "A piece of advice? Move your cattle back to your own land and get them behind a fence. You were warned about this months ago, again and again. And now the Wolf Trust is expected to reimburse you?" I shake my head and start walking back for the car. Behind me I can hear Evan apologizing and explaining some of the prevention methods—again. I feel bad for my outburst; the poor man's lost something he loved. But he could have prevented this, and he didn't even try.

I see Duncan's truck approaching along the track and hurry to reach my car before he arrives. He knocks on the window just as I am starting the engine. Reluctantly I lower it, aware of how big my stomach must look. My coat will hopefully hide the worst of it. "Hey."

"Wolf?" he asks.

"Yep."

"What do we do?"

"About what?"

"About the wolf."

I frown. "Nothing, Duncan. It's one cow. They'll be paid for it. More kills will come. You should be getting your people used to the idea instead of giving them hope of recourse."

I roll up the window.

It doesn't take long for word to spread about the cow. No time at all, in fact. And as though this is a war, the return fire is swift. The hush, over.

The smell reaches me first, even before I've seen it. This is the molecule that would repel me while at the very same time attracting predators. I know it's a chemical reaction but my body fills with adrenaline nonetheless and there is nothing I want more than to turn and run in the opposite direction. Instead I carry on, and see.

Our base camp cabin is draped in a vermillion cape. Splatters arc across walls and windows with what can only be called a delighted savagery. It frightens me, as it was meant to, and that makes me angry, as most things do.

I reach for my phone, even though it's barely dawn. No service. Never any service. I have to walk out into the field before I can make a call, and even then Duncan's voice drops in and out. I manage to communicate that he needs to come.

Duncan arrives still half asleep. I didn't think to warn him not to bring Fingal, and now the dog darts from smear to smear, trembling with joy.

"Quite a thorough job they've made of it," Duncan mutters. I wait while he limps around the small building, snapping pictures on his phone. "Did anyone break in?"

"No."

"Are you sure? Did you check inside to make sure nothing was taken?"

"Nothing taken. Door was still locked."

"They're just trying to scare you."

"No shit, Duncan."

"Leave it with me. You okay?"

I nod and he hops back in his car. Fingal doesn't respond to being called because he's having conniptions licking the animal blood so I jog over to him and pull him gently away by the collar. "Come, fiend." He gives an excited yelp and launches himself up into the back of the truck.

"I'll call you with any news," Duncan says. He's looking at me and I have to consciously avoid touching my swollen belly. It's taken a long while for me to start showing. These days, naked, I'm obviously very pregnant. With thick woolen sweaters and a loose overcoat, I'm fairly sure you can't tell. I look sloppy, but that's not unusual for me.

"Thanks," I say.

By the time the team arrives I've only managed to scrub the front door clean and there's a river of sweat pouring off me.

"What the *fuck*," Zoe says. "I'm going to be sick."

"Who did this?" Evan asks.

"We've been expecting it," Niels says.

"Um. No one warned me?" Zoe says.

"Not specifically."

"Was there an animal here?" she asks.

"You mean aside from . . ." Evan gestures to the blood.

"Yeah, a living animal."

"Duncan's dog was here," I tell her.

Zoe gives a moan, and scratches her arms. "I knew it, I'm breaking out. I am so not cut out for this wilderness shit." She runs inside, presumably to take an antihistamine for her animal hair allergies. She shouts from the doorway, "I'm not coming out again until that's all cleaned off. In fact probably not even then. I live in here now."

"How is that different from usual?" Evan mutters. Then he moves closer to me. "Let me do this, boss. Niels and I can handle it, you go in and get started on the day."

I shake my head and keep scrubbing.

He lowers his voice. "Probably not the best idea in your condition."

I stop. "What?"

"Nobody else knows. I just have three sisters and a whole lot of nieces and nephews."

It's not that I'm keeping it as some big secret, it's just that I try my best not to think about it, and that means not talking about it. So no one except Mrs. Doyle—and now Evan—know about it. I hand him my sponge and wordlessly head inside. For just a moment I pause, hand on my belly, on the firm swollen bump there. There is a universe within.

Once the cabin is as clean as we can get it, I send Evan and Niels out to find the packs and download their latest GPS data. We need to know which wolf killed the cow. The Tanar Pack is busy hunting the spotted deer with enormous antlers, and a very long way from Seamus and Claire's farm. I doubt it was them. The Glenshee Pack are the closest but have stayed near their den while their pups are young, and they'll probably remain there for months to come. We'll have to think of a plan to collar the pups at some point. Number Ten's data shows that she remained with her pack, which wasn't what I expected to see. Of all the wolves, I would have put money on it being her. Meanwhile the Abernethy Pack have been happily ensconced in their forest to the north. Which leaves me with no explanation.

The next attack is far worse than the first.

Halloween is afoot. The streets are draped with hanging lights and spiderwebs. Grotesquely carved lanterns sit on doorsteps and corners. Ghoulish spirits peer out from windows and finger bones reach up out of their graves of dirt. The Scots love their monster stories; here the macabre is relished.

I am driving through town when stopped by a crowd of people on the road. My first thought is that it must be a kind of street party. But as they part for me I see that there is something strung up on the town sign, and it is not like the other bits and baubles. A gray smudge. A lolling tongue. My guts bottom out.

Old Number Fourteen, the gray wolf who survived all manner of threat and led his family from the pens to safety. Decapitated, his head hanging from a noose, all four paws cut off and draped around the four points of the sign.

I stop being a woman, a human, an animal, whatever I was. I am fury dressed in flesh.

Tonight come the hungry ghosts, in from the fields, seeking shelter from the approaching winter. Give them gifts of food and warmth to appease their desire for revenge. The boundary between this and the Otherworld is thin. Such are the old beliefs of Samhain, the Gaelic harvest festival to mark the beginning of the dark half of the year, the coming of the cold. A huge bonfire is lit at dusk in a field outside of town. People from all over the Cairngorms arrive dressed in spooky costumes. Once they would have killed a cow; I can almost smell the primal Pagan scent of its blood on the air. I move through the disguised bodies with a hunger of my own.

It turns out the monster I'm searching for is stupid. He kept Number Fourteen's body, perhaps to illegally sell the hide, perhaps as a trophy, and he kept the radio collar that had been around the wolf's neck. Maybe he pulled it apart, maybe he put it underwater, thinking that would be enough. But they are almost impossible to destroy and so it has continued to send its mortality code to our system, and this is how I've found him.

His name is Colm McClellan. He is thirty-one years old, divorced, and has two kids who don't live with him. He's not even a farmer—but he does enjoy hunting. I followed him from his house tonight and have watched him lead his children through the festival, feeding them sweets and letting them run around the crackling flames.

He wears a wolf mask.

Ways to kill a man. Push him, unseen, into a bonfire.

A body brushes against me in the crowd. A hand takes mine, distracting me. I pull my eyes from Colm to see Duncan's face in shadow.

"Are you all right?" he asks me.

I try to move past him but he stays me.

"Inti. I'm sorry about what happened."

I look at Duncan. "Are you? I thought you wanted the wolves gone as much as the rest of them."

"Don't say that. You know I've been shifting. You were shifting me. I wasn't sure, but now I am."

"What are you sure of?"

"That whatever you've brought here to us is good."

It stops me. "What made you sure of that?"

"You did," he says.

He lets go of my hand, but only to trace his face with a finger. I shiver; he knows I can feel it. His fingertip running a fever from my forehead to my cheek to my lips. It doesn't feel like a trick; the distance between our bodies feels like the trick because we share the same skin, the same muscles, the same bones and their marrow. I could be swept away so easily; there is a tide wanting to take me. For a split second in time he is everything, he is the whole world, and the little one inside me a universe for us both, but I gave myself to a universe long ago, one that held only my sister and me, and I don't know how I will survive this. I think Duncan sees something in me that isn't really there.

"Have you found who did it?" I ask.

"Not yet. I will." Duncan leans close to my face. "I'll get him."

He won't, though. Because I'm going to be the one to get him.

Colm drops his children at their mother's house and then heads home. I follow a couple of car spaces behind. He lives on the edge of town. He has a large back shed, but parks his car in the driveway and goes inside.

I have a crowbar. I bought it from the hardware store.

In the dark I cross to his car and I smash the crowbar into his windscreen. Over and over. Then I smash his windows, one by one, and the rear windscreen too. He is coming outside now. Shouting at me. While he calls me all manner of filthy names I swing at his leg and feel his knee crunch. Colm screams, I scream. I almost fall, the pain erupting like light before my eyes. But I breathe, and lean on my crowbar, and when the sensation of shattered bones passes I feel something else. The knowledge of what I have inflicted, and it's a rush, heady, disturbing. I could keep going but instead I walk past him to the backyard. I use the crowbar to open the poorly locked shed but inside I don't find the remains of Fourteen's body. I find only his radio collar, discarded in a bucket along with other waste.

I phone Duncan.

"I have an address for you. And a name."

"Inti, tell me you didn't—"

I give him the information and hang up, and then I wipe the crowbar clean of my prints—what little good this will do I don't know—throw it to the ground with a clang, and leave. *You bitch!* Colm shrieks. In my rearview I see him sprawled in his front yard, getting smaller and smaller.

At home I take a bottle of wine from the cupboard and I walk with it out to our paddock. I swallow a few swigs and lie on my back in the cold grass to watch the enormous full moon above. The sky is so clear, so boundless, I fall into it.

Tears trickle into my hair.

Footsteps in the grass, and a body next to mine. My sister takes the wine bottle from my hand and drinks from it, before placing it out of my reach and then lying beside me in the dark.

Our fingers twine. From somewhere nearby there is the soft snort of a horse edging closer.

"Do you think we have any control," I ask, "over what we are?"

She doesn't retrieve her hand to reply, she leaves it in mine.

"I think most of me got left behind in Dad's forest. And now I'm all the things I hate."

I close my eyes and my hair is wet with salt, I am made of it.

Her hand moves now, and fast. *No,* she signs. Then signs it again, *No.*

I roll toward her, curling into a ball. Poison pours from me and I have not cried like this since it happened, because I had no right to cry like this when my sister was the one harmed and even she couldn't cry.

Aggie holds me, she holds me so tight, her lips to my temple, kissing me over and over, and when her fingertips drum a pattern on my spine I am returned to our tiny bodies in Dad's shed, when she brought me back that very first time, as she does now.

She gasps, tilting my chin, and we both look up to see what the sky does, how it dances green and purple and blue, the colors too brilliant to be in *Werner's,* and I am crying still but now it is for the beauty of the world, and for its gentle pull, for the mystery of it and its timing, for its deep, deep knowing, when I was so close to the edge and now I am returned, and I wonder if this is what Aggie sees each time she comes back to me.

23

I am charged with assault and malicious damage to property. Colm is charged with the killing of Fourteen. Neither of us spends a night in jail, but we land heavy fines.

Over the next weeks a trail of livestock is left dead. Most mornings I wake to calls from Bonnie telling me to get out to the next farm to inspect the next sheep or cow carcass half-devoured, and calls from Anne Barrie.

"Fix it, Inti," Anne says. "Do it now, or all our jobs are on the line."

I could follow the ravens to the kills, if I wanted; they travel in great flocks to crowd the skies above the carcasses. And with each new kill my dread grows. The wolf, whichever one it is, has learned that it can feed on livestock. Wolves don't like the taste of penned animals, they like game meat, and they like to hunt it. It's called their prey image. Sheep and cattle, as vulnerable as they are, are not part of that prey image. They're a last resort to a starving wolf. So I must discover which one has a hunger so urgent that it would ignore its own instincts, and why.

I think I already know which one it was. I think I must. And as soon as we prove it, we're going to have to kill her.

Today the Tanar Pack are on the move, drawing east toward the edge of Red's property line, which is just about the worst place they could be heading. If the people of this town are determined to make this a war, then I need to make sure they aren't given any extra ammunition, and the wolves aren't helping themselves, circling so close to Red's land. After dark I leave my sister watching TV and drive to Red's property. I don't turn down the driveway but park beside the fence of his front paddock. I've brought the rifle from the weapons safe and remove it from the trunk, then I head onto McRae land. I don't pass where Nine was killed, but I think of him. I go through fences, reaching down to unhook gates and then re-hooking them behind me. One thing I learned from spending time on Dad's land: never close a gate you find open, never leave open one you find closed. I don't know where Red has the sheep tonight, but eventually I find them in an eastern paddock, heavily fenced and as far from the tree line as his property will allow. I appreciate that he's being careful with them, unlike a lot of farmers who still refuse to fence their livestock. A kind of defiance, I guess. Cutting off noses to spite faces.

I walk to the edge of the sleeping flock, their wooly bodies hunkered down to protect their lambs against the cold, and I sit on the grass. Eyes trained on the edge of the forest, rifle ready over my lap. If wolves come for these sheep it will be from among those trees, and I will be waiting for them.

Breeding male Number Two, leader of the Tanar Pack and now the strongest alpha male of all the wolves we set free, is Werner's velvet black. The color of obsidian. The only black wolf in Scotland. A swallowing black; the blackest black of deep night. He is an enormous creature, so big, at two hundred pounds, that he could belong to his cousins' species, the larger Alaskan timber wolves. He moves with a stunning fluidity that comes from such strength. His power is utterly animal.

I have been coming here night after night, and this night, the fifth of my shepherd's watch, I see only his golden, unblinking eyes, and I know it's him.

He stands in the cover of forest and watches us.

He watches me.

Awaiting his moment.

His pack will be gathered behind him, ready to move when he tells them to. Three hungry, adult wolves who can smell these creatures and their pulsing warm blood, and don't yet know them from any other. They will spread out and flank us, moving quickly and silently to take down a sheep at the edge of the flock. They could take one each, if they chose, and then kill the rest with ease. These slow, unprepared herd animals stand no chance against the nature of such predators.

I have always worried more about the plight of the predator than its prey. Predators spend their lives starving slowly. Every hunt could be their last. So if it was just me here, I would let the wolves feast. But this is a world carved by humans. Feasting on the wrong animals will see the wolves dead. So I draw my rifle, loaded with bullets, not darts, and I aim at Number Two.

The shot cracks out into the night, echoing off the hills. His moonlit eyes are gone now. Fled with his family to hunt somewhere safer, I hope, scared off by the shot I sent above him. I stay where I am anyway, just in case.

The sheep are awake and running. They head in a ramshackle group for the fence line and bundle together, bleating their outrage, wondering what the hell is going on.

Five minutes later a quad bike zooms across the paddock. "What the fuck are you doing?" Red kills the engine and swings off the bike. "What'd you shoot?"

"Nothing," I say.

"You better speak plain, girl."

"I shot at a fox."

He stares at me in the dark, trying to make sense of me, of my gun. We are barely outlines. "You were watching over them?"

I nod.

His shoulders sag. He mutters something under his breath I haven't the faintest chance of catching. Then, *"Why?"*

"Because I don't want to see dead sheep any more than you do," I say.

Red rubs his eyes. "Leave it to me, now. You shouldn't be out here this late, missy, not in your shape."

I turn away, wishing he hadn't guessed at my pregnancy. I feel exposed.

"Did you get it, then?" Red asks.

"What?"

"The fox."

"No, sir. But it knows to stay clear, now."

"How do you know it knows?"

I glance at Red. "Animals learn their lessons. They're smarter than people that way."

In the morning I head out to the Glenshee Pack. I know where the Tanar Pack is, after they graced the border of Red's farm last night. And I've been searching for the Abernethy Pack, too, finally catching sight of it yesterday. Ash's pups have grown enormously at about six months old. They almost look like adults, a bit scrawnier, their paws still a little big for their bodies. The runt of the group—Number Twenty—is still the smallest, but her siblings defer to her. She is becoming more purely white as she ages, even whiter than her mother. As I watched her dominate her larger brother with a quick nip to his mouth, a quick nip to mine, I marveled anew at the complexity of the power dynamics between wolves. They are capable of recognizing personality traits, of knowing that inner strength is as powerful as physical. Dominance often has nothing to do with size or aggression.

It's cold today. I'm glad to be in the hide. Wind shrieks along the bare mountains around me, batters at the small hidden structure. If I didn't have this shelter there's no way I could be out here in weather this fierce: I'd be swept off my feet.

I draw my binoculars to watch the Glenshee Pack.

Do I imagine the sorrow in their bodies or am I humanizing them? It is true, certainly, that wolves mourn their own. I don't think I am imagining their grief over lost Number Fourteen. There is something subdued to them; they don't play. Even the pups seem muted. And it's not just Fourteen who is missing. I can't spot Number Ten either. Her data tells me she's here, or was very recently. But as I adjust my binoculars I spot an unusual object in the grass, and recognize Ten's radio collar. She has chewed free of it. She could be anywhere.

"No," I sigh, on a breath. Here is the proof I was dreading.

Of course it was you.

The wolf who fears nothing, not even humans.

I dream of the buck deer rutting in the forest; of the sound they make when I walk through early mornings, that mighty clash that echoes for miles through the fog.

Clash, go their antlers as they throw their bodies at each other. *Clash.*

I wake with a start.

Clash.

Not antlers, but there is something smacking against the window. Something wet. It is being swung like a sack into the glass and the clash is more of a *thunk*.

What the fuck?

There's someone out there. I dart into my sister's room and pull her out of bed. Flatten her to the floor so we can't be seen through the windows.

There are voices now, several of them, howling like wolves.

"Shit shit shit shit shit. Stay here, don't move."

I crawl back into my room and grab my phone. The figures are all around the house now, I can hear them banging on the doors and the windows, trying to get in. One of them walks with a bad limp, I can see his silhouette and no, no no no there's no way it's him, please don't let it be him. But as I watch, his face catches the moonlight and it's not Duncan, it's Colm McClellan, whose limp I created myself.

There's no damn reception on my phone and I could throw it at the glass in frustration. After collecting my sister from her room we both run, hunched double, to the bathroom and into the tub. There's a bar of service in the very corner here, and I hold the phone in place until it's found. My finger goes to dial 999 but stops, and presses the button for Duncan instead. He's closer.

"Inti?" he answers, sounding groggy.

"He's here," I whisper. "Colm. He's with men and he's trying to get in."

"I'm coming."

Aggie is crawling into the kitchen. "Wait!" I scramble after her. She goes for a knife in the drawer and I realize this is a good idea, and get myself one too. We huddle on the kitchen floor and it hits me that this is just how I found her the other night when she thought she'd heard someone outside and I told her she was being crazy but Jesus, maybe she was right.

Or maybe we're both crazy.

A window smashes above us, showering us in glass. I press a hand over my mouth. Aggie's eyes are too wide. I think mine are the same.

The sound of a car engine revs. Some of the figures bolt but a couple remain. I get to my feet so I can see through the cracked window. Duncan is here. He is unarmed.

"You're under arrest, Colm," he says. "The lot of you. Get in the truck."

"Fuck you, ya greenie fuckin' traitor," Colm shouts, and runs at him, despite his walking stick and broken knee, and I think he must be in some sort of psychosis because that is just insane behavior. I sink back to the floor so I won't see what happens, and my sister and I hold each other and I have had enough, I have truly had enough violence for a thousand lifetimes.

Someone opens the front door and walks inside, and it's Duncan, but I can't work out how he did it until I see that the glass of the door has also been broken and he's reached in to unlock it. Even this spikes my pulse because now anyone can get in.

Duncan sees us and comes toward us. I don't know what happened outside but he has overcome the men somehow. My body reacts; it fears him. "Don't!" I say, and he stops. I don't understand the fear, couldn't explain it, even to myself, but it is here, and it is loud, and I don't want him in here.

"Are you okay?"

"Just go, Duncan, please."

"I need to get you to hospital, get you checked out, love."

"We're fine, nothing happened. Just please."

I can't stop imagining him and Stuart, how his fist beat Stuart near to death under the orb of a streetlight. I can't stop seeing him in the woods that night and I want it out of my head, I want him gone from my space, from my life.

His eyes go to what I can no longer hide, even huddled as I am on the floor. My swollen belly. He sees it, he recognizes it, and he's coming toward us again, and now I am not just sickened, I am rearing up in alarm.

"*Back off,*" I say.

Duncan stops, stunned. "Sorry."

Aggie moves her body between us protectively, her hand out to ward him off and I think here is my sister, and because he is looking at her too I also think thank god, she's real, she's alive, I'm not mad.

"Please don't be afraid of me," Duncan says. "Either of you. I'm just here to help. They're dealt with, all right? Those pricks, they're locked in the truck. They weren't gonna do anything, they were just trying to scare you."

Good fucking job they did.

His eyes keep going back to my belly. "Is that . . . ?"

"Get out, Duncan!" I shout.

I am still, but for the vibrating core of me. I wait to see if he will come at me again. Would I have time to reach for the knife?

The devastation on his face almost cuts through my certainty that there is some threat here. "It's all right, I'll go," he says, "you're safe," and then he does go.

Aggie and I hold each other. Does she feel as fierce as she seems? She is more real in my arms than she has been in years.

She pulls away and signs, *He's the father.*

I nod.

Don't let him in again.

I meet her eyes. I thought her fear was madness but there is nothing insane about learning from your experiences. Her vigilance might be the sanest thing in our lives.

"I won't," I promise.

Later I learn that the sack used to smash our windows was full of what remained of Fourteen's body.

24

had a plan, a desperate one. If Aggie couldn't leave her husband then I would become her, I'd play the old game and don her disguise, and I would end this toxic marriage of theirs, I would leave him for her. And I would only tell her after it was done, so she wouldn't try to stop me.

I spent the day with Aggie, remembering what it was like to slide inside her skin, to see the world through her eyes. With a great deal of passion, and a temper that sparked wantonly. I'd seen enough of her with Gus to understand that power was at play constantly between them, that it was a never-ending game of one-upmanship that bordered on flirtation, a walk on the knife edge of anger and desire.

When it was time I dressed in Aggie's clothes and did my hair and makeup like she did hers. It was a costume, it was armor, and the truth was that slipping back into Aggie was the easiest thing I'd ever done. I felt at home, somehow.

I sent him a message from Aggie's phone and met Gus in the city after work. We had a drink at a bar and I took up a deliberateness to the way I moved, to where my eyes rested, to how I arranged my expression, because that was Aggie. Composed—bored, even—until she wasn't. Gus was tired and stressed out, but I could tell he was focused on me. Studying me. I didn't let it make me nervous; instead I enjoyed it as Aggie would, knowing she had control. I enjoyed being desired, the truly forbidden shiver of lust over my skin I had long ago renounced but was now given full rein to embrace.

I didn't know how to broach the subject delicately, how to warm up to it, so under the dim lights of the bar I blurted, "Inti and I are moving out."

He stared at me, and there was a flash of something in his eyes but he didn't move or speak for so long that I began to feel a shift beneath my feet.

"I thought," Gus said very slowly, "I had made myself clear." His hand moved to my thigh and squeezed it a bit too hard, and harder again. "If you try to leave me, I will find you, and I will kill your sister."

I thought I'd misheard him.

And then the truth, too horrific for me to have guessed at, was made clear. There was no game between them. Only true danger. Only a monster hiding behind the handsome face of a man. And I had been blind to it.

"Come on, let's go home and have a bath, relax, it's been a long day."

I was shaking so badly I could hardly walk but he steered me out of the bar and I knew then what a joke I was, thinking I had any control here, thinking Aggie had any. The power was entirely his, and he was using it to hold her hostage. I understood now why she'd tried to get me to leave.

He drove us home and all I could think, as he talked about work, was how I had to get out of this car, I had to get out, I had to get out, I had to open the door and roll backward onto the road and I had to run, just fucking run but of course I couldn't do that, not without Aggie.

He led me to their bedroom. I was frozen. I needed to speak up, to tell him it was me but nothing was coming out of my mouth except a dry croak. He closed the door and still I was frozen. I had never known fear like this, so liquid, so hot. And then he took my throat in his hands and he squeezed, cutting off my air. This was what he did to her. Did he do it every night? In this room with only one wall between us?

"I thought you understood," he said, as he choked me, "how fucking much I love you."

He was a madman. And he was going to kill us.

"Stop," I managed to gasp, but he didn't.

The door burst open and there stood Aggie, and Gus dropped his hands from my throat so I could take a shuddering breath and stagger away from him.

"What the fuck?" he demanded.

"Busted," she said, and smiled.

"You swapped?" There was something frantic in his eyes then and my heart was fleeing my body, we had to get away, he was going to lose it. And then he burst out laughing. He roared with laughter. "That was pretty damn good, I gotta admit. I had no idea."

Like this was all a big prank.

"You had me going, Inti," he tells me.

"And I guess we proved whether or not you'd be able to tell," Aggie said and my head was spinning because what the hell was going on, it was like they were both in on the amusement and then I saw Aggie's hand make a sign behind her back. She hadn't signed anything in years.

Go.

She was protecting me. She'd gathered enough of what I'd tried to do and was trying to defuse things. But how could I leave her alone in this room with him? How could I ever leave her alone with him again?

Aggie kissed her husband, and it was me kissing him and I could have been sick. Her hands, she was signing again. *Trust me.*

And so, like the coward I was, I left her. I went to the bathroom and I *did* throw up until there was nothing left in me. And then I sat, stiff as a board on the end of my bed, listening for any sounds through that wall. I sat listening until the first light of dawn.

25

Tonight Mayor Andy Oakes calls a meeting at the school about the dead livestock, and we wolf-folk aren't invited. I don't like to imagine what they're saying without us there.

I use the distraction to get groceries and, as I hoped, the aisles are empty. I wander aimlessly, lost in thought and having to retrace my steps. The staff flash me looks and mutter to each other. I'm so preoccupied by this that I push my trolley into a huge display of canned dog food, sending the cans thundering noisily to the ground and rolling every which way.

I scramble on my knees to gather them up while two young cashiers hurry to help me. A girl and a boy, no older than fifteen.

"I'm so sorry," I say.

"It's okay, we'll do it," the girl says kindly.

"Really, ma'am, you rest yourself," says the boy.

I give up, sinking onto my bum. It's hard crawling around when your belly protrudes to the size of a bowling ball. The growth seems to be speeding up, while my energy levels plummet and my back aches. For the first time this morning I Googled whether this was normal, all of it, and discovered that the size of my belly is actually smaller than average. Aggie said the baby is the size of a rockmelon. I put the phone down in a cold panic the second it started telling me things like how the baby can see light now, and coughs and hiccups and *dreams*.

"Are you the wolf lady?" the girl asks me.

I nod, expecting some sort of . . . I don't know, reprimand? But the teenagers stop gathering cans and look at me with excitement.

"What are they like?" she asks. "Have you touched one?"

We're in the last aisle and there's no one else around. I lean back against the shelf. "Plenty."

"When they're babies or grown?"

"Both."

This delights them no end. They crowd a little closer.

"Have you been bitten by one?"

"No, not a real bite. They chew and snap when they're little, but that's just play."

"Did they get to know you?"

"Of course. Wolves are family animals. If you raise them, they'll be loyal until you set them free." Sometimes even after.

"Why don't you keep them, then?"

"They're too wild for that."

"The ones here," the girl asks. "Are they really dangerous? 'Cause I saw one one night and it just ran away, so quick you could barely make it out."

I choose my words. "If you keep your distance there's nothing to fear. But never try to touch or feed them."

"What if it's close?" the boy asks. "I mean, like, if we're hiking and it's just there, suddenly."

"If you come across a wolf in the forest and it doesn't flee from you, I want you to remember one thing. Never run from it. If you face a wolf you will scare it. If you run, it will hunt you."

They gaze at me, thrilled. I really hope they're not about to go looking for a way to test that advice.

"The one I saw . . ." the girl says softly, "it was beautiful."

I nod.

"Sorry some people are being so shite," says the boy. "But that's not everyone. There's a whole lot of people who love the idea of wolves in Scotland again. The way it used to be."

I smile. "Thank you. That means a lot."

I let them pull me to my feet.

It's started snowing when I get outside, having forgotten to buy anything. I look up at the sky, watching the slow sway of the flakes. It's true, fluffy snow, almost weightless and glowing in the moonlight.

My car is the only one parked here and there's someone leaning against it. For a split second it's Gus, the tall broad shape of him, and then he turns and it's not Gus, it's Duncan, and I suck in a lungful of air to try to calm the pulse that still won't calm.

I stop a few paces from him. He's blocking the driver's side door. Is he doing that intentionally, so I can't leave? Jesus, I need to get a grip on myself.

"I need to ask . . ." Duncan pushes a hand through his hair, which is getting longer, scruffier and more silver. In the neon light of the grocery store he looks sickly, his eyes hollow. A wave of concern fills me.

"Is it mine?" Duncan asks.

I suppose I've been expecting this question, dreading it. Although it is slightly offensive—I don't know how many guys he thinks I was sleeping with.

"No," I say. "Inasmuch as it isn't mine, either. I'm giving it up."

"Is that a roundabout way of saying it *is* mine? That you and I—we made it together?"

I don't reply.

"Can I . . . I'll help you, Inti. You don't have to do this alone."

"You don't want kids," I say. "You told me yourself."

He lets out a breath, a kind of laugh. "That was true once, before I met you. By the time I said it, it was already a lie."

Oh god.

"You don't have to give it up," he says.

I can barely get the words out. "I want to."

"Why?" he asks.

I close my eyes, feeling dizzy. "Because there's nothing good in me anymore, Duncan. I'm just angry, and that's all."

"That is such rubbish," he snaps.

I walk past him to the car and reach for the door handle but I can't make my hand work to open it, I just stand here trying to remain intact.

"I didn't kill Stuart," he says abruptly. "I didn't think I needed to say it but it seems I do."

I meet his eyes. "I don't think I believe you." There's nothing else that makes sense. "You were out there," I say, done with hiding what I know.

"Lainey called you, telling you where Stuart was. And you went out to find him."

"And failed," Duncan says. "I didn't find anything."

"Then why did you lie about her call? Why bother, if not to protect yourself?"

"To protect you!" he exclaims. "I didn't find anything that night, Inti, but you did, didn't you? You were out there. If you walked from my place to yours then you were out there same time he was."

There are snowflakes in his eyelashes, there are some in mine, too, softening the world. I can't remember any words.

"I keep asking myself the same question," he admits. "If you did it, would it matter to me? And that goes against everything I've ever held on to."

"It would matter. It matters," I say. "Death gets under your skin, it stays with you. That's what you said."

Scratch, goes the little person inside, *scratch* go her tiny fingernails. *Not now,* I beg her. *Please, little melon, not now.*

"All that matters to me is keeping my sister safe. And I don't trust you not to hurt us," I tell him bluntly. "I don't trust anyone."

"I've been there, Inti."

"I know you have, and it doesn't go away."

"You're wrong," he says. "It goes if we let it. I made space for you."

"You think it matters that there's love?" I ask. "Love only makes things more dangerous." I get in the car.

"Inti."

My windscreen wipers fight the flurries of snow as I drive from the carpark. But it isn't long before I must pull off the road, unsure I can keep driving. I watch the snow fall in the headlights.

The little person inside me moves again, she spins with such force that I gasp. I press my hand to her and feel her hand press back to me, and like that, she has reached so far beyond all the things I knew, all the guards I built, that she has found me, she has seen, and there will be no more hiding.

26

The drive from Denali to Anchorage was long, and I'd been making it less and less often. But tonight I needed my own bed so I made the trip, only to find men in the house again. It was becoming a common occurrence. Gus was miserable, and he was furious with his wife, who was frightened of him, and was trying to get through the days without "provoking him." But he wanted her to be as miserable as he was, and me, too, by extension. So he often filled the house with men who drank with an almost defiant need to get drunk. I hated it, and usually escaped back to work. But tonight I was too tired, my day had been too grueling, and I just needed to sleep.

James, his cousin, was visiting from Sydney. He hated me unreservedly, for the offense of having slept with him once and not again, and even though he'd been staying in my house he'd barely spoken a word to me all week. The rest were a mix of Australian friends and the surgeons Gus knew from work. There was a weird kind of competitiveness between the Americans and the Australians, each keen to prove they could drink more and behave worse. The Australians always won: this particular group from Gus's rugby days were well practiced at being dickheads.

I tried to sneak past but there was the usual call for me to stay for a drink, just one, which always turned into several before I could escape. Tonight I didn't have the energy to fight it, so I sank onto the couch next to someone called Robbo and took the beer.

Soon there were more beers, then tequila, then cocaine.

I didn't need any of it to feel drunk, wired, sick. I needed only to be here, watching. I wished Aggie would come home, I wished it desperately. I felt far too old for all of this, I felt as though I had stepped out of my real life into some twisted toxic dream of adolescence. Why did I live in a house with a man who enjoyed this? Why was my sister *married* to him?

Fear debased me into sitting there, into taking the drinks and smiling along and all the while my mind had a hypervigilance, it raced with strategies of how to get out of this situation without offending anyone.

I watched Gus now, doing shots. He was ignoring me. It would be all right. They would get drunk enough to pass out and I'd go to bed. James sat on my other side, squeezing me tight. His breath smelled foul and his limbs were sloppy. I watched the men around me rile each other up, bulls stamping their hooves and snorting, and I stayed quiet and took the path of least resistance. Ride it out, don't make a fuss. The last thing I wanted to do was cause some sort of scene. There was an edge of unpredictability to them, they seemed intent on losing themselves and destroying things and I didn't want to be in their eyeline when an idea came to them.

The door opened and there was my sister. I was flooded with such relief that I almost burst into tears. She took one look at what was going on, clocked my expression, and turned to her husband. "What's the game, darling? Deal me in." Then Aggie reached for my hand and pulled me up from the couch.

James grabbed my other wrist. "Come on, Aggie. Don't be a killjoy. She's enjoying herself."

"I just need to talk to her and then we'll come back and play."

I could barely hear her over the thumping music, the laughter and booming voices. James let me go and I hurried with Aggie to the kitchen.

"How much have you had to drink? Can you drive?" she asked me.

I shook my head.

"Go upstairs and lock your bedroom door."

"Come with me."

She nodded and we were about to go when Gus arrived. "Two for the price of one," he said. His pupils were big black holes.

"We're going to bed," Aggie said.

"No you're not. You love to play. So play."

She and Gus shared a long look.

I told myself to relax, just relax, it wasn't that big a deal, nothing was happening. There were people here. Nothing could happen in front of other people.

Aggie pulled her husband back into the living room so that he wouldn't remember or care that I was here too, so that I could escape upstairs while I had the chance. I locked my bedroom door and called the police. I made a complaint about the noise and waited for them to come. It took twenty minutes or so and I stuck my head out the window to listen to Gus answering and telling the officers he'd keep it down, and then they left. And the party continued.

I called them again and this time I told them a fight had broken out and people were in danger but when they came back they could clearly see that no one was fighting, and what was I meant to do? What could I say if I phoned them again? Nothing had actually happened. Maybe Aggie was enjoying herself down there. Maybe she knew how to manage this situation. But Mum taught us the warning signs and there had been a million. I had spent my life resenting her for seeing the worst in people but as I stood in my room, listening to the noise from below, I realized how naïve I'd been to assume I knew the depths of what people were capable of.

You were meant to leave, when you saw the warning signs, but what if you couldn't? What if he was too dangerous to leave? What if your sister thought staying meant protecting you? What if she was right, and this was how we survived him? By mitigating the risk?

I heard a thump from outside. I unlocked my door. Gus was taking Aggie into their room. James was following. She was barely conscious but she flashed me a look as she disappeared behind the door, not of control, but of terror.

Every doubt vanished. I knew unequivocally that staying was no longer an option. That there was no longer any way to defuse. Something very bad was about to happen and my sister needed help.

I surged forward. "Hey!"

Gus glanced at me. "Stay out of this, kid."

"It's okay, Inti, go to bed," Aggie said from within.

"Or you can join us, if you want?" James suggested.

"You're not doing this. I'm calling the cops."

"Jesus, relax," James said, and then he twisted my wrist until my phone dropped to the floor. He stomped on it with the heel of his boot. Laughed. Told me again to relax, they were just having some fun. Went into my sister's bedroom and shut the door.

I threw myself at the door. *"Let her out of there, you sick fucks!"*

When they didn't answer I ran downstairs and told the men that Aggie needed help, that Gus and James had locked her in the bedroom, but instead of helping they laughed and turned away, and not one of them would lend me their phone.

I ran back upstairs and I started kicking the door, trying to get the handle loose, I threw my shoulder against the timber over and over. I would get this door open even if I had to tear it apart with my hands and teeth and destroy myself in the doing.

"Deal with the bitch, would you?" I heard James say from inside.

The door opened and I was faced with Gus, too big to push past, too strong to do anything about. "You really want in?" he asked, and I didn't know what he was asking me except that I did. "You want to see this?" What happened in this room was going to happen regardless of my efforts to stop it. There was nothing I could do, not against the size and strength of them, not when there would be no help from downstairs, not after my phone was destroyed.

All I could do, it seemed, was be with my sister so she didn't have to be alone.

He let me inside, and Aggie was naked on the bed and really out of it, drunk or stoned or something, and James was holding her down by the throat, he was holding me by the throat, and when Aggie saw me she tried to sit up, she shouted to get me out of here, to let her go, she shouted at them to stop, begged for them to stop until James swung his fist and punched her so hard in the face that she was knocked out.

When I opened my eyes I was lying on the edge of the bed. A bed that was moving.

My clothes were still on, and no one was touching me.

But. I turned my head.

My sister's face was level with mine. Her eyes were closed.

"Aggie," I said, and she opened them.

I took her hand and squeezed as tightly as I could and I was appalled at the hatred Gus must have inside him, the humiliation, the rage. How had I not seen this in him? Except I had, hadn't I? I'd seen it, and still I'd trusted it would never get this bad because this bad was unfathomable. I thought of all the moments that had led to this and knew there were a thousand that could have shifted just a little and I might have saved us from it. All those moments when I knew what he was, when I recognized the monster and still did nothing, even tonight, when I sat on that couch and I thought to myself that this was a bad situation and I didn't fight to leave, I didn't want to make a fucking *fuss,* and everything inside me was on fire and I would never stop burning. I wanted to kill him and James both, brutally, only I couldn't stand and fight because they had us both pinned to the bed, and I could feel the trauma they were inflicting on her body, taking turns one after another, and seemingly with an effort to cause harm, an effort to destroy and humiliate. I couldn't stand and fight because I was made wrong, because I was weak. I couldn't protect her the way she'd done for me our whole lives. She saved me from this but I couldn't save her. And as I held her eyes, as I held all of her with all of me, I wasn't enough against this tide, I couldn't keep hold, she was leaving me, she was gone.

I sit under the shower and try to disappear. But there is a little one and she is wriggling inside me and sending me back into the worst thing my skin has known, back into that night, over and over, to that bed as it moved and my unforgivable stillness. These are the memories that live in my body.

When they were gone, James and the rest of the men, Gus sat on the floor with his head in his hands. He didn't try to help his bleeding wife. I struggled upright, dazed but unharmed, and used my sister's phone to call an ambulance, and then I did what I could for her but in the end that simply meant stroking her hair the way she loves, over and over, even though I didn't think she could feel it.

Her body barely survived. And when she woke, she'd gone elsewhere, and she'd taken all the strongest pieces of her, even her voice.

27

We've been searching for Number Ten for two weeks when Evan finally walks through the front door of base camp and says, "We spotted her."

"Hallelujah!" Zoe says.

I've been taking to the sky with Fergus to get eyes on Ten. Winter has well and truly set in, unseasonably early, just as everyone knew it would. It is late November, but the world is white. Without her tracking collar Ten's been invisible to our tech, and days of searching by plane reaped no reward either. By now she's learned the sound of the plane and knows to stay hidden. So I sent Evan and Niels to track by ground, wanting to be out there myself but knowing my belly has gotten so big I'd be useless. At thirty-six weeks pregnant, little one has made up for lost time and is growing at an alarming pace. She is due in one month, on Christmas Day.

In any case, pregnant or not, it's hard going out there in such thick snow. Easier to track in it, certainly—the wolves are slower, their prints clearer. But they are wild creatures and we are something tamer. We've forgotten how to move through the wilderness as though we belong to it. This is Number Ten's domain and we trespassers in it. My hope of finding her has been dwindling with each passing day, but when I speak to Bonnie I always tell her we are close, we are getting it done, we just need her to stall the hunters a little longer so we can take care of this ourselves. Even though it makes me sick to my stomach, I have assured her that when we capture Number Ten we will put her down: it will be this, and only this, that will save the rest of the wolves from Red and his friends. The single rogue wolf must be dealt with to protect the species.

"Where?" I ask now.

"At the base of Cairn Gorm mountain."

"Why didn't you bring her in?"

"I tried. Missed her. She got away and we couldn't find her again."

"Are you kidding me? Why didn't you follow her tracks?"

"It's a blizzard up there!" he replies. "There were no tracks!"

My temper eases as I see how tired and cold Evan is. He and Niels have been out there for days. "Sorry," I say. "You did well to find her at all. Go home and take a shower. Get some sleep."

As Evan stomps out I tell Zoe to download Evan's locations so I can take a look at where he spotted Ten. He's right about it being a long way away. Deep in that wild heart of the Highlands, where I first suspected the wolves would feel called. It'd take days just to ride out that far in adverse weather. I don't think I can ask Evan to go out again tomorrow, he's reached his limit, and Niels is shit at tracking even when it's not in the middle of a blizzard. Plus all our horses are exhausted and Ten could be long gone from that spot by the time anyone gets back up there.

"This is a goddamn nightmare," Zoe says, watching the hope leach out of me.

"It's okay. It'll be okay. I'm going to make some calls, see if I can get some old colleagues out here to help us. We just need more manpower. Ten can't cross through the mountain range in this weather so my guess is she'll circle south, back toward her pack. We can cut her off closer to home, where the conditions aren't as bad and we have more bodies to help."

I grab my phone and see that I have two missed calls from Duncan, which is weird, but I don't have time to worry about him right now. I've been dealing with Bonnie on the wolf front so anything he has to talk to me about can wait. I get on the phone and organize some of my Denali colleagues to fly out here as quickly as they can. Most have work of their own they can't leave, but a few are eager to help, saying they've been watching the progress of the project on the news for months.

I leave past the stables. We've moved Gall here for the winter, not having stables at home to keep her warm. I feed her a couple of apples, then do the same for the other exhausted horses who've been traipsing around the country for weeks. I brush each of them down and make sure their hooves are all right, before returning to Gall and stroking her neck.

"I wish I could take you home," I tell her softly. "Aggie's been missing you." She presses her nose into my cheek and I close my eyes, breathing in the warm scent of her.

I drive home over icy roads.

Aggie doesn't respond to my entrance. I assume she's in bed, where she's been all day, but instead of trying to convince her to come out for some food I leave her in there; I can't face her silence tonight. So much for thinking she might have turned a corner. Colm's attack has sent her spiraling back down the hole, and to be honest I don't feel entirely free of that same hole.

I'm in the process of taking off my winter layers when there's a knock just behind me. Bonnie is gray-faced. "Come in," I tell her, pulling her into the warmth. "Are you okay? What's happened?"

"I need to ask you something."

"Okay."

Her nervous energy is alarming.

"Sit down. Can I get you anything?"

"No, I'm fine, thanks."

"Is this about Colm?"

"No. We're keeping a close eye on him, you don't have to worry."

I sit in the armchair opposite hers. My sister doesn't come out from her room. The thought darts quick like a tiny bird: that's because she's not really there. She's dead.

No, she isn't. Duncan saw her. He did.

"I had a visit from Red McRae," Bonnie says.

"Okay."

"He said you came to see him, and said something that stayed with him."

I try to think back to that conversation.

"Apparently you thought Duncan was involved in Stuart's death."

"What?"

"That night before he went missing. You spent it at Duncan's."

"Yeah . . ."

"You told me you were there the whole night. But I realized I never asked you if Duncan was there the whole night."

My heart beats hard in the tips of my fingers and toes.

"Was Duncan with you from the time you left the pub to daylight hours of the following morning?"

I don't say anything because I don't know what to say.

And then, somehow, I do. He told me he didn't kill Stuart. And as utterly idiotic as it may make me, even after everything Aggie and I have been through, every lesson to the contrary, I think I finally believe him. "Yes," I reply.

"Oh." She sighs, and I can see this conversation is costing her a lot. "Then what made you think Duncan had anything to do with it?"

I breathe out. This is what I wanted—to figure out the truth of what happened to Stuart so I could tell someone and shift the blame from the wolves. This was the whole point of what I did, burying him like that. And now that someone is sitting here willing to listen to me, all I can think about is how to lie convincingly. Just as I can't let the wolves go down for this, neither can I let someone innocent take the blame.

I shake my head. "I was pissed off with him. I've been pissed off for a while now. He didn't tell me he was sleeping with Lainey and I felt like I'd been used or whatever. I was running my mouth with Red. But as much as I'd love to take him down a peg, Duncan was with me in bed all night. That's all I know. I'm sorry I wasted your time."

She doesn't say anything for a good long moment. Watching me. It is an unnervingly frank gaze and I think this must be how she gets people to confess to things, to get out from under that gaze. I hold firm.

Bonnie gets to her feet. "Okay, thanks, Inti. I just wanted to follow up about it."

"Sure, thank you."

Once Bonnie is gone I can't think what to do. She didn't believe me, of that I am sure. Her cop nose has caught a scent and she's going to follow it, whether she has my information or not.

I pull on my coat and hat and scarf. "Aggie, I'll be back soon," I call as I head out. Maybe this is why he was phoning me today; I feel bad now for not returning the call when I had service. I have to at least let him know I've made him a suspect again. Warn him that Bonnie might be coming after him.

Rather than walking through the cold on aching feet, I drive the short way to Duncan's cottage. The lights are on and his car is here. But when I knock there's no answer. I knock a few more times and then find the door unlocked. Inside I call his name, expecting Fingal to come bounding.

Only he doesn't, there's no one here.

Which is strange.

The woodstove is crackling as though it has recently been stoked, and that's not something Duncan would do right before he was about to go out, he wouldn't leave the flue open like that, it could burn the house down. His wallet and keys are sitting on the coffee table. His car outside. I stand in his living room and try to work out where he is, how it could be that he's not standing next to me. Did he take the dog for a walk? Leaving everything as it was?

I walk outside and stand in the dark. "Duncan?" I shout.

Silence.

And then a whimper.

Something in me goes cold.

I draw my phone from my pocket and switch on its torch. Then I walk, slowly, into the dark. The snow before me is white, untouched, and then I see it disturbed by footprints, and then again by streaks of red.

The color of cherries and the heads of cock goldfinches. And of arterial blood.

I see Fingal first. His stomach open. His lungs moving rapidly because by some miracle he is still alive. His eyes are open and gazing up at me as I move past him, aching, wanting to stop but compelled by the other body, the larger human body that lies a few feet away.

Duncan, too.

His throat is open. All of his blood seems to have come free, onto the snow. All of mine.

I clutch at my throat to hold it closed, and I can't look, but I have to. I will look, and I will just have to feel whatever I feel because that will not be the last time I look at him.

I sink, shaking, to my knees. Reach for his face. And look. He opens his eyes and it shocks me so much that I cry out.

No sound comes from Duncan's mouth but I have spent a lifetime

understanding silent languages. In his eyes are words of fear and plead-
ing and love.

"It's okay," I say. "You're okay," and what an absurd thing to tell
someone who is spilling like this but it doesn't matter, I am moving without thought to press his throat closed, to press snow into the wound and
pack it tight. It hurts and I can hardly breathe but I will not let my condition be the master of me, not here.

My dog, his eyes say.

"Fingal's all right," I tell him. "He's alive."

Duncan's grip on me is so strong. He is shaking me.

"I understand," I tell him. "I won't leave him here." Because he must
have tried to save Duncan.

My hands are slippery with his blood, he is all over me, and the smell,
it's dizzying. I remember to phone an ambulance but there's no reception,
I can't get a signal yet again, the remoteness of this place, the isolation of
it will be the death of us all.

"I'm getting you to a hospital, Duncan."

My dog, his eyes say.

"I won't leave him. Can you stand?" Of course he can't fucking stand,
his throat's open. "I'll have to drag you, okay?" I put my slippery hands
under his armpits and grab hold as best I can, then I start dragging his
weight back along the snow. It's very difficult, far more so than I thought
it would be. It would be difficult even were I not eight months pregnant
but right now my muscles shriek in refusal. This is too much, too impossible. And not. It's just getting a person to safety. I can do that. Fingal is
here, we are passing him, and I say, "Don't look, Duncan, don't look,"
but he does, of course he does, and something in him breaks as he sees
his dog lying there, gasping for breath. I say, "He's still alive," but it's
cold comfort because we both know nothing survives having its guts torn
open by a wolf. Duncan cries the silent pain of grief but I keep dragging,
I have to keep dragging. He is so heavy, my hands so slippery, I drop him
constantly but I pick him back up each time and drag him on, I will drag
him forever if I have to because in each staggering step I know a thing
with all my soul, that I have been wrong, that he didn't kill Stuart and

also that it doesn't matter either way because there is a greater knowing within me, and that is the depth and breadth of how I love him.

I look down at his face and see that his eyes are closed, he's out. A sob leaves me but when I search his wrist for a pulse I find the faint memory of one. He's still breathing somehow, his heart still beating. We reach the car. I open the back door. Climb in, turn around, awkward as a whale on land, and reach down for him. My *back*, as I pull him up and onto the seat, god it hurts. I've bitten my tongue and can taste iron. There are spots in front of my eyes, and his throat as mine, but there is a sort of numbness setting in now, that sensation fatigue that switches me off, and finally he's in the car, I've managed it.

I'm about to hop in the front when—

My dog, said his eyes.

I turn back for Fingal. I won't leave him. Not when he fought to save Duncan's life, when he has died in the trying and isn't that the way of animals, to break your heart with their courage, with their love. I scoop him up and hold him to my chest. He's lighter than I thought he'd be. A slight creature under all his hair. His eyes are still open and I look at him as I hurry back to the car. "Good boy," I say, over and over, "darling boy," as he slips away.

I place him gently on the front seat. His eyes are closed now. The panted breaths ceased.

I speed along the black road for town. I drive way too fast but not as fast as the car will go, knowing the roads are winding and perilous at night, knowing I won't save Duncan's life if I crash this car.

At the hospital entrance I yell for help, and it comes, carrying Duncan onto a stretcher and wheeling him away to where I can't see him anymore. I sink onto a plastic chair in the waiting room until a nurse arrives and leads me through the doors, and I think she's taking me to Duncan but she sits me on the end of a bed and checks my pulse and also listens to the heartbeat of the baby. A doctor comes soon and does an ultrasound, and when I explain that I haven't been to a doctor before, not during my pregnancy, he is shocked and starts to say all kinds of things about how irresponsible I've been and how many things could have gone wrong, but a part of me switches off and I can no longer hear him. I stare at the ceiling and think about the wolf.

It just wasn't making sense—who killed Stuart. If Lainey didn't do it, if I didn't and Duncan didn't, then who did? Who could have?

The answer has been here all along, the entire town saw the answer but I refused to. I was too stubborn, too willfully blind, keener to accuse the man I love than to accuse the animals I brought here. Even knowing, as I did, that there was one wolf among them who did not fear humans, one wolf more aggressive than the rest, one wolf unwilling to be caged. And now Duncan has paid for my denial.

I'm told he's gone into surgery. That he will be in there a long time, and that it will be a miracle if he lives out the night.

First I go to the base camp to look through the old data. We lost Number Ten for a good while after she fled the pen. She ran north. Toward us. We knew that much, so then why didn't it occur to me to check? Because I didn't want to see it.

But I check now. I look at the pings from those dates and though there is no location on the night of Stuart's death, there are two on either side that are close enough to allow her to have reached him in the blind spot between.

At home I prepare. Red and his hunters will be doing the same, when they hear. The stroke that lit the match. All the evidence they need, now that two people have been mauled to death. They will mount a hunt for the wolves, every one of them. But this isn't the only reason I'm moving. Or the truest one. The truest reason is that I lay still once before. I let a terrible thing happen and I didn't put it right. I wasn't strong enough. So I fill a pack with supplies. Food and water and matches and pairs of socks and extra gloves. A sub-zero sleeping roll. A box of bullets. I put on as many layers as possible, though I don't need as many as I might once have, with a little oven in my belly to keep me warm. Snow boots, a hat, gloves.

Aggie appears in her pajamas as I am heading out. I see her sign from the corner of my eye.

Where are you going?

At the door I look at her.

"To kill a wolf."

28

Before the court cases began, before, even, the investigation had got under way, Gus remained free to do what he pleased, and he had decided he wasn't going to give up on seeing his wife in the hospital. So I waited until his next failed attempt to get past security, and I followed him home. From my car I watched him go inside, saw his silhouette in their bedroom window. From the kitchen I took a knife. My hands were so moist I could barely grip it. My mouth too dry to swallow. I wasn't sure I could go back into the bedroom, but the moment passed and I did. I moved quickly. I had not killed things before by choice but this was different. For this creature I had no pity and I had no fear of killing myself in the process.

He was on the bed. Eyes closed. The police would arrive later that night, wanting to arrest him, but for now he lay unbound and unpunished.

I was on top of him and under me and the blade was to his throat and to mine.

Gus opened his eyes.

He was afraid, I saw it so clearly. It felt good. He'd made me into something that enjoyed his fear. I pressed the knife until it broke the skin; it stung and a droplet of blood slid down my neck.

"Inti," he said.

"Don't speak."

"I'm sorry."

"Don't." It came out as a snarl, a growl from the base of my stomach and out through my teeth.

I was going to kill him.

He could see it, and he started to cry.

It was appalling. "Don't," I said again. I pressed the knife harder, cutting a clean line across his throat and it hurt, it really did hurt, and it tricked me with its pain, it made my whole throat close up in panic.

"She'll never have children, did you know that? She hasn't spoken since and maybe she'll never say another word again. You did worse than kill her. You tortured her, you debased her, and you left her alive to remember it."

And finally, the question to which I could not fathom the answer, the question I would spend sleepless nights asking.

"Why?"

But he didn't answer me, would never answer because maybe he didn't know why, maybe that was the true horror of it, that there would never be an explanation to make sense of this. He stopped crying and I saw him detach into that cold inner world of his, and I knew this for his coping method, one he had imparted to his wife. I wished I could kill him more than once.

But as I went to slice open his throat, my hand didn't move.

And I knew with perfect clarity that I couldn't do it. Even now, I wasn't brave enough. I wasn't my sister, who spent her life smashing books of poetry into the noses of cruel boys for me, to protect me, and pulling triggers so that I wouldn't have to.

"Did you ever love her?" I asked.

He didn't answer and I was glad because the question stopped meaning anything to me. It didn't matter either way.

It's all just meat. All just fuckin' meat.

"We're never going to see you again," I told him. "Because if I ever see your face, even for a second, I am going to kill you. *Do you understand?*"

He nodded once.

I lowered the knife.

I need a horse. Ten is in the mountains, beyond where the roads end. None of our mounts are rested, none but Gall. As I saddle her and secure my pack and rifle I realize I am nervous. I haven't ridden her since the day we met, on the ice. The day she broke her leg and her spirit, and I am all too aware of the fact that it was not me who tamed her enough to be ridden since. But Aggie has been riding her and with each day Gall has become calmer and more confident. I don't want to endanger little one but I think that if Duncan was right about trust then animals must surely respond in the same way. Maybe this horse needs me to have faith in her. Or maybe I am about to be thrown.

I think of how she let me lower her onto the ice and drape myself upon her, how she rose to her feet and climbed that steep riverbank despite her injury, and my hands go to her nose as they've done a thousand times, I feel her tremble with eagerness beneath my palm, I feel my palm against the warm, throbbing beat of the pulse in her neck and mine, and know we share a need to plunge free.

I mount. She doesn't snort or stamp, giving me no indication she's uneasy. I use my thighs to reduce the jostling motion, nudge her forward and fit my movements to hers. There is a fluidity between us for which I thank my dad, for all those years on horseback and for his understanding of the love that could pass between a rider and her mount. And then we are away, dissolving into moonlit forest.

Dawn peeks over the horizon as we arrive at the edge of the Glenshee Pack's den territory. The night has been cold and long, our passage frustratingly slow when a car trip would have taken a couple of hours at most, but I had no vehicle with which to bring Gall and without her I could not have gone on from here. The sun turns the white ground sparkling and its warmth fills my muscles with energy. I doubt Ten is still here but I will check regardless. From the hide I watch the pups enjoy the morning light, and my chest aches to see them playing so joyously. I feel their teeth graze my skin, their tongues lick my face, their paws batting me to the snow. I can feel their pelts pressed to me, their warmth, their strength, their certainty mine. To be so at home in your body. To be at ease, and powerful. A shiver of desire moves through me and I am almost there, I think I can feel it, their power, the togetherness of them, the family. Little one kicks, her foot stronger than I could have imagined, and I think she feels it too.

I have to leave here. The pull to stay is strong, the feel of them too visceral. I feel wolf; I am forgetting myself.

There is no sign of Ten, so I must go north toward the mountain where she was last spotted. Her pattern has been to travel out from the center of the park to make her kills and then head back to its center. Maybe she feels freer there, where there are no roads or houses or people. Maybe she is smarter than we know, and she understands that this is where she is safest, where we cannot reach her.

Gall and I ride a long time, following valleys and ridges through bleak windy hills. Our altitude climbs and drops and climbs again. We are searching the mountain range and there is no cover as we go up the edge of one, down the edge of another, no respite against the freezing sleet or biting gales. The hours lead us into night once more, those witching hours I dread. We stop to eat and drink at regular intervals, and to rest. The breaks in the monotony of the ride help hold back the shadows. But in the dark I have no chance of seeing tracks or scat, or remains of prey, so when we come to a stretch of ground without snow I build a fire, then lower Gall to the ground and sleep against her body to keep all three of us warm.

I think of Duncan and my anger fuels me. And I *am* angry at Ten but this is foolishness and in the end I know it's myself I am most furious with. For not dealing with her sooner. For not seeing these attacks as a sign of the darkness to come. We took her from her home and dumped her in a foreign land and we expected her to adapt but I think that was too much to ask. Maybe she is as angry as I am.

Morning breaks on the second day and within it I find the tracks of a handful of what I think are fallow deer.

My dad's words in my ear. *There is no hunting a wolf. They are cleverer than we are. So instead you hunt its prey.*

Sometimes, and only because I have looked at so many over the years, I think I can detect the very faint paw prints of a wolf *inside* the tracks of the deer. Here lives the difference between a wolf and a dog, or indeed a wolf and most other animals. The elegance and efficiency of specifically seeking compacted snow—snow that other animals have done the hard work of compacting—is a clever way to reduce the energy she must use. But I am on her trail now.

After some time we follow the deer tracks along the length of an icy river to the edge of a huge frozen loch. It glitters blue-white in the sun. The tracks part around the edge of the loch.

And on its other side, just like that, stands a wolf.

She watches me. A smudge of tawny brown. I can imagine she is daring me. Then she walks, casually, out of sight.

No matter how much I need to reach her, I'm not stupid enough to take a horse over a frozen lake with no idea how thick the ice is. I nudge Gall and we start around the loch, still at a walk. I won't be goaded into a trot or a run; my certainty will simmer long and slow. I don't need to rush. I have her now. With patience, I *will* kill her.

I pick up Number Ten's tracks. They are clean and stark in the snow. We follow them easily toward the base of the mountain. She must be aware of my scent. Must know I'm coming after her. But I can see she isn't running, she walks calmly as we do. Something ancient is stirred within me as we step on and on. I draw the rifle from the saddle and load it with a bullet, but keep the safety on and the muzzle pointed skyward. Gall's steps become mine, the rhythmic movements of her body thrumming through the pulse in my veins.

The creature ahead lets out a howl.

The language of the most territorial creature on Earth, warning me to back off or continue at my own peril.

She howls again and again and it begins to shift from a warning to a taunt.

Gall's ears flatten but she walks on calmly. My fury has none of the same calm. The wolf is provoking it into something frenzied. There is violence in me, in my hands, which vibrate with the need to exert some kind of control, some defiance, and if it is revenge for the things that have been taken from me then fine, I will have that too. I am done with falling prey. I will be predator, at last. I will forget the walls and the self-protection and I will become the thing I hunt and feel it all.

Snow begins to fall; soon the tracks will be covered. It doesn't matter. There's a clearing ahead and she's on the other side of it. I can hardly see her through the blizzard that is beginning, but she's there, motionless and watching. I swing off the horse, who is restless now that the wolf is so near. I can't risk her throwing me.

I face Number Ten as I did once, but that was in a cage and this is very far from that cage. She didn't back down from me then. This time I have the rifle to my eyeline, aimed at her chest. This time I'm ready, waiting for her to attack. She took something beloved from the world. From me. Once I wasn't strong enough to make things right but I am now, I will be.

I turn off the safety.

She doesn't ready herself to attack. She just watches me.

My hand on the trigger stalls.

The tidal wave passes through.

She's not a person, who understands right and wrong. You can't be angry with an animal, can't hate it, get revenge upon it. That doesn't make sense. She didn't kill because she was cruel. She killed because there are instincts in her body telling her to do so, to protect against threats, to survive, sustain herself, live on.

Everything leaves me in a rush so that all that remains is a great and profound sorrow.

I pull the trigger.

Because whether I feel it or not, whether I love her or not, she has attacked two people. Because if she isn't put down they all will be. Because this is my job, an awful part of it. But not because she deserves punishment or because I want revenge.

My eyes are closed. I will be less when I open them again.

I stand very still, coming to terms with all the ways I could have avoided this. It is devastatingly clear to me now what I should have done from the start: I should have included the farmers in this process, worked with them instead of treating them as the enemy. They might have shown me animosity but the stakes were so high, I should have risen above it, led the way toward cooperation, toward the sharing of this planet. No one can meet your trust if you don't offer it.

Ten is still breathing. I cross the clearing to her. The bullet went through her neck; I can feel it in mine, sharp and radiating.

I sink to the ground and place my hand on her forehead, stroking her soft fur. "I'm sorry," I whisper. "I'm so sorry." Her eyes look up at me and I open myself to her completely, lay myself bare for her to see, and she does, and dies.

All creatures know love.

I stroke her for a long time.

It's the cold, in the end, that makes me move. It is not because I want to leave her. I don't, not ever. I have brought a canvas to wrap her in. Once she's protected by this I lower Gall onto her knees so I can pull Ten's body onto her back. I am distantly astonished Gall is willing to carry this load, but she was always brave. The wolf isn't as heavy as she looks, a fine creature, lean in form. She seems almost delicate now that her ferocity is gone, stolen. Not for the first time I hate my job, the humanness of it. I would leave her out here to feed the other animals, to feed the earth, if I didn't need to show Red and the hunters proof of her death, if my job didn't require me to study her remains.

I swing up onto Gall's back once more, settling myself just in front of the wolf so I can feel her fading warmth against the base of my spine. And then comes the cramp.

I've had cramping before. This is . . . louder.

Little one is squeezing me from within. There is pressure and discomfort and then it's gone. I start riding for home with a thought in the back of my mind and a louder thought that no, it's too early for that. I couldn't possibly be so unlucky.

Unless it's my fault. The movement of my body, the swelling of my soul. Calling something forth before its time.

Not now, little one, I tell her. *Just hold on.*

But the cramps continue, growing in intensity and frequency until I can't lie to myself anymore, this is happening. The only question is whether or not I'll make it home in time. It's meant to take many hours, isn't it? *Days* sometimes?

It is a shorter journey home than it was to get here. We have been circling closer and now I can cut straight back through Abernethy Forest, to my house and then beyond it the town, the hospital in which Duncan lies. This is the last stretch but it is still a long one. The forest reaches ahead and yet I am immensely grateful to be within its shelter.

The trees whisper.

Keep on.

A little further now.

The pressure becomes too much and I have to get off the horse. I have to move. I pant and swear and walk in circles. It is bewilderingly uncomfortable, so uncomfortable it seems impossible my body can maintain this feeling but it does, and I stop having reasonable thoughts, start trying to make bargains with the sky and the roots, can't work out what the hell I should do or how to make this stop but I definitely, definitely need it to stop.

I can tell Gall is nervous but I don't have the capacity to worry about it, until I let out a long, low moan, the moan of a cow, and she jerks in alarm at the sound and then she's off, trotting away and leaving me here and I certainly have the capacity to worry about it now.

So I walk. In between contractions, for as long as I can until the next one hits. My skin is so raw that even my clothes hurt, and I'd give anything to take them off but I'm lucid enough to know that would be very stupid. I have to start thinking about this baby. I've been so stubborn. I am a coward. I've put her in harm's way because I was terrified of how I might love her and how I would be swallowed by her, and I couldn't allow being so disastrously vulnerable and so I made her vulnerable instead and that is unforgivable.

I speak to her as I walk through the snow. I say all the things I might have said over the last eight months if only I'd been brave enough. I will her to live and then that seems foolish because it is her will to live that seizes my body every few minutes, her strength despite my efforts to ignore her. As I lower myself onto all fours in the snow I know I must be as calm as I'm able, must reach for strength that will be worthy of hers.

I'm not sure how much time has passed before I need to take off my pants. I'm struggling not to push, I don't know how to push and yet I can't not, I have to. I've never been more frightened. Never calmer.

I take off my boots and pants and underwear, leaving my socks, and I make a bed on the ground with my coat. The trees above and around. They sway. I am home here, and so glad. It is right that I'm here after all. It was always going to be here.

The pain starts to take over and swell up from within me, exploding in a mighty roar that startles the birds from the trees. She is tearing through me and everything is clenched so tightly I forget to breathe and there are spots in front of my eyes and I think the human body is a failure of evolution because it was not meant to withstand this, our shape is wrong, our capacity is wrong, and yet women do this every day and they survive and so that's what I'll do, I will do this and survive because afterward I will need to get the baby to safety.

With my fingers I feel for her head, there is certainly something hard and wet there but I have no way to tell if it's her skull, I must hope. I am moving still, unable to find the right position, on my back is a nightmare but on my hands and knees I can't reach to catch her, so in the end I stand up, leaning my forehead against a tree. It holds all of me up, and I bend my knees and reach down to catch her. Within me is a certainty I have never known. This is my pain. It is no trick, not stolen; it belongs to no one but me. This is my body, my child. I can feel her and she is *mine* and in this moment the truth of that is so powerful I am able to give a mighty push. Her head and shoulders force their way out and then the rest of her slips free, my hands catching her by the leg and swinging her up into my arms. She is a bruised shade and covered in bloody, pussy muck so I lower my mouth to her face and suck her airways clean. She takes a huge breath and she is breathing into my lungs, lungs we share, and I thought my condition was a trick, a curse, a burden to carry but in this moment it is a *gift*. She opens her eyes.

And looks at me.

I am halved and doubled at once.

I sink to the ground on my makeshift bed and place her on my chest, against my skin, and I guide her to my breast so she can latch on. She does it straight away, with very little struggle. I vaguely feel the placenta coming free of me, but I'm too intent on her face to take much notice of it. She is so tiny. I don't know if she's getting anything out of my unprepared breast. I bite her umbilical cord with my teeth, and then I wrap her in my thick thermal undershirt. I can't bear to put her down, to let go of her for a single second, but I have to get dressed or I'll freeze to death. So I lie her down and clumsily draw on my clothes and then press her to my chest inside the warm coat. I have no strength left in my body, my legs are almost paralyzed with weakness. I am bleeding quite a lot, and this scares me but there isn't time now to rest, I need to get her somewhere warm, somewhere she can be looked after. So I find what little strength I have left and I get to my feet and I start walking.

She sleeps in my arms, this little creature. We are both calmed by the smell of each other. I give her what warmth I have. Leaving a trail of red behind.

At some point I realize I have been following a figure up ahead, keeping my steps timed to his.

"Dad," I call, and he stops. Turns.

"My girls," he says, with such love.

"Where did you go?" I ask.

"Into the forest."

I swallow this aching thing in me. "Did it look after you?"

Dad smiles. "It did."

I close my eyes.

"Isn't she beautiful," he says, by my side now. "Keep going, darling."

"I'm so tired."

"I know you are. But I'll show you the way."

I follow my father through the trees until eventually he is swallowed up by the falling snow.

As night falls I must stop. I have been moving too slowly, I haven't made enough progress, and now it is too cold to move at all: my body won't obey. I try to make us a fire but Gall left with my matches and my hands are shaking and too stiff to make use of my fingers. So I hunker down against the base of a tree and I press my body warmth around my daughter, whose calm I take courage from.

"We'll start walking again as soon as the light changes," I whisper to her. "We'll walk forever if we have to. I won't ever stop. You're safe, little one."

I'm bleeding even more now, but I will get back up again soon.

It's the scent of them that reaches me first. In the dark of the earliest hours comes the feather-soft musk of their approach. This is their forest, and they too have been alerted by scent, the trail of it I've left behind. I open my eyes. I haven't slept, but have lain in a frozen kind of limbo, slipping back and forth.

My first conscious thought in hours is: This night is too cold to survive. We're going to die here.

The second is: The wolves have come.

My will to fight is immense. I will stand and run at them, I will scare them. If they don't scare, I will fight them with my hands and my teeth, I will tear at them, I will make of my body a shield, I will do *anything*. I will not let them hurt her.

But the immensity of a will is still nothing, not compared with the body. The body is master of us, and it can only be asked for so much. I try to stand but nothing happens. I try to yell but only a rasp comes loose. The cold is too deep, I've lost too much blood.

The wolves melt from the trees. Their eyes reflect the moonlight.

I turn and cover my daughter with my body, and I look down at her in this little cocoon. *Survive,* I urge her.

The air catches in my lungs.

But she doesn't attack me, this smallest of the wolves, nearly grown now but still white as the day I held her in my hands. She lies her body next to mine. And as the rest of her pack move to join her, pressing their warmth around us and saving us from the cold, I lower my face into the white of her neck and I weep.

29

When I wake to dawn light, they are gone, and I am left to wonder if they were real. The infinite mystery of wolves. I am delirious as I stagger to my feet. Little one has been asleep a long time now.

I walk. Step after painful step. I'm amazed there is any blood left in me.

Soon I hear a sound. I know that sound. It's a horse. My body collapses to the ground and this time I won't be getting up again.

It doesn't matter. She has found us.

Have I imagined her?

She swings off Gall and runs to me and she's here, my sister is here, and so it doesn't matter that I won't get back up. There is no life in which she will let harm come to little one. She protects.

Aggie kisses my cheeks and forehead and she scoops the baby into her arms. Her arm, which has blood seeping through its sleeve. I am confused, don't understand her blood.

But she says to my daughter, with her voice, "Little one," and I am crying again, and she is, too.

"Take her," I say.

Aggie meets my eyes and we don't need words. She knows what's within me, the very farthest reaches of me. I can't get on a horse, not hemorrhaging like this, and even if I could it would be too slow to try to carry us all. It's time that matters now. It's little one, and she hasn't moved in a long time, far too long. And so Aggie nods, and she places her coat around me and kisses me again, and she says, "I'll come back for you. Just hold on."

I hear her voice in my mind long after she has carried my daughter away.

In the dream I am sitting before Duncan's fireplace and Fingal's head is in my lap. There is twisted furniture all around. And his large hand is stroking my hair, slow and gentle, his lips against my temple.

"You know what happened," he whispers, breath to my ear.

I do.

I know it now, at long last.

"Ho!"

The shout comes from a long way away. Maybe another world away. I have been slipping between two for hours; the veil is paper thin.

I resist that shout, happy where I am. The fire is warm. His touch everything.

"Up ahead!"

Inti, he says, and I say, *Duncan,* and we both say *don't go* but it's too late, I am gone, returned to the cold.

How long have I been out here? How long since Aggie left? Did she make it back in time? The sky is spinning. Snow clouds turn in circles. There are flakes falling on my face, into my eyelashes, onto my lips. I can taste them on my tongue.

A face appears.

It's Red McRae.

My hope stutters out. I think he will leave me here. An end to his problems. But he lifts me into his arms and says, "It's all right, sweetheart, you're safe now," and I hold on to him as he carries me home, thinking I know nothing about hatred or love, about cruelty or kindness. I know nothing.

30

I wake to find my sister in bed with me, and a baby in between.

Aggie has been watching us both as we sleep. Our hands are linked and hers is so warm. Now she smiles at me, and I smile back.

Later, when things make sense again, she moves to the chair so I have room to try to breastfeed. I've been sewn up and given a blood transfusion, and left on a drip. My body hurts but mostly it just feels exhausted. Little one has been given fluids and warmth and has been monitored, she has some jaundice and I'm not producing much breastmilk, but she is, miraculously, in reasonably good health.

She is tiny, with thick dark hair and the prettiest little face I have ever seen, and beloved.

Aggie tells me she'd been watching for my return when Gall showed up carrying her burden. Aggie lowered the wolf from the horse's back, then turned her around again and followed her path back to me, far more quickly than I was able to travel on my journey. It is strange to hear her speaking. I'm not yet used to it, and at the same time it seems as though she never stopped.

We are quiet awhile, listening to the beeps of the machines that drift in from the hallway, and I marvel at the way it feels to breastfeed, at the intimacy, even when she's not getting much. The trying, apparently, will help.

"What happened to your arm?" I ask Aggie.

"A dog," she replies.

I look up at her, frowning. "What?"

She doesn't answer, and I remember my dream, and know.

The story comes in small morsels, as much as Aggie can say at a time. She uses signs as well as her voice, because signing is not a habit she will shake in a matter of days, maybe not ever.

It goes like this.

When Lainey drops Stuart at the end of the road, she thinks she is leaving him to go after Duncan. But instead he walks for my house. It is me who has publicly accused him of abusing his wife. It is me who is vulnerable; Duncan is too strong a target for Stuart's already-humiliated rage.

Aggie wakes in the night to a furious hammering on the door. There isn't a doubt in her mind that it's what she's been waiting for: Gus has found her. She takes a sharp knife from the kitchen, as she would do several more times in this very same kitchen when needs arose, and she looks through the window and sees a man. Her husband, come to finish her. She decides she will finish him first. She feels a thrill. A need. And fear to obliterate the rest, to swallow it all whole.

The man is shouting. Saying her sister's name, spewing abuse. How dare I stick my nose into his business.

There is a jolt of cognitive dissonance as the man's face changes before Aggie's eyes. This is not her husband, but it is *a* husband, one who has been harming his wife. I'd been talking about him, after all. Talking and talking to a woman I thought couldn't hear me, but as it turns out she was listening all along and she did not like the sound of Stuart Burns. She had seen him, as I had, sitting in his car beyond the boundary of our house, watching us.

When the man gives up and walks away into the forest, Aggie follows him. She is very frightened, more so now that she's outside, but she gathers her courage. She was fierce once. And she has always been more comfortable with rage than I have.

She calls, "Stuart."

He turns and says, "What?" Like it's normal to be addressed out here in the dead of night. He recognizes her, thinks she is me. He advances, thinking to teach me the lesson he came here to impart. But before he touches Aggie some instinct makes her arm jerk. She stabs and slashes with her serrated knife.

Then she turns and walks home. Simple as that.

What neither of us realized is that there was someone watching from the road, thinking she was me.

There is a long quiet as we both return from that night forest and its ghosts. I feel myself shiver, and wonder how I didn't guess sooner. Little one has tired of feeding and fallen asleep.

"Promise me you'll never tell anyone," I say to Aggie. "If he's ever found, we'll let them think it was Number Ten who killed him, and I'll admit I was the one who buried him because I wanted to protect my wolves."

Aggie looks at me for a long moment, but she doesn't reply. *And Duncan?* I want to ask. But I already know the answer and I can't bear to hear it spoken aloud. Something in me will perish along with him, when I know for certain that he is dead, and she the one to do it.

I can already picture how it must have happened.

Aggie sees that I'm afraid of him and that's all it takes. The tried and tested practice of her life. She walks the same path through the forest once more, further this time. She takes the knife. She waits outside his house for him to emerge. He lets his dog out first, maybe. Fingal is barking, he can smell someone in the trees. Duncan follows to see what the fuss is about. Maybe Aggie has intended only to threaten him, she means to keep him away from me, but maybe the dog panics her and the man is advancing and so she lifts her knife and slashes Duncan's throat. The dog attacks, sinking his teeth into her arm. She is forced to cut him, too. And runs, leaving them both where they fell. My shadow sister.

"I was so tired of feeling afraid," Aggie says, and she does, she sounds so tired. "I didn't want that prison for you, too."

I understand. It's why I told her I'd killed Gus. To free her.

"Why that night?" I ask. "What made you go to Duncan's that night?"

"He came to our house," she says. "Earlier that day. You were at work, I didn't answer. He was knocking and knocking and calling my name, saying he wanted to talk to me and I just . . . I knew he wouldn't ever stop trying to get to you. Not unless I made him."

Oh, Aggie.

"I love him," I say.

She blinks, and then her mouth forms a soft *oh* of surprise. *No,* Aggie signs. A refusal.

"I do. He never did anything to deserve fear. It was Gus who did that."

Aggie closes her eyes. Terrible pain passes through her. *I thought it was happening again.*

So did I, I sign in return. But, as it turns out, we were the ones who couldn't be trusted.

There is a knock at the door. I twist in bed to see Red and Douglas McRae poking their heads politely into the room. "Okay to have visitors?"

"Yes, come in."

The two men shuffle in. Douglas is holding a bunch of flowers, which he places on my side table, knocking over a cup of water in the process. "Look at this little lassie," the old man says, sweeping my daughter into his arms and cradling her with practiced ease. I blink in surprise. All right then.

Red is looking between my sister and me. "There's two of you."

I introduce them and Red gives Aggie a polite nod. She looks him up and down with cool appraisal.

"Word is you shot the wolf yourself," Red says to me.

For the crimes of having attacked two people, crimes she did not commit. I will never forgive myself for this mistake, but in the end, Ten would have had to be destroyed anyway, because she drew a map of dead livestock and the fury of man is absolute.

"She's at home," I say. "You can go and see for yourself if you need the proof."

He shakes his head. "I believe you. I've called off the hunt."

"Thank you."

Red is shifting uncomfortably and I wait to see what's bothering him so much. "Did she . . ." He hesitates. "Did she show fear, when it ended?"

I am surprised by the question, and search his face. "No." My throat prickles. "She was very calm."

"Mine too," he says. "The big male." And then he admits, softly, "The moment I pulled that trigger, I knew it was evil I'd done."

I close my eyes. The bed moves as my sister sits beside me and takes my hand.

"The way I see it," Red says gruffly, "you and I have some things to talk about. None of this is going to work unless we start talking."

A great weight lifts off my chest. "I couldn't agree with you more, Red."

Later, after I have slept a little, I watch my sister with the baby, rocking her gently by the window.

"I'm sorry, Aggie," I say. Long overdue.

She looks at me.

"I'm sorry I didn't stop them. I'm so sorry I didn't fight."

"You couldn't have. They were doing it to you too."

I shake my head. "That isn't real."

My sister holds my eyes. "You came in to be with me. They were doing it to you too."

"You went so far away."

"You were with me. You're always with me."

I say, "I didn't kill Gus."

Aggie takes that in. She breathes out wearily, then lowers her cheek to little one's. "Okay. That makes sense."

"I tried, Ag. I'm sorry." I hate him so much for what he's done, for what he's taken from her. And from me, too. So much time, wasted in fear of others.

"I love you," she tells me.

"I love you."

I look at my daughter and she helps to fortify me.

"Is Duncan . . . ?"

Aggie says, "He's waiting for you."

With little one in my arms, my sister wheels me into his room. It's on another floor. He is hooked up to a monitor and drip. There are thick bandages around his neck. His eyes are closed, face pale. Aggie pushes me to his bedside, as close as she can, and then she leaves us.

The sun moves beyond the window, casting us in warm evening light. We wait for him to wake. Maybe it's the soft sounds little one makes, but soon he opens his eyes. When he sees us his tears slip down his cheeks.

There is a pad and pen on his tray. He writes something and holds it up. *You saved my life.*

I swell with the knowledge that he was right. He was so right. He could have become his father but he chose to become his mother instead. We all have that choice, and most of us make it. There is cruelty to survive, to fight against, but there is gentleness more than anything, our roots deep and entangled. That is what we hold inside, what we take with us, the way we look after each other. I look at little one and I tell Duncan, "You saved mine, too."

They said I might not speak again, he writes.

I smile. "There are languages without words, without voices. I'll teach them to you."

His hands as he takes her are so tender they tremble.

"Gently," I say.

31

We are home now. There are tangled birds' nests between us but there is little one to think of. I don't know how we will find our places in each other's orbits because there are not only two of us now, but four.

Duncan has written a statement declaring he was attacked by a wolf, as everyone thought. They don't look further into the type of wounds he was given—a sharp blade instead of animal teeth, a slice not a tear. They don't question, because he is the police chief and because this is the outcome that makes sense to them, a crime that has already been punished. I killed the monster, after all. Number Ten lies dead upon a lie. Upon my mistake. She will become legend and the wolves will suffer for it, because it was not them who came to this place and spilled blood. It was my sister and me.

And Duncan was the first to figure it out. After he met her and saw how similar we looked, and how unwell she was, it sparked a theory. Fergus called him a bloodhound and he is, he guessed it all, and still he has done his best to protect us, and that is not something I will soon forget.

Tonight, as Aggie bathes little one, Duncan and I sit before the fire and he runs his hands through my hair, and it is my dream awoken.

He writes on his pad. *She needs to be in a facility. She could still be a danger to others.*

I meet his dark eyes. "I can't, Duncan."

He puts his pen down but I know it will not be the end of this conversation. The policeman in him. The protector. He is just like her in that way.

I phone Mum, unsure how I could possibly put into words all that has happened, knowing I must.

She answers quickly. "There you are, sweet girl. I've been calling and calling. I have something to tell you both."

This surprises me, so I hold off my own tumult.

"Jim and I are getting married."

I laugh. "How's that, Mum?"

"Well, I was trying to figure out the same thing myself, and I did have a thought. Remember how I told you about the timeline? About making a timeline to solve your case?" Mum asks.

"Yeah."

"My thought's got to do with that. Yeah, people do bad things to each other. And we remember those stories, we remember the pain, but we remember it because it stands out. It's the blip in the timeline, the thing that doesn't fit, and that's because the rest of the timeline, which is our whole lives really, is made of kindness. That's what's normal, it's so normal we don't even notice it."

I smile.

"Mum," I say. "Can you come to Scotland?"

"I thought you'd never ask."

Aggie and I walk Gall around the paddock while Duncan cooks dinner with our daughter in a sling on his chest. We are both watching the sky to see the lights again, but they don't return for us, not tonight. The stars and the moon are alone up there.

After a long while I speak into the quiet.

"I saw Dad," I tell her softly. "When I was in the forest."

Aggie searches my face. "How was he?"

I smile. "He was Dad."

"It stills calls to you, doesn't it? The forest?"

"Always." But my eyes fall on warm Blue Cottage and what it holds. "It's quieter now."

"I think I get it, finally," Aggie says with a smile. "How you belong there. How we both do."

You wake early. There is heavy fog. Your horse is waiting for you, as she has always been. You lead her out toward the hills.

You have been healthy, looking after our little family—even Duncan, though there is something heavy and irrevocable between you. You took something precious from him and he knows you were sick, but still. Life is strange, we do our best. He is very good at forgiveness, he learned young. You have been happy, I know you have. There is purpose now, and we have let Gus go. So then why?

You walk up and along a ridge to watch the sun rise golden. Gall's snorts are warm, her mouth tickling your palm. It is beautiful up here; it is vast. With the waking world at your feet you are free.

Maybe it's guilt for the violence. Maybe it lives in you in a way you can't ignore.

Maybe you think you'll come between us, or simply want to make space for something new. Or because it doesn't go away, it never goes away, that pain, even in the midst of this new life.

Maybe it's because you can finally be sure I'll be all right without you.

I don't truly know why. But I wake one morning to find you gone.

You have left a note on the table.

It reads simply, *Gone home. x*

And you have taken Gall.

I leave little one with Duncan and I go out searching. I track what I can, but the trail disappears. I call your name with a voice broken by grief, but I have done this before and I know its end. You have gone the way Dad did, like the animals do. You have gone into the wild to die.

Or maybe, you have gone to live.

Epilogue

On a cold night last month, Ash, leader of the Abernethy Pack, lay down to sleep and didn't wake. Her family lay around her, keeping her warm as she passed away. She was nine years old. The first to build a pack in this new world, the first to bear pups and protect them, alone, against all manner of threat. She guided them through this land and taught them to survive. She never mated again, not after the death of Number Nine. She had only one litter of pups but they have all proven to be strong and brave, and she had a gentler passing than most wolves are afforded.

The Abernethy Pack has a new leader now. She is as white as her mother was. She is smaller, and even stronger, if that is possible. I love her with every atom of me and perhaps, in some deeper world than we know, in some place more beautiful than we can see, she loves me in return. She saved us, once. And it cannot be said that there are no mysteries within a wolf.

Last winter I went out with my tranquilizer darts and I removed every radio collar we'd placed so the wolves could truly be free.

It is spring now, and the hills have changed color. The deer are on the move. Things are growing again. The wolves have come home. And by some miracle, or perhaps it's simply the natural way, the people of this land are becoming accustomed to them. With no more incidents since the death of Number Ten, a kind of quiet has fallen over the Highlands, and I suspect, when I see locals using binoculars to patiently watch for sightings, that the wolves are working their way into the hearts of the Scottish people.

My daughter squirms in her sling over my back. She would prefer to be walking, but I want to reach the crest of the hill before I put her down to explore. The sky is gray with rain but then it mostly is, here in the north of the world. It makes the earth lush, helps it to grow.

We reach the survey grounds I first inspected years ago, this stretch of hillside I have walked time and again, hoping to see new growth. I pull her from the sling so she can run freely through the heather. She laughs, as in love with the wilderness as I have ever been. She was born here, is bound deeply. Even if we leave—there are other forests to save, other wolves to return home, the trembling giant has been calling—a part of her will always belong here.

Something catches my eye and I squat to look at it.

"Come and look," I say, and she runs to see, tracing her fingers over the brave new shoots we have been waiting for. "Willow and alder," I say. Then I show her how to press her ear to the ground. "Listen," I whisper. "Can you hear them?"

Acknowledgments

I wrote this novel out of a sense of profound distress over the loss of our natural world. I wanted to imagine an effort to rewild a landscape, such as the ones brave conservationists are attempting throughout the world. To them I say a heartfelt thank-you, for the courage it takes to try to turn back the tide.

I'd like to specifically thank the extraordinary team at Yellowstone National Park. After seventy years without wolves, in 1995 they achieved the almost impossible feat of reintroducing these essential predators to an environment in crisis, and have breathed new life into the land. I took a great deal of inspiration from these women and men, but also from the wolves themselves, and their incredible stories.

Thank you endlessly to my agent, Sharon Pelletier. You are such a rock for me, always so generous, insightful, and supportive. I'm so very lucky to have you on my team.

An enormous thank-you to my wonderful, tireless editor, Caroline Bleeke. You are a wonder of a woman. You took something small and shy and tentative and saw a way to help it bloom, and I'm so grateful for your cleverness, kindness, and honesty. Your dedication is humbling, and you are so very good at your job.

Thank you to Amelia Possanza, publicist extraordinaire! You work miracles, AP, you really do! And to the whole team at Flatiron—Katherine Turro, Keith Hayes, Jordan Forney, Marta Fleming, Nancy Trypuc, Kerry Nordling, Cristina Gilbert, Megan Lynch, and Bob Miller—you are all an absolute dream to work with, and I can't thank you enough for taking this second ride with me!

Thank you to the wonderful Nikki Christer, my Australian publisher; publicist Karen Reid, and the whole team at Penguin Random House

Australia. You've all gone above and beyond for me, and I couldn't feel luckier or more grateful that this novel found a home with you. Nikki, thank you for being such a tireless advocate for these books and the messages they're trying to share, I'm truly so lucky to have you.

Thank you to Charlotte Humphery and the Chatto & Windus team for your amazing work in the UK. CH, you have an eagle eye and I'm so grateful for it!

Thank you to Teresa Pütz and her German team at S. Fischer, for providing my books and I such a fantastic German home.

A huge thank-you to Addison Duffy, my film and TV agent at UTA, for your tireless work in bringing my novels to life on the screen. It has been such an exciting ride, and a dream come true, so thank you!

To my friends. Sarah Houlahan, Charlie Cox, Rhia Parker, Caitlin Collins, Anita Jankovic, Raechel Whitty and all my wonderful book club ladies—I am so lucky to be surrounded by such generous, intelligent, hilarious, strong and kind people. Honestly each one of you blows me away. Thank you for being you.

I want to thank my father, Hughen, whose farm is a testament to cruelty-free and sustainable farming, his attitude one of sharing the land and feeding it. This is the way forward, and it makes me so proud to see, Dad. To you and Zoe, Nina, Hamish, and Minna. Thank you for your love and support; like my gratitude, it is endless. To my brother, Liam; my grandmother, Ouma; and my mum, Cathryn. I will never be able to thank you enough because I can't put into words how grateful I am to you. I wouldn't be doing this if it weren't for you. I don't think I'd have the courage.

And to Morgan. You are my home. I love you.

Lastly, I must again acknowledge the wild creatures and places in this world, which inspired every word of this novel. The gentle they have shown us far outstrips anything we have ever shown them in return. Though Scotland has not yet passed an initiative to reintroduce wolves, it's my hope that they—along with the rest of the world, and especially my homeland of Australia—will further embrace the essential work of rewilding, and maybe in doing so, we will begin to rewild ourselves.

About the Author

Charlotte McConaghy is an author based in Sydney, Australia. Her U.S. debut novel, *Migrations*, was a national bestseller and is being translated into more than twenty languages.